Also by J. G. White:

Operation Saint George
ISBN: 978-1-84963-339-0

About the Author

JG White was born and raised in London and Kent. He served in the Royal Marines during the 1960s. He went to London University and trained as a teacher. He taught in secondary schools for twenty-five years: he was a Head Teacher for ten years. He is now retired and lives in Nottingham.

This book is dedicated to the memory of my good friend, who suggested the idea for this book.

Roy Peacock
(1944 – 2013)

J.G. White

NEVER SURRENDER

AUSTIN MACAULEY
PUBLISHERS LTD.

A CIP catalogue record for this title is available from the British Library.

ISBN 9781786126771 (Paperback)
ISBN 9781786126788 (Hardback)
ISBN 9781786126795 (E-Book)

www.austinmacauley.com

First Published (2016)
Austin Macauley Publishers Ltd.
25 Canada Square
Canary Wharf
London
E14 5LQ

This book is a work of fiction, except in the case of historical fact or persons. Names and characters are the product of the author's imagination and any resemblance to actual persons living or dead is entirely coincidental.
Please note that this book contains an excerpt from JG White's forthcoming adventure story. This has been set for this edition only and may not reflect the final content of the new book when published.

Acknowledgements

I am deeply indebted to a number of former Royal Marines and soldiers who have helped me with the research for this book, especially those who found themselves at the sharp end. They are too numerous to mention here but I am most grateful to all of them for their time and their memories.

However, as unfair as it may seem, I must extend a very personal thank you to Mr Alan John Dacre of Woodbridge, Suffolk. Without his inspiration and enthusiasm this book would never have seen the light of day.

To all my friends and family who told me that *Never Surrender* would be a very demanding book to write, I can only say how right they were. It was but I thoroughly enjoyed every minute of it.

I also wish to extend my grateful appreciation to my publishers for their help and encouragement, and for having the commitment to publish this, my second book.

Lastly, my thanks must also go to my better half, Kathy, for her help and support.

Finally, I hope you, the reader, will find this story as fascinating as I did when writing it.

JG White

"We shall fight on the beaches, we shall fight on the landing grounds, we shall fight in the fields and in the streets, we shall fight in the hills; we shall never surrender."

Winston Churchill
Prime Minister
1940

Prologue

An Italian by the name Pantaleoni Manzioni arrived in London from Naples in 1906. A friend already living in the great city had sent him the necessary money for the sea voyage, steerage class of course. Pantaleoni, or Leo as he was known, was thirty years old. Accompanying him was his beautiful young wife, Rafaella Palumbo, who was just twenty-two. Accompanying them was their six year old daughter Maria Maculata. They had all walked from the hill top village of Ravello, high up in the hills above Amalfi on the Neapolitan coast. Neither the mother nor the child wore any shoes. Acute poverty had driven them from their families to seek a better life abroad.

In London Leo worked hard and long hours hauling large blocks of heavy ice around the city for those who could afford it. Within a short time he had progressed to selling ice cream from a handcart. Finally, he had saved enough money to buy a small shop on Tower Bridge Road which he opened as a grocery store. He quickly realised that he would need to specialise in something if he was ever going to be successful. By using his connections to the old country, he began to import Italian wines and olive oil. His business grew quickly and within a couple of years he opened two more shops, one on Beresford Square in Woolwich and the other in Deptford High Street. Then, two years later he opened three more shops, this time at the Elephant & Castle and in Lewisham and Peckham. He was riding high and life was good, in fact too good to last. In 1918 his beautiful wife died in the 'Great Influenza Pandemic'. He was heartbroken. However, two years later his daughter fell in love and married an Australian diplomat Barton J Dacre. Having heard of Leo's wine emporium, Barton had come south of the River Thames from the City to find exclusive wines. It had been love at first sight. Then disaster struck the family for the second time. The newly wed husband was killed in a terrible accident in Italy whilst climbing in the Dolomites, just eight months before his child was due to be born. To compound this tragedy Leo's daughter, Maria Maculata, died in childbirth later that same year which left a grief-stricken Leo with the task of bringing up his grandson, Alan John.

The war to end all wars (1914-1918) had been over for some time. In the late 1920s and early 1930s thousands of ex-servicemen were still trying to settle back into a home life only to find instead unemployment and poverty. Many people who had been in gainful employment also found themselves out of work. The period known as 'The Great Depression' spread its tentacles everywhere; hardly a home or family was not affected in some way or other. Even those who had wealth and had thought themselves safe from financial disasters suddenly found out that they were not immune. It was the same story across much of the world particularly in North America and Europe. In Germany and Italy the political situation, exacerbated by the massive economic decline, contributed to the rise of Fascism and, in particular, the Nazi party in Germany. Leo, and many of his generation, viewed this development with a growing sense of dread.

Leo found his business contracting. Gradually he had to sell off his shops one by one until he was left with just one in Tower Bridge Road, the first he had opened. Despite everything, he still managed to make a good job of bringing up his grandson. He sent him to good schools, the best he could afford, and encouraged him to visit the family home in Ravello. As far as he could, Leo shielded the lad from the harshness of those lean years. He didn't spoil the boy, far from it, but made sure his needs were well met. They naturally became very close during Alan John's formative years, as he grew to maturity. Although Leo found it was not easy being a surrogate parent and mentor, he loved every moment of it. He was pleased to see that the youngster grew to be tall and strong, with a well-balanced personality and a fine sense of right and wrong. His parents, he thought, would have been proud of him.

By the late 1930s, Leo's business gradually began to recover but he had learnt his lesson, albeit painfully. Instead of expanding once again, he put all his energy into just his one shop by focusing on improving the quality of his fine wines and olive oil. Thankfully this was appreciated by the ever-increasing number of highly satisfied customers.

PART ONE

Per Terram – By Land

Surname	Christian Name(s)
DACRE	Alan John

Official No. CH/X 06821	Description of Person				
Rank: Marine 1st Class	Stature	Feet	6	Ins.	1
Date of Birth: 1st August 1922	Colour of	Hair	Brown	Eyes	Hazel
Town/Village: Ruislip		Complexion		Fresh	
County: Middlesex					
Trade/profession: Scholar	Marks, scars or wounds	None			
Religious denomination: C of E					

Unit or Ship	Rank	Trade/Tech Qual of SQ	Capacity in which employed	Dates (from-to)	Remarks as to professional/instructional ability, special qualifications, awards, characteristics, etc.	Signature of Head of Dept., etc.
RM Depot	Mne 2nd	-	Recruit	Feb 39 - Sept 39	Best all round recruit in his squad. Awarded King's Badge. Marksman	J Bateson Capt. RM
Chatham Division	Mne 2nd	-	Trained Soldier	Sept 30 - May 40	Further training in Royal Marines Company. Excellent potential	V Taylor Capt. RM
RM Company	Mne 1st	-	Trained Soldier	May 40 - Nov 41	Underage; unable to go to France with Company. Volunteered for small boats: to Dunkirk on Gypsy Rose. Awarded Legion d'Honneur. Detatched duties London.	H Derry Major RM OC Coy

Next of Kin	Relationship:	None
	Name	
	Address	

15

Chapter 1

The sound of the motor cycle roaring into life woke the neighbours. It was 6.30 a.m. and Dacre AJ, aged just seventeen, was in a hurry. He had borrowed his friend's 350cc B.S.A. motorcycle and was keen to get going. It had taken him several good hard kicks on the starter lever to get the monster going. He adjusted the mixture control on the handle bars until the engine was running sweetly. He eased his way out of the backyard of his grandfather's wine and olive oil emporium which was located on Tower Bridge Road in South London. Then, mounting the motorcycle he set off towards the Old Kent Road which formed part of the arterial A2 main road. There were few other road users about at that time in the morning. Hunched behind the handlebars, dressed with goggles, a cap on backwards and a leather flying jacket, he opened the throttle and accelerated towards New Cross and Shooters Hill. He was heading for the naval port of Chatham in Kent.

The last few months had been a horrid and most painful time for the seventeen year old. His beloved grandfather had died suddenly just before Easter. They had been particularly close as his grandfather had brought him up since he was a baby. He had never known either his mother or father. Tragic circumstances had deprived him of the love to which he had been entitled. His father, Barton J Dacre, himself an orphan, had been born in Sydney, Australia. He had died in a climbing accident in Italy, eight months before the child was due to be born. His mother, Maria Macolata (nee Manzioni), sadly died in childbirth leaving his maternal grandfather to bring him up.

The death of his grandfather had been a real shock to him and was totally unexpected. It had shaken the young man to his very core, particularly when he realised that of his family he was the only one left. After the funeral, which took place on a very wet and windy day at Kensal Green Cemetery attended mostly by business acquaintances and some customers, Dacre AJ realised that he was the one who had to take charge of his life. The first thing that he did was to tell the Head Master of his public school at Mill Hill that he was going to leave at the end of that term. He had endured school rather than enjoyed it. Later in his life he would be the first to admit that this period of time had laid the foundations for the man he was to become.

The school occupied a glorious position, high up on a long ridge overlooking London to the south. It was blessed with elegant buildings and was set in some of the most beautiful and well maintained grounds to be found anywhere. Whilst it did not pretend to rank along-side the schools of Eton and Harrow, it was, nevertheless, extremely well thought of and had been producing young men of quality for the country and the empire since 1807. He had liked all the sports which the school provided, especially cricket and rugby, and he relished the occasional opportunity to go rock climbing, skiing, sailing and canoeing. He had even joined the school's Cadet Force, dressed in their World War 1 army uniforms, and had quite enjoyed the rudimentary marching and drilling under the watchful eye of a retired sergeant. However, he was the first to recognise that he was not, and never would be, a scholar. It was true that he had a certain flair for foreign languages. Naturally he was fluent in Italian as he and his grandfather had spoken it all the time at home. Spanish, French and German just seemed to come to him naturally.

At one time he had briefly considered a career in the Diplomatic Corps like his father before him. His knowledge of languages would certainly have helped but he felt it would be too sedentary for him. His Head Master, Mr Roberts, had tried to persuade him to stay on at school. He assured Dacre AJ that he was destined for an early entry into the Advanced Certificate Examination and then on to either Oxford or Cambridge University on a sporting/language blue. It was all mapped out and it was, after all, what his grandfather had wanted for him. But no, he realised that he had had enough. He had endured the school's social regime of 'fagging', where younger pupils acted as the servants of the older boys, part of the tradition of being at a public school. Eventually, as a sixth form prefect, he had chosen not to have a 'fag'. It was, he felt, inherently demeaning for the younger pupils and certainly led to bullying by some of the older boys which for him had been extremely unpleasant. It was likely that he would have been made Head Boy the following term, in which case he would certainly have had the authority and power to bring about some change.

However, it was not to be. He had decided to join the Royal Navy. Several of his school friends had fathers who were serving officers and one or two 'old boys', who had enlisted, returned to the school from time to time, although, he suspected, it was mainly to show off their uniforms. Dacre AJ had been intrigued by the stories they had told and although he was not naïve enough to believe everything he heard, it did seem like an interesting life and one that might well suit him. Besides, he quite liked the idea of a girl in every port. He had heard also, via the 'old boys' network, that the school was to be moved north to Cumberland because, with the possibility of war, HM Government needed to make use of their buildings.

As soon as he had formally left school Dacre AJ took himself down to the small fishing port of Whitstable, famous for its oysters, on the North Kent coast. His grandfather had not only left him a small legacy but also a little house in nearby Tankerton, on the cliff tops overlooking the sea. This had been his grandfather's retreat and holiday home for as long as he could remember. Dacre AJ spent several months there, building a sailing boat in the garage from a kit he had ordered from the London store, Gamages. It had been, he supposed later, a form of therapy, focusing his grief at the death of his grandfather into the discipline and routine of boat building. As in all things he undertook, he was single minded about the project and never let up. Some days he would drive himself to work seventeen or eighteen hours, non-stop.

His next door neighbours, the Miss Grahams, Lil and Sue, fussed over him like two mother hens. What wonderful people these two elderly sisters were. Both were in their mid-fifties. Sue was small and birdlike, frail looking with short, white bobbed hair. She worked from home, setting a weekly crossword for the *Times* newspaper. Previously she had lectured in Mathematics and Logic at the University of London. Lillian, or Lil as she liked to be known, was the more robust of the two, bigger and rounder, with her long hair plaited and tied up in a bun. She worked for the War Department, something clerical she always said, and would travel up to London daily by steam train from the little station at nearby Swalecliffe.

Dacre AJ always thought that there was more to Lil than met the eye. She had that certain air of authority that suggested she was used to giving orders rather than receiving them. To the youngster they had both seemed ageless and he loved them as if they were his own family. Between them, they kept the lad well supplied with hot food, soups and sandwiches and would tut-tut at the late hours he kept, all to no avail.

By the time he had finished the project and had applied the final coat of varnish, he knew he was ready to move on.

He did not even bother to launch and test the boat. That could wait for another time. He said his goodbyes to Lil and Sue and, setting out, he returned to London fully intent on joining the Royal Navy.

The miles flashed by as he passed through Welling, then Bexleyheath, onto Dartford and finally Watling Street, the ancient Roman Road that had once connected Portvs Dvbris (Dover) to Londinivm (London). It had started to rain. Despite his leather flying jacket he was cold, particularly his hands because he had forgotten to put on any gauntlets. He gritted his teeth with determination. He wasn't going to stop for shelter. The town of Strood passed by quickly and then he was heading down into the old town of Rochester and onto the bridge over the River Medway. Halfway across, he noticed to his right hand side several sea planes bobbing at anchor in the large river basin. The sign over the waterside hanger simply said SHORT'S.

The naval port of Chatham arrived none too soon. Dacre AJ was soaked to the skin and his teeth were chattering uncontrollably. He made his way carefully through the town and down to the Naval Base and Dockyard, taking care to avoid the wet manhole covers that were set into the road. It had only been last week, when testing out his friend's motorcycle that he had skidded on one of these and ended up lying in a gutter. It had all happened so quickly. A large red London bus had pulled up alongside him and the driver had leant out from his cab and shouted, 'What's your name mate, Death?' Dacre AJ had learnt a valuable lesson that day.

Arriving at the Recruiting Office, which was directly opposite the main gates to the Naval Base, Dacre AJ found that it did not open for another half an hour. Leaning the motorcycle against a nearby wall (for some reason or other the stand didn't work) he went and sat on the office doorstep. He huddled up and tried to conserve some of his body heat. As a mountaineer and climber he had recognised the danger signs of getting too cold. Rain water dripped from his sodden clothing and formed small pools around his feet. Fortunately ten minutes later a very attractive young woman dressed in a naval uniform opened the front door and handed him a very large mug of hot, sweet tea – what a life saver! She smiled down at him.

'It won't be long now,' she said.

She smelt of lavender water and talcum powder, just wonderful he thought.

At precisely 11.00 a.m. the heavy doors opened. Dacre AJ got up stiffly from the front step and stumbled into the recruiting office. He was not impressed with what he saw. It was dark and dismal and the walls were covered with faded posters of distant foreign ports. There were two desks, one of which was unoccupied. Behind the other stood a very tall Royal Marine in an immaculate dark blue uniform that buttoned up to the neck. Around his waist he wore a white belt with brasses and an ornate buckle that sparkled in what little light there was. On his arm were three gold stripes on a red background and on his chest a row of medal ribbons. He was taller than the youngster by a good three inches, which put him at about six foot four. He was broad in the shoulders and narrow at the hips, and his uniform fitted him like a glove.

'Well, young man, what can I do for you on this wet and miserable day?' he asked.

'Please, sir, I have come to join the navy,' replied Dacre AJ.

The marine held up his right hand making a distinctive stop sign.

'Now then, I am not a 'sir'. I am a Sergeant of Marines.' He pointed to the three stripes on his arm. 'It has taken me twelve years to get these; so if you would be so kind?'

There was a twinkle in his eye and a slight smile just touched the corners of his mouth. Dacre AJ realised that he had made a gaffe and hoped it would not be held against him.

The sergeant continued, 'Well as you can see my opposite number isn't here so I'm afraid you can't join His Majesty's Royal Navy, well at least not today anyway. Instead, why don't you consider joining the Royal Marines? Sit yourself down and let me tell you about my Corps and why I think you should join.'

Such was the persuasive nature of the Recruiting Sergeant that thirty minutes later Dacre AJ was fully convinced that he wanted to be a marine. He handed over his school report and a letter of recommendation from his Head Master. The sergeant took them both and read them through most carefully.

When the sergeant spoke, his voice carried just that amount of authority that commanded immediate attention and respect. At the same time there was just a hint of kindness.

'Well, young Dacre, I must say that you come highly recommended. There are plenty of opportunities for men with your skills and experience. In my opinion you should do very well in this Corps of mine.'

There were some enlistment papers to be completed and because he was underage and had no parents a local Justice of the Peace was sent for who, after questioning Dacre AJ about his reasons for joining up, signed the papers in absentia. Then, receiving the King's shilling, he was duly enrolled as a Marine Second Class. This was followed by the taking of the solemn oath to serve his King and Country for the next twelve years. He was then officially a recruit in His Majesty's Royal Marines and he felt about ten feet tall.

The sergeant explained that all 'Royals' are sworn men because they take an oath to the sovereign whereas those in the navy do not. 'We call them 'pressed men' which, of course, they are not any more. It's just a little conceit that we have which gives us a nice feeling of superiority.'

The sergeant paused with a satisfied look on his face.

'Now on your enlistment papers I am required to put down your former occupation. Since you are not employed I shall put down 'scholar'. Are you happy with that?'

The youngster smiled ruefully and nodded his head in agreement. He thought to himself, so much for those teachers who said he would never make it as a scholar. He had and it was official!

Mill Hill School Report   **Easter Term 1939**

Pupil's Name: *Dacre, Alan John*   Form: *Lower Sixth*

Subject	Comments	Grade	Teacher
Mathematics	*Average performance, no real flair, basically competent.*	C	DJ
English	*Satisfactory, could always do better.*	C+	HS
Geography	*Works well, good at map reading and navigation.*	B+	JC
History	*Has shown some improvement over the year.*	C+	MB
Latin & Greek	*For someone with a natural ability in languages this is a disappointing performance.*	D	JB
Languages	*Has a wonderful ability orally in Italian, French, Spanish and German. Written work less so.*	A-	AB
Games	*Excels in all sports, especially cricket and rugby, school captain in both. Outstanding climber, canoeist and dinghy sailor.*	A+	GG
Form Tutor	*Will never make a scholar. However, is a prefect with natural authority, looked up to by younger boys. Might have been elected Head Boy next term.*		JD

I fully endorse the above.

Signature of Head Master:

M Roberts

Mill Hill School
The Ridgeway
Mill Hill Village
NW London4th April 1939

To whom it may concern
Reference for: Dacre, Alan John

Dear Sir,

I have absolutely no hesitation in recommending this young man to you. Whilst he will be the first to admit that he will never make a real scholar, he has a number of other outstanding qualities.

He was an exceptionally gifted prefect who was respected by his peers and looked up to by the younger boys. He is an outstanding sportsman and captained both the First XV Rugby and the First XI Cricket team. He is a talented mountain climber and skier and is an excellent canoeist and sailor. In addition he has a natural talent for foreign languages. He is fluent in Italian, French and Spanish with some German.

Next term I am sure he would have been elected Head Boy, such was his popularity. He was also a keen and active supporter of the school's Cadet Force. It was highly likely that he would have gone up to either Oxford or Cambridge on a language/sporting blue.

I recommend Dacre AJ to you without reservation.

I remain, sir, your obedient servant etc.

M. Roberts, Head Master.

Chapter 2

The 12.30 p.m. train from London Victoria steamed slowly into the rundown station of the coastal town of Deal in Kent. This small seaside town was the alma mater of the Royal Marines. Here at the Depot, marines had departed fully trained to serve in the Royal Navy's fleets and on land around the world, defending the far flung outposts of the British Empire.

When the hustle and bustle of steam, passengers, whistles and flags had died away, there remained some twenty or so young men standing on the platform, each with a small suitcase or valise. They looked around, unsure of what to do or where to go. As the steam and smoke finally cleared Dacre AJ was the first to spot a Royal Marines corporal standing stiffly to attention with his pace stick under his right arm.

Dacre AJ nudged the lad next to him, 'Here we go.'

His companion looked up and simply replied, 'Aye.'

The corporal having quickly and efficiently organised the new recruits into two ranks led them off the platform and out of the station as speedily as he could. It was as if their shabby appearance had to be hidden from the curious eyes of the locals who, in reality, must have witnessed this charade dozens of times before. Following the JNCO, the group marched or rather straggled through the back lanes of the town towards the barracks. Clearly they were not smart enough to be seen by anyone, including other marines. At last they reached their destination. The corporal produced a large key to an old iron studded door set into a very high stone wall. As they passed through the gate in a single file it occurred to Dacre AJ that this was his point of no return. Once inside the group was directed to a small parade ground in front of the Globe Theatre. It was a smaller edition of the 'holy of holies', the main parade ground, which they were not to use until they could march like marines. Standing in the middle of the Theatre Parade was a marine drill sergeant waiting patiently. The corporal brought the group to a halt and turned them to face the sergeant.

'Good afternoon, gentlemen. I am Sergeant Derek Robinson and this is Corporal Richard Varley. Never ever address us as 'sarge' or 'corps'. We are going to be your squad instructors and we will be with you for the next six months. It is our job to turn you into proper Royal Marines. We will do this come rain or shine, with or without your co-operation. Dacre AJ thought that he sounded like the recruiting sergeant who had signed him up in Chatham, but then he supposed that all sergeants had that similarity, that firm authoritative no-nonsense voice, which was why they were sergeants. He then told them about their settling in period which would last until the squad was up to strength with another forty recruits.

The whole group was then marched to a nearby barber's shop where they lined up to await their turn to be shorn. An old service cap was placed on each head in turn and whatever hair showed was shaved off. Seeing what was left on the top of their heads, most of the young men had that removed as well.

Dacre AJ had had a haircut just a couple of days earlier. The barber looked at his hair and said to the corporal, 'There's nothing here to cut!'

Without bothering to look for himself, the corporal simply replied, 'Just cut his hair, George.'

The barber looked more closely and then said, 'I'm telling you, there is nothing here to cut!'

This time the corporal glared at the barber. 'Cut his damn hair, George, or get another job!'

Dacre AJ had his hair cut. He had also learnt another valuable lesson: you never argue with the squad corporal.

When everyone was ready, the group was marched to a communal shower block and heads. Here they were ordered to strip naked. Nobody appeared to be shy about their nakedness and soon everyone was under the hot showers, scrubbing each other's backs with a strong smelling carbolic soap. Clearly cleanliness was a high priority in the marines. They were then supplied with large white towels and told to get dressed again in their civilian clothes. From here the recruits were marched down a gravel path, out of sight of everyone, to the clothing store.

As they were marching along, the sergeant explained that the Depot was made up of four barracks. The East Barracks, towards which they were going, was originally built as a hospital but was used mostly by the quartermaster for stores. It was also where the tailors and the cobblers had their shops. The Royal Marines Band Service were quartered here also and made use of the available space for band practice. Then there were the North Barracks which was where they would live, eat and drill. The South Barracks which had once been used by the cavalry was where the officers and the sergeants had their messes, as well as a collection of offices. It also had the gymnasium and the playing fields with an assault course. Lastly there was the Infirmary which had a fully equipped hospital and a school. Most of the barracks were Napoleonic and over two hundred years old, although there had been some improvements over the years such as the recently added dining hall and galley.

At the clothing store the recruits entered ten at a time. Inside there was a long waist high counter, the top of which was covered in a grey linoleum worn through in places. Behind the counter stood ten elderly men, the stores assistants, dressed in long brown overall coats. Behind them were rows upon rows of shelving holding all manner of clothing and equipment. At the far end of the store stood the Quartermaster Sergeant, a big man with a big moustache and an even bigger stomach. He was holding a clipboard. In a well-practised manner he began reading out a list of clothing. As he did so the men behind the counter began taking items from the shelves to make a pile of kit in front of each of the recruits.

'Three pairs of socks (grey), three pairs of underpants and vests (white), three shirts (khaki) one with a separate collar. One ceremonial tunic, blue no. 2 uniform and trousers with red stripe, one blue serge uniform no. 3 and trousers, two blue and red service caps and one white cap cover for summer use only.'

The QMS paused briefly to draw a breath.

'You are lucky men because you are going to get the new battledress which has just been delivered as well as the new 'fore and aft' khaki cap. It is not to be called a forage cap!'

Dacre AJ looked at his neighbour and winked.

The QMS continued, 'One great coat army style, two pairs of denim fatigues, one Wolsey pattern white pith helmet with brass fittings.'

The pile of clothing in front of each recruit was getting larger and larger. The recruits looked at each in utter amazement.

'One tin mug, one set of knife, fork and spoon, one pair of braces, one corps belt, one white belt plus rifle sling and bayonet frog, all to be blancoed and brasses polished. Three cap badges, two sets of collar dogs and two sets of letters RM all to be cleaned and polished daily.'

The QMS paused for a breath. It was clear to everyone in the store that he was enjoying this, especially the shocked looks on the faces of the recruits. The old men behind the counter had seen it all before dozens of times. For them it had lost its novelty a long time ago.

He continued, 'One hussif, needles and thread for the use of darning, etc., one clasp knife and lanyard, two pairs of shoe brushes – one large, one small, one clothes brush for the use of, one button stick brass to keep the metal polish off your uniforms.'

The QMS paused again before the final lap.

'Two pairs of army parade boots for drill, one pair of ship's leather boots, one pair of shoes black, one pair of sandals navy type for the use of on HM ships. One pair of white pumps gymnasium, two pairs of shorts sporting, two rugby jerseys (one white and one blue). Three sheets white, two pillowcases, two towels and two pairs of pyjamas and one pair of white gloves ceremonial. One type block name, one large kit bag beige (navy model) and one kit bag small, army green.

That's it, gentlemen. See you all in three weeks' time when you will be issued your field equipment.'

Dacre AJ and the others just stared at the mountain of kit in front of them. Then they quickly packed everything into the two kit bags in order to allow those waiting outside to take their turn.

As they were moving out of the store Corporal Varley warned them, 'You are advised to keep a sharp eye on your kit. Any lost item will have to be replaced and you will have to pay for it.'

Once outside they were allowed to 'stand easy' and talk quietly. The lad next to Dacre AJ introduced himself as

Stuart McFee. He was from Glasgow. They shook hands. 'Just call me Jock'. His accent was as broad as his smile. Dacre AJ introduced himself.

'Was that you who nudged me at the railway station?' asked Jock.

Dacre AJ nodded.

'Aye I thought so. You're quite sharp aren't you? I mean you seem to have your wits about you. So what do you make of all this then?'

Dacre AJ thought for a moment or two before answering.

'I think it's going to be like a game. They know the rules and we don't. It's up to us to learn them quickly and then try to beat them at their own game.'

The Scotsman was silent for a moment or two.

'I like that idea and I like you. You've got a good head on your shoulders. If you are agreeable let's team up and play the buggers really hard.'

Dacre AJ readily agreed. He had taken an instant liking to this lad from over the border.

'This is going to be better than I expected,' said Jock.

By this time the other ten recruits had rejoined their comrades outside. The sergeant brought them all to attention and then said. 'If you require other things such as boot polish, metal polish, blanco (white and green), toothbrushes, tooth powder, etc., you can purchase them from the NAAFI shop when it opens this evening.'

Chapter 3

The twenty recruits were on parade facing the barrack block that was to become their home for the next six months. The time spent in the clothing store had been an interesting experience. They struggled back heavily laden, each of them carrying two kit-bags. However, no-one had complained which, thought Dacre AJ, was a good sign.

The sergeant began to allocate rooms by name. Dacre AJ and seven other lads found that theirs was on the very top floor. Picking up their kit bags once again, they trudged up the steep, stone stairway to the top of the building. On the way up the youngster noticed how worn down the stair treads were, he supposed by countless pairs of hobnail boots over the years, doing just what he was doing. The room they had been allocated was large, airy and light because of its high ceiling and its numerous windows. There were twenty iron-framed beds. Each bed had a thin mattress, one pillow, two blankets and a blue and white coverlet on which was emblazoned the Royal Naval insignia. Above each bed there was a shelf and some stout wooden hooks. Beside each bed was a large steel locker and in the centre of the room were some tables and chairs, together with several spittoons. At each end of the room there was a large pot bellied, black, cast iron stove, sitting in a white grate. By mutual agreement the men chose eight beds at the far end of the room. No sooner had they begun to unpack their kit when the door opened and in marched Corporal Varley.

'Gather round!' he ordered. He tapped the floor with his pace stick. 'This will be known as the deck and these are the bulkheads.' He pointed to the walls and the ceiling.

'Everything in this room will be washed, scrubbed and polished daily. Water can be found on the ground floor. If it stands still – clean it; if it moves – salute it! Understand?

'First I will show you how to make up your bed pack which you will do every morning, except Sundays. Then I will show you how to make your bed using hospital corners.

'Reveille is at 0630 hours each day except Sunday, when you can have a little lie-in until 0730. Church parade is at 0900 and it is for everyone except Romans and Jews.'

He paused and looked at them questioningly. Nobody responded.

'Now I will show you how to lay out your kit for inspections and lastly how to set up your lockers. Watch and learn!'

The well-practised demonstration lasted just twenty minutes.

'You will shower and shave every day without fail. You will be clean and smart at all times.

'The stoves may be lit only at the weekend. You will find coal and kindling downstairs in the courtyard. They will be cleaned and polished by 0700 hours each Monday morning.

'You will also take your turn at cleaning the showers, heads and stairways.

'Check the company noticeboard every-day for guard duties and the like and for the dress of the day. Your evening meal will be at 1800 hours.

'Tomorrow morning you will parade in fatigues at 0845 on the Theatre Parade and carrying what are going to be your best pair of boots. Now enjoy your first evening as Royal Marines.'

Without another word he turned and marched out of the room.

To say that everyone was slightly shell-shocked with all instructions they had received was an understatement. Dacre AJ decided to take the initiative.

'Come on everyone, since we are going to be room-mates for the next six months or so let's sit down and introduce ourselves.'

The eight of them sat down, all feeling slightly self-conscious. A silence descended on the room, no-one really wanting to go first.

The Scotsman was eventually the first to break the silence.

'Oh hell, I'll have a go. I'm Stuart McFee, but call me 'Jock'. I'm from the Gorbals in Glasgow. I'm twenty years old. I was born in 1919. I am six feet tall and I weigh about twelve stone. Before joining up I worked in the docks on Clydeside as a riveter's mate. My father was a drunkard and my mother was a whore!'

The group sat very quietly taking in what the Scotsman had said. One or two were shocked at his brutal honesty, others less so, but all respected this man baring his soul to a group of strangers. The man to his right went next.

'I'm David Edwards from Plymouth in Devon. You can call me 'Jan'. I am twenty-three years old. I was born in 1916. My father was a Royal Marine as was his father. I am six feet three inches tall and weigh thirteen stone. I'm not married but I have a girlfriend. Before enlisting I worked at Devonport Naval Base in the stores.'

The man sitting to his right introduced himself. 'My name is John Thomas. I know what you are all thinking.' Everyone laughed with him. 'My parents had no imagination. So call me 'Taffy'. I was born in Builth Wells in Wales in 1917. I'm twenty-two years old. I'm six feet two tall and weigh nearly thirteen stone. I'm not married and don't have a girlfriend. I worked on a hill farm and I am good with animals, especially dogs. Oh, and please, no jokes about sheep or Wellington boots because it might well be true!'

Everyone laughed again.

The next lad followed. 'I'm Peter Davis or just plain 'Pete' to you. I'm twenty-one and I was born in 1918. I am five foot ten in height and I weigh just eleven stone. I am not married but I do have a girlfriend back home. Before I joined up I worked down the pit as a coal miner, having left school at fourteen. I thought that there must be a better life than the one I had so I enlisted. Out of the frying pan into the fire I would say.'

Everyone laughed, several agreeing with him. It was noticeable that the atmosphere was changing: it was becoming more relaxed and friendly. They were beginning to enjoy finding out about each other.

'I'm Jack Samson. I answer to either Jack or 'Jacko', I don't mind which. I am twenty-seven years old. I was born in 1912. I am five feet ten inches and I weigh eleven stone. I am ex-army. I served four years with the Middlesex Regiment and saw service overseas in Palestine. I also did a bit of boxing in the army. I was married with two children but my wife ran off with another man and took the kids with her. I haven't seen them for nearly two years. I know quite a bit about routines in the army, so if I can be of any help at any time, just ask.'

Everyone said a 'thank-you'.

'My name is William, William Cann, but call me 'Bill'. I am twenty five years old. I was born in 1914. I am a direct transfer from the Royal Navy. I enlisted in 1936 and I trained as a stenographer, don't ask me why but it just seemed like a good idea at the time. I haven't been to sea. My three years was spent in HMS *Drake* which is a 'stonewall frigate'' or shore base to you land lubbers. My height is six foot one and I weigh twelve and a half stone. I am not married and don't have a girlfriend, yet! But I am looking, I am always looking!'

'My name is Brian Lloyd. I'm from Liverpool so you can call me 'Scouse', although I usually answer to 'hey you.' My father was Irish and my mother is English. I am unmarried. I am six feet tall and I weigh twelve and a half stone. For the past two years I have been training with the Army Reserves. So, like Jacko, I know a bit about soldiering which I am happy to share with you all.'

Dacre AJ was the last of the group to speak. 'My name is Alan John Dacre but I answer to AJ. It would seem that I am the baby of the group since I am only just seventeen. I am six foot one tall and weigh about twelve stone. I can speak several languages and I am quite good at sports and outdoor things like canoeing. I have joined up straight from school but I'm no scholar. I actually intended to join the navy but a very large bull-necked marine sergeant in the recruiting office persuaded me otherwise, so here I am.' The group joined him in laughing. 'I'm not married and I don't have a girlfriend. In fact,' (here he felt himself begin to blush) 'I have never been with a girl.'

This revelation was greeted by a shocked silence. His new-found friend, Jock, looked at him questioningly and with a frank directness asked, 'You're not one of those are you?'

It took Dacre AJ a couple of seconds to understand what his friend was implying.

'What? No! Of course not! I did go to boarding school I know but it's just that I have never had the opportunity.'

There was an audible sigh of relief from everyone. The Scotsman looked at his new friend with a mixture of fatherly concern and admiration.

'Well, my young friend', he said. 'When we get to go into town we must see what we can do about losing you your 'cherry'.'

To this all of the others clapped and cheered.

Bill Cann, the ex-sailor interrupted. 'When we go into town it is called 'going ashore', like it is in the navy.

Somebody in the group said, 'These marines have some strange traditions.'

'Whatever,' said Jock. 'As soon as we get to go ashore our first job is to get you sorted out, young AJ.'

At that moment a bugle call sounded from the parade ground. Everyone looked up. It was Jacko who explained it was the mess call for the evening meal, Come to the cookhouse door, boys, come to the cookhouse door.

'Time to go and don't forget to bring your eating irons with you,' he said.

The dining hall was large, very large. It seated nearly three hundred men on long tables with wooden benches on each side. At the far end was a counter where the cooks dished up the food onto tin trays. A section had been closed off for the corporals and trained soldiers. As the small group entered, the whole place went deadly quiet, all eyes turned towards them. They were clearly the new boys.

On the far side of the hall someone started to stamp his feet. Slowly, the stamping spread from table to table until everyone in the hall was beating out the time in perfect unison. The noise was deafening. Even one or two of the cooks could be seen banging their ladles in time. Then the noise just stopped as if somebody had suddenly turned off a switch.

Dacre AJ was suddenly aware that Sergeant Robinson was standing beside him, immaculate in his best blue uniform and peaked cap, his pace stick held firmly under his arm. He had not said a word or given a hint of a command. His sudden appearance had been enough to silence the three hundred pairs of boots. He turned and spoke, not unkindly, to the group.

'It's alright, lads. That was your welcome to the Depot. Next week you'll be doing the same thing to some other poor sods. Now go and get yourselves something to eat.'

The food was good, hot and plentiful. More than one of them went back for seconds. Some of the lads had never seen so much food in a week let alone for one meal.

After they had eaten their pudding, Dacre AJ decided he wanted a mug of tea from the nearby urn. As he went to get up, Jacko looked at the ex-sailor Bill and nodded. Both of them then firmly but without attracting any undue attention pushed Dacre AJ back down into his seat.

'That's not a good idea,' said Jacko quietly.

The Scotsman looked across the table with surprise, tinged with the start of anger that his new-found friend was being manhandled.

'Oh aye and why is that then?' he asked aggressively.

Jacko, Bill and Scouse all sniggered whilst the others looked on totally perplexed. Then they began to pretend to argue as to who should tell the rest of the group. Meanwhile Jock was getting more and more angry.

'For fuck's sake will you three stop your blathering and tell us what the hell is going on – for crying out loud!'

Jacko stopped laughing and put a mock serious expression on his face.

'They put something in the tea to stop us recruits from getting too horny. If you or any of us are planning to get some female company when we get shore leave then don't drink the tea, at least not from here.'

The Scotsman looked around the table at the others who had been stunned into total silence as the penny dropped.

'The wee buggers!' he said. 'My plans for you AJ were nearly fucked up, that's for sure. Well I never! Thank you, lads, for saving us from a fate worse than death!'

Everyone laughed.

'It's standard practice in all training establishments across the three services. They always say that they don't but everyone knows that they do,' said Scouse.

'So where can we get a safe cup of tea from?' asked Dacre AJ.

'The NAAFI should be alright', said Bill. 'We can get one on our way back to our room.'

Chapter 4

Chartwell, Kent. Winston Churchill sat behind a large mahogany table in his study which was next to his bedroom. He was still wearing his pyjamas and dressing gown. As was the custom amongst certain people of the upper classes, he and his wife Clementine had separate bedrooms. She was an early to bed and early riser sort of person whereas he was the opposite, often working well into the early hours of the morning. Last night had been no exception. His Chief Secretary, Mrs Violet Pearman, had been allowed to go home at 2.00 a.m. Churchill had telephoned for a taxi himself, had thanked her and wished her goodnight.

It was 10.00 a.m. Churchill had had his usual four hours' sleep in his large four poster bed and, on awakening, a good breakfast. Mrs Pearman sat quietly in her usual place at the corner of the table with her notepad and pen on her lap. She was bright eyed and alert considering her few hours of sleep.

On the opposite side of the table sat Anthony Eden. He was cultivated, good looking and extremely well dressed in a smart double breasted Savile Row suit. He sat crossed legged smoking one of Churchill's Turkish cigarettes. He might have preferred the more popular Virginian cigarettes but as Churchill couldn't abide them he wouldn't have them in the house. Eden was relaxed and at ease in the great man's presence and not at all overawed by him or his reputation. It was true that they were both outspoken on appeasement but they were not allies or even really friends. Whilst they often disagreed with each other, there was a sort of mutual respect. Eden felt flattered that Churchill had asked him to visit and had wanted his views on developments in Europe. Having recently resigned as Foreign Secretary he was, he considered, in a good position to advise this most senior of politicians.

Churchill's first cigar of the day, a Corona Coronas, was already alight, the smoke curling up towards a dirty brown-stained ceiling. Not a window in the room was open.

'Thank you very much, Anthony, for coming down to see me at such short notice. Whilst we do not agree on everything, I just want to say that I do value your opinion. As you may know I am shortly due to go to France to inspect the Maginot Line.'

Eden nodded his head; he had already heard the news.

Churchill continued. 'Well, like you, I am not happy about this whole business with Herr Hitler. I just don't trust him. I have been urging the government and Prime Minister Chamberlin to be more pro-active. Last year I suggested conscription but they chose to ignore me. It is only recently that a call-up has been started for men between twenty and twenty-one years. Better late than never I suppose. Now, Mr Chamberlin seems to be set on appeasement which neither of us has any time for. What I would like you to do is to remind me of how we got to this intolerable situation. I need to be fully informed before I go to France.'

Eden sat quietly for a good three or four minutes, thinking things through, sifting the facts and putting events into order. Churchill didn't seem to notice the delay. His cigar had gone out and since he never ever re-lit one, he reached for a fresh one.

'Well, Winston, as soon as Herr Hitler and his thugs came to power he made it very clear that Nazi Germany was going to be a world power. Once they had shrugged off the Treaty of Versailles they began re-arming. Of course we and the French did the same. However, the Germans were more organised and, therefore, were more effective. Most of our re-armament has focused on the navy and the air force, not the army. In fact I would go so far as to say that the British Army is totally unfit to fight a real war in Europe. For a long time our politicians and some officers at High Command have thought that if there were ever to be another war against Germany, then our contribution to such a war would consist of naval and air forces. How anyone ever thought that we could avoid sending our soldiers to fight alongside the French is beyond belief. Nevertheless, the fact is that we have had no large-scale battle exercises with troops. Indeed, I venture to suggest that the Army is actually unfit even to take part in any realistic exercises. They have an inadequate signals system, virtually no administration and no organisation for high command. In addition, vehicular transport is, in many cases, practically non-existent and civilian vehicles have to be hired or requisitioned. The lorries that they do have are old and often in need of repair. Infantry equipment is either poor or out-dated and, for the most part, we are still relying on World War One hand-me-downs.'

Churchill interrupted. 'How do you know all this, Anthony?'

'Like you, I make it my business to be well informed. I still have some contacts in the military who are not afraid to share their thoughts and concerns with me,' he replied.

Churchill sat silently for a several minutes, mulling over what Eden had said.

'I believe you and your friends are right and that we may well rue the day that we allowed our army to become so dysfunctional. As you know, I have my own concerns.

Indeed, I have mentioned them several times in the House. Please continue, Anthony.'

'Thank you. At present, German air strength is twice our number despite our best efforts. In the Far East, Japan is set on a policy of expansionism and at the moment its attention is on China. But who knows, it may well be the whole of the Far East. Despite heavy fighting they are now firmly established on the Chinese mainland.'

Churchill interrupted again. 'My views on the Japanese are similar to those I have of the Nazis: I just do not trust them! I believe the Americans need to be very watchful. It's a good job that we have 'fortress Singapore' as our base in the Far East. It is virtually impregnable. At least that will be safe!'

Eden nodded in agreement and continued. 'The conference in Brussels failed to stop the fighting, and now Japan and Germany have signed a non-aggression pact. It's only a gesture, I know. Our government wanted to send a fleet but Roosevelt felt that economic pressure was the way to stop Japan. Ironically the USA has almost no army to speak of, yet has a massive navy particularly in the Pacific.

'Of course the political situation in mainland Europe is constantly changing. Germany marched into Sudetenland and was welcomed with open arms by the German-speaking population. I supported Chamberlain in his efforts to preserve peace through reasonable concessions and I did not protest when Hitler re-occupied the Rhineland. I realise now that I may have been wrong about that. The agreement at Munich, however, is where the policy of appeasement came into its own and, which you and I agree, is a great mistake. The Prime Minister was determined to act first and to satisfy Herr Hitler's demands before he made them. So before we knew it, the German speaking areas of Czechoslovakia were handed over to Germany. Ostensibly there was an agreement between the four powers: France, Germany, Italy and Britain. However, it was a devil of a job to persuade the Czech government to yield to Hitler's demands and an even greater challenge to get France to agree to abandon their Czech allies. In the end they only yielded because of the threat of war which they were desperate to prevent. Then, of course, our Prime Minister came back with that piece of paper signed by Hitler which is being called 'peace in our time' and which I suspect will prove to be of little value.'

Winston Churchill interrupted yet again. 'Two things occur to me, Anthony, which I must share with you. Firstly, I was saddened when you felt that you had to resign as Foreign Secretary. I understand why you did and, in your place, I might well have done the same thing. However, like me, you are now outside the cabinet which I believe is a disadvantage both to you and the government and the people of Britain. Secondly, I completely agree with your assessment of Munich. However, Mr Chamberlain may well have bought us some much needed time in which to prepare for war because in my view war is inevitable. If that was really his intention then I think he may have been extremely clever.'

Eden thought about what Churchill had said before replying. 'You may well be correct, Winston, on both counts, only time will tell. Shall I continue with my assessment?'

Churchill nodded in agreement.

'With Czechoslovakia broken up, Herr Hitler has turned his attention to Poland. I think he expects a repeat performance. However, the Poles are determined to remain independent. Of course Germany is now increasingly seen as the aggressor and people are beginning to realise that they will have to be stopped.'

There was a knock at the study door and Churchill's valet, Sawyer, popped his head in. 'I am sorry to interrupt you, sir, but Mrs Churchill would like to see you when you have a convenient moment.'

'Do you know what it is about?' growled Churchill.

'Bills for the woodworm treatment, I believe, sir. Mrs Churchill is in the dining room.'

'Thank you. I'm sorry about this, Anthony, but when Clemmie calls I have to go, especially if it is about money and the house. Will you be staying for luncheon?'

'Thank you for the invitation, but no, I have to be back in town this afternoon for a meeting.'

'We'll meet again soon, if you are agreeable, so that you may continue with your discourse,' said Churchill.

'Most certainly, I would like that. I am at your disposal, Winston.'

Chapter 5

At precisely 0840 hours, Dacre AJ and the other recruits
assembled on the edge of the Theatre Parade, each of them
clutching a pair of boots. They had already learnt that a
good marine is always five minutes early. After a brief
inspection by Corporal Varley, they were marched across to
the cobbler's shop in East Barracks. The cobbler went to
some lengths to explain that their boots would have an
additional sole put on together with a fair number of steel
studs, all of which would have to be cleaned and polished.

'This is to help you march like proper Royal Marines,'
he said with a hint of a smile on his face.

The recruits spent the remainder of the forenoon back
in their barrack rooms stamping their names onto each
piece of clothing and kit. Once that was finished everything
had to be laid out on their beds in a prescribed manner for
their first kit inspection that afternoon. Each piece of
clothing had to be folded to a particular size and placed in a
specified position on the bed. Each piece of kit was also
allocated its proper place. At the foot of the bed boots and
shoes were neatly lined up, all spotlessly clean. Dacre AJ
began to wonder at the point of all this fussiness but then
realised it was all part of the game. Everything they were
told to do was all about testing their resolve whilst at the
same time instilling a sense of discipline, something they
were surely going to need in the future.

In the next bed space Jock was having difficulty getting his clothing and kit into straight lines. Dacre AJ could hear him cursing in his broad Scottish accent.

'What's up, Jock?' he asked.

'These buggers will no line up straight, no matter how hard I try. They are always crooked.'

He was right, they just didn't look straight. Dacre AJ studied the problem for a second or two.

'Give me the reel of cotton from your 'hussif' will you,' he said.

Taking the reel he tied two lengths of the twine to the top and bottom of the bed frame, just the right distance apart.

'There that should help. Now just make sure that you line up your clothing and kit against the two lines and everything should be nice and straight.'

Jock looked at this with a frown on his face. 'Are you sure that we need to do all this, you know, be quite so precise?

'No, to be truthful I'm not sure. But remember what I said about seeing everything as being part of the game. Just see it as part of the challenge.'

'Aye, I'm sure you're right. Many thanks! You know, AJ, you are quite a clever bugger for someone who is still a virgin.'

Dacre AJ flushed a little as he smiled at his friend's compliment.

After lunch, the eight recruits stood to attention by their beds as Corporal Varley went through each person's kit. Using his pace stick he prodded and pushed certain items around and in several instances he flicked a piece of clothing across the room, followed by a tin mug that clanged against a wall, which for some reason or other had offended his sensibilities. When it was the Scotsman's and

Dacre AJ's turn, he took ages scrutinising their carefully folded clothing in their very straight lines. His only comment was, 'Well, we might just make marines out of you yet!' With that he left.

The two of them looked at each other, burst out laughing and shook hands.

'First round to us I think,' said Jock.

'Maybe, but let us not count our chickens too soon,' Dacre AJ replied.

Over the next few days, the new recruits were mainly employed on fatigue duties, helping to keep the barracks spotlessly clean. At least one recruit was sent to paint the 'last post' much to everyone's amusement. They were all learning fast. It was during this time that the remainder of the squad arrived at the Depot, bringing the total up to fifty men. They were all allocated their regimental numbers. The recruits were divided into three groups. The first group were given numbers beginning with CH/X for Chatham, the second group were PLY/X for Plymouth and the third group were PO/X for Portsmouth. For the remainder of his career Dacre AJ would be known as CH/X 06821.

The following morning's parade was taken by Sergeant Robinson. It began with a blistering attack on how they stood to attention.

'In all my life I have never seen anything so pitiful, so abysmal, so terrible that it hurts my eyes. You're a bleeding disgrace! Now then, I am going to tell you this once and only once, and woe betide anyone who doesn't do what I say. Now stand up straight, stomachs in, chests out, shoulders back, heads up and chins in!'

He then proceeded to check the position and stature of every single man, pushing and pulling each one until he was perfectly satisfied. For most of the recruits it was agony being forced to stand in this most stylised position.

Muscles were aching or screaming in pain. One or two recruits began to twitch in an effort to relieve the pain but they received the sharp edge of the sergeant's tongue.

'Stand still in the ranks! If I see anyone move, I'll have you standing here for the whole forenoon!'

When he had finished his inspection he returned to the front of the squad.

'This is how you will always stand and also how you will march. We are not at home to Mr Slouch or Mr Slovenly, and you had best learn that and learn it bloody quickly if you want to stay in this man's army!'

He then stood the squad at ease and then easy, much to everyone's relief.

The sergeant then called Corporal Varley to the front of the squad. Using his pace stick he pointed to a small round badge on the corporal's right arm, just below the shoulder.

'This, gentlemen, is the 'King's Badge'. It was instigated by His Majesty King George V on a visit here to the Depot in 1918. He directed that the best all-round recruit in the Senior Squad should be awarded his cypher. He also directed that in the future all senior squads were to be known as 'The King's Squad'. Why am I am telling you all this? Because I am hoping that somewhere in these ranks in front of me somebody is going to rise to the challenge and become your 'Kings Badge Man', which will make me proud and you even prouder! We shall see?'

Back in their barrack room much of the conversation focused on the award of the King's Badge.

'I quite like the idea of going for this,' said Dacre AJ.

'Aye, so do I. It's got a nice sound to it don't you think?' said Jock.

'I expect Jacko and Scouse will have a go. Their knowledge of the army should give them a head start.'

'I should think so,' replied Jock. 'That just means you and I will have to work that much harder if we are to stand a chance.'

'So we are going to give this a go?'

'Aye, right enough! You and me together, and may the best man win!'

They shook hands on the agreement.

In the afternoon they were given their first and only lesson in how to clean their kit. Corporal Varley had gathered the recruits around the tables in the centre of the room. Here he showed them how to strip and blanco a white belt, rifle sling and bayonet frog. Then he showed them how to clean the brasses by burnishing them with metal cleaner and cardboard, and how the ornate buckle could be cleaned with an old toothbrush and how the intricate detail could be picked out with a pin. Next, they were shown the secret of how to re-assemble their belts so that no blanco or finger marks got on the newly shined brasses, and how to use the blade of a clasp knife in order to push the brasses up to the buckle.

Then came their boots. The corporal showed them how a heated spoon handle could be used to burn off all the pimples on the leather and then how to burn shoe polish on.

'There are,' he told them, 'No short cuts to good old fashioned 'spit and polish'.'

The toe caps, heels and uppers of the boot would all have to be worked on and take hours and hours of real persistence. The black paint of the lace holes was scraped off to reveal the brass underneath. These were then polished. The bootlaces were strips of square leather. These were always removed from the boot in order to be polished and when re-threaded must never be twisted. The underneath of the boot was also blackened and polished and each stud was cleaned using metal polish and a matchstick.

The whole process of cleaning kit was long and laborious. It seemed to have as much value as when they were told to strip and shine the tins of metal and shoe polish.

Dacre AJ and Jock kept themselves going by constantly reminding each other that everything was a challenge. 'Never give up, never surrender' became their mantra when things got really tough.

There were also lessons in how to keep their uniforms clean and smart. Certain tricks of the trade were passed on such as soaping the creases of trousers and jackets and then pressing them with a very hot iron and a damp cloth, taking care not to scorch the material. If the uniform was inadvertently scorched, they were told how to use a silver coin to remove the burn marks. The brass buttons on their blue uniforms and greatcoat, cap badges, collar dogs, letters RM, holding pins and gates all had to be polished every day without fail until they shone brightly.

They were now at the end of their third week and whilst things were not getting any easier most of the recruits found that they had got into the swing of things by applying certain little routines that made life a little bit more bearable. There were exceptions, of course, and more than one recruit found himself doubling around the Theatre Parade or doing extra drill or cleaning out the heads. Physical Training had been introduced which took place either in the gymnasium or in the drill shed. The instructors were relentless in developing those muscles that they never knew they really had.

One evening, when Dacre AJ and Jock were in the unusual position of having a bit of time to spare, they visited the wet canteen for a glass of beer. They got talking to an old soldier. His three long service badges on his sleeve and a row of medal ribbons all indicated that he had been in the marines for well over twenty years.

'You lot have got it easy,' he said. 'In my day, when I was a recruit, we had to wear boards strapped to our backs to make us stand up straight. I've seen grown men reduced to tears it was so bloody painful. Then there was the leather stocks that we had to wear around our necks as a punishment. That made us keep our heads up, I can tell you. That's where the term 'Bootneck' is supposed to come from. Our training really was tough, not like you lot have got it now. In those days marines really were marines. You were either a 'blue' marine or a 'red' marine, in other words Royal Marines Artillery or Royal Marines Light Infantry. No! You lot are too bloody soft for my liking. You'll not amount to much and that's for sure.'

With that he did up his top button, put on his cap and marched out into the night air.

Jock stared after him. 'Did you see that AJ?

'No! What?'

'On his sleeve he had a King's Badge. He must have been one of the first to receive that award. I wonder what made him stay in the ranks instead of going for promotion.'

Back in their barrack room Jock asked AJ the question that had been troubling him.

'Do you think that we have got it soft then?'

'No! Not really,' replied Dacre AJ. 'I think it's all relative. In another ten or twenty years' time I'm sure we'll be saying the same sort of thing.'

'Yeah, maybe. I'm not so sure,' said the Scotsman thoughtfully.

Several nights later Dacre AJ and Jock were sitting on their beds bullying up their boots. The other recruits in the room were equally busy, cleaning and polishing. For some reason or other Jock was in a black mood.

'Why the fuck are we doing this? If it's not our boots then it's our buttons and badges we're polishing. Then comes our white gear. And as for that bloody pith helmet I can never get the blanco even, it always seems to be streaky.'

Dacre AJ listened to his friend with sympathy. It was hard. They were often up way beyond midnight bullying and cleaning and it didn't really seem to get that much easier.

In the forenoons, the squad was continually drilling on the Theatre Parade, marching, marking time, turning about, saluting and so on. At first they were clumsy and awkward but gradually they began to get it together. They could step off together, their heels striking the ground as one, and they could halt without the embarrassment of colliding with each other.

In the afternoons, the squad would parade in a variety of uniforms to be inspected by a whole host of officers. First was the Company Commander followed by the Adjutant, then the barracks' Second in Command and finally the Commanding Officer. At each separate parade, the tailor would be there with his triangle of chalk marking the uniforms that needed modification according to the particular inspecting officer. These uniforms were then returned for alteration, after which they were re-inspected by that same officer. And so it went on, day after day, until everyone was satisfied that these recruits could actually dress and look like proper Royal Marines.

By now it was the beginning of the fourth week and once again they were marched across to East Barracks, to the store that issued the field equipment. This time it was a full set of green webbing, a belt, shoulder straps, ammunition pouches, plus back pack, bayonet frog, rifle sling, water bottle, gas mask, a pair of anklets, a waterproof cape, two mess tins (one large and one small), a steel helmet with netting and an entrenching tool with a webbing cover – a small collapsible spade which, they were informed, was for digging their own graves in some foreign land.

The QMS looked at the recruits steadily and then announced in a loud voice, 'All of this equipment will be blancoed green and the brass fittings will be polished until they shine. Make sure that you strip down and clean your water bottle stopper. They can go rusty and that means you could become ill by drinking unclean water. Then you will not be able to perform your duty which is to fight and kill the enemy!'

As they were marching back, Jock commented, 'More bloody gear to clean and polish, as if we haven't enough to do!'

Dacre AJ was smiling. 'Fight the good fight, Jock. Remember, it is all part of the game. Nil desperandum!'

'What the fuck does that mean?'

'It's Latin. It means 'never despair'. But I prefer the expression that one of my teachers told me which is 'don't let the buggers get you down'! Just see it as another challenge, Jock!'

'Oh aye! Another bloody challenge, he says!'

However, Corporal Varley ended their whispered conversation abruptly with, 'Silence in the ranks!'

Every day the drilling became more intense as each new manoeuvre was taught, practised and mastered. Dacre AJ and a couple of other recruits even perfected the idea of sleeping whilst marching. It wasn't that they were fully asleep, more that their eyes were closed and they were semi-conscious. It all went well until one day the squad changed direction whilst on the march and Dacre AJ found himself on the edge of the parade ground all by himself, much to the amusement of the rest of the squad. Even Sergeant Robinson had a chuckle to himself.

One afternoon a week the whole squad was marched across to the school house in the Infirmary Barracks where they had classes in arithmetic, English, corps history and map reading. This was to prepare them for the necessary educational tests and qualifications needed in order that they might move up the ranks with promotion, something that the Royal Marines prided itself on. Dacre AJ found it all pretty basic and tried not to show how boring it all was since his level of schooling was way beyond what was needed here. However, it was in the evenings that he came into his own. Almost half of his room-mates had only just completed their elementary education so he suddenly found himself in great demand, carefully explaining what they had learnt that day, going over and over it, again and again. Word of this spread to other rooms and, indeed, to some other squads, and before long he had a group of about twenty men all hanging on his every word. Somebody managed to scrounge a blackboard and some chalk in order to make things easier.

His friend Jock had been watching all this commotion with a great deal of admiration. One evening when class had finished he said to Dacre AJ, 'You know, AJ, you're good at this teaching thing. You should really think about taking a commission and transferring to the Royal Navy and becoming a 'schoolie'. I know you could do it.'

Dacre AJ was so surprised that at first he didn't know what to say.

'No, I don't think so. I don't mind helping out squad mates and even others. But doing it full time? Not on your life!'

Word of his success had even spread to the instructors with the result that one day Sergeant Robinson took him to one side and explained that if he ever wanted to go for a commission the sergeant would be more than happy to put his name forward.

Chapter 6

Chartwell, Kent. Winston Churchill stood by the window of his study looking down into the garden. He had redesigned much of the layout and with the aid of his two gardeners had begun to turn his plan into reality. Progress had been good and he was pleased with the results.

Anthony Eden who was sitting quietly by the large table, coughed gently.

'Shall I begin, Winston,' he asked. 'Only I see that your secretary isn't here.'

Churchill turned away from the window to face Eden, his face was clearly troubled.

'Mrs P has been taken ill and will not be joining us, so I am afraid that we shall have to proceed without her. Please continue when you are ready, Anthony.'

'As I mentioned the last time I was here, in recent months Britain and France found that there was very little that they could do to curb Germany's policy of expansionism. Indeed, at that time Mr Chamberlain saw Russia as the greater problem and that German expansion in the east might be a valuable barrier against communism. So Germany was encouraged as long as it took place in an orderly manner. Indeed, Lord Halifax took just such a message to Herr Hitler, that everything could be settled in Germany's favour as long as there were no far reaching disturbances.'

Churchill interrupted, 'So of course Herr Hitler and his Nazis just walked straight into Austria completely unopposed.'

Eden continued. 'Of course, part of our strategic problem is that the Prime Minister, together with the French Government, believe that the Maginot Line is so secure that they need not worry. Plus, of course, the French have the largest army in Europe. When you go on your visit, Winston, it is vital that you see for yourself just how secure this Line really is. For my part I think it may not be as secure as we have been led to believe. Added to this is the fact that Mr Chamberlain believes that we have similar protection afforded to us by the Royal Navy.'

Churchill nodded in agreement and growled, 'As for the Maginot Line, I suspect you may be correct. War, as we know it, has changed even in the short space of time since the last do! I will do my very best to find out what the situation there is really like.'

'Earlier this year, the Prime Minster visited Mussolini to see if he could patch things up, but to no avail. It was quite clear that Il Duce and his fascists were looking for a war.

Incidentally, Winston, did you know that Mr Chamberlain increasingly calls on the King both to advise and inform him of the international situation.'

'No I did not! But I am not surprised. Under the British Constitution the King has the right to be kept informed and to advise his prime minister. I hope his Majesty has made full use of that right and that Mr Chamberlain has listened to him.'

Eden drew a long breath and went on.

'This summer, the Government has been in talks with the Russians. Someone has at last realised that it is better to have them as allies rather than the enemy. However, quite sensibly the Poles want nothing to do with Russia. Their view is that once the Russians are in, even as allies, they will never get them out. The Russians even proposed a triple alliance between themselves, France and Britain. However our government was not in favour, so deadlock has resulted. Then just this week Ribbontrop flew to Moscow and agreed a non-aggression pact between Germany and Russia. You can imagine the outcry that has resulted.'

Churchill just shook his head as if in despair and let out a heartfelt sigh. He waved a hand for Eden to continue.

'Setting all this to one side for a moment it is worth clarifying the situation with regard to Poland. The British Government clearly fears German aggression in the west, maybe in Holland or, God forbid, even in France. Initially I was against strengthening her but I now realise it is inevitable. Talks have already taken place between Anglo-French staff but as yet nothing has been decided. Britain needs Poland for a possible second front should France be attacked and yet Mr Chamberlain is desperate to avoid war. So he is in a cleft stick situation. Herr Hitler, I think, expected that Britain and France would persuade Poland to give in, so he made no further demands. He just sat and waited. Since the British and French governments were so anxious to appease Hitler, they eventually agreed to his claims over Poland. However, the Poles refused to yield even an inch of their homeland and the two governments were, to say the least, embarrassed by their obstinacy. Mr Chamberlain realised that if they did abandon Poland then the Poles would either simply give in or fight to the end, albeit briefly, since they are no match for the might of the German war machine. So either way a possible second front would be lost. Eventually realising this, The Prime Minister, having ignored the advice of his Chiefs of Staff, actually wrote out a guarantee of support to Poland in his own hand. He gave this to Colonel Joseph Beck, the Polish Foreign Secretary, who accepted it most gratefully.

Churchill got up from his chair and began to pace about the room, back and forth, trying to take in everything that Anthony Eden had told him. He lit a cigar and then gave a chesty cough.

'Anthony! If you had a crystal ball to gaze into, how would you see things developing from here on?'

Eden reached over and helped himself to a Turkish cigarette from the elegant box on the table. He lit it with the Ronson table lighter and inhaled deeply. He paused before answering.

'I am almost certain that Herr Hitler will get tired of waiting and will invade Poland. Britain and France will have no option but to support the Poles and will therefore have to declare war on Germany.'

Churchill thought about this briefly. 'That is exactly my reading of the situation. How soon do you think it will be before we are at war?'

'Anytime now Winston, anytime now!' replied Eden.

'If that is the case then I hope that they can find some work both for you and me since they are going to need all the help that they can get!'

Churchill paused and lit another cigar.

'Will you stay for dinner, Anthony?'

'Thank you, Winston, I would like that.'

Churchill rang a small hand bell on the table. His valet appeared almost immediately.

'Ah Sawyers! Will you please tell cook that we have one extra for dinner this evening and please tell Mrs Churchill that Mr Eden will be joining us.'

'Yes, sir!'

With that the valet quietly left and closed the door.

'I always dress for dinner but you need not worry about that, you are fine as you are. It is a little tradition that I have. By the bye, perhaps it would be better if we did not discuss the current situation at table. I would not want to upset Clemmie!'

'I agree, Winston, better to talk about other things now. There will be more than enough time to talk about war later!'

Author's Note: Hitler had planned to attack Poland on the 26th August. However, on the 25th the Germans drew back because they were not fully ready. There followed six days of desperate negotiations, Britain still trying to get some concessions from the Poles. By the 31st August, Hitler would wait no longer and on the 1st September 1939 at 4.45pm he ordered the attack. There had been no ultimatum or declaration of war. Poland immediately appealed to her allies Britain and France. They sent a letter of protest to Berlin. Mussolini put forward the idea of dividing Poland up, in a way similar to that of Czechoslovakia. The French Foreign Minister Bonnet eagerly accepted this idea principally because France wasn't yet fully mobilised. Lord Halifax, the then British Foreign Secretary, also agreed. However, Parliament recognised the validity of the Prime Minister's hand written pledge and declared that it was a matter of honour to stand by the promise to Poland. It was clear by the 2nd September that the government would fall if war was not declared. Accordingly, the British Ambassador in Berlin presented an ultimatum to the Germans. After two hours there was no reply from them. On the 3rd September Britain and France declared war on Germany. Later that day Mr Chamberlain made his radio speech to the nation informing them that once again Britain was at war with Germany.

Chapter 7

This was the beginning of their fifth week of training. It was a bright sunny morning. The sky was cloudless and it promised to be a very warm day. Dacre AJ and his fellow recruits had been up since 0630 hours. Today was the squad's most important test in basic drill competency. Rig of the day was battledress, fore and aft hats, white belts and, of course, parade boots. Uniforms had been pressed and re-pressed, white belts had been blancoed and the brasses polished until they gleamed in the light. Their boots, whilst not yet fully up to the standard required which would take a lot more time and effort, still looked good. The recruits had checked each other over most carefully to make sure that no-one let the side down. They were going to be inspected by the most senior drill instructor, simply known as the First Drill. Hearts had sunk when the recruits had first heard this news. The First Drill had a fearsome reputation and was the terror of the parade ground. He had been known to fail squads time after time until he was perfectly satisfied that they could march as well as any Royal Marine. They were to be put through their paces by Sergeant Robinson in front of the First Drill and if, and this was a very big if, all went well they would be granted their first shore leave at the weekend.

On this occasion the squad was allowed for the first time onto the most 'holy of holies', the main parade ground. As the junior squad, they were to be positioned at the far end nearest to the dining hall, well out of the way of the more senior squads and in particular the King's Squad. They marched to the edge of the parade ground in pairs, their arms swinging in line with their shoulders. Once everyone had arrived Corporal Varley began organising them into their usual three ranks. There was a little bit of good natured pushing and shoving as they all tried to get a position next to Jacko, Scouse or Bill. The squad had quickly learnt that these three veterans, with their long service stripes, marksman badges and at least one medal ribbon between them, always attracted the attention of the inspecting officer or SNCO. They would always stop to find out where and when these men had gained their badges so that the person next to them was barely looked at. Today was no exception and by luck Dacre AJ found himself standing next to Scouse who, unlike the other two, had the long crossed rifle badge of a qualified sniper on his arm rather than that of a marksman.

The Commanding Officer was Colonel W.R. Philips RM and this was his parade. Both he and the other officers were perambulating up and down the pathway that ran along the edge of the parade ground behind the inspecting dais whilst the RSM formed up the parade. His mighty voice, echoing off the buildings behind him and which carried effortlessly across the parade ground, brought every one of the four hundred men present to attention, recruits, instructors and bandsmen alike. The RSM called for the markers to fall in. Immediately the right hand man of each formation sprang smartly to attention and, counting the correct pause, stepped off and marched the regulation paces to their front where they halted perfectly in line with each other. Sergeant Robinson and Corporal Varley were standing on either side of the squad. In stage whispers they offered their advice, 'Listen to the RSM. Balance on the balls of your feet. Remember, heels down hard.' An air of expectancy descended over the whole parade. Then without appearing to shout, the RSM gave the order for the parade to advance. As one, every man stepped off as each formation marched onto their markers and halted. Whether by luck or judgement everyone got it right. It was a most impressive display of drill and discipline of the highest order.

A bugler sounded the officer's call, who then marched to their designated position. The RSM reported to the CO that the parade was ready. He then ordered his officers to inspect their squads. As was his right, he would inspect the King's Squad. The First Drill marched across the parade ground to Dacre AJ's squad. Sergeant Robinson had already turned the squad to the left so that they were facing the dining hall and had put them at 'open order'.

The inspection seemed to take an inordinate amount of time. Several men were told to remove their belts so the inside could be checked for cleanliness, and more than one recruit was ordered to remove his hat so the brass holding pin of the cap badge could be checked that it had been polished. Boots were also carefully inspected both for twisted laces and that the underneath had been blackened and the studs polished. Eventually the inspection was completed and the First Drill surprisingly declared that he was satisfied. By this time the remainder of the parade had dispersed with the exception of the King's Squad who were practising for their passing out parade. Since they had seniority, Dacre AJ and his squad mates were marched into the drill shed, a massive hanger-like building located at the opposite end of the parade ground. The next hour and a half sped by as the squad was put through a routine of precision marching, counter marching, saluting, changing step, breaking into slow and then quick time and so on. All was going well, each man of the squad giving it his very best effort. One or two off-duty instructors had come out to watch and could be seen nodding their heads in appreciation of a good performance. At last they finished and Sergeant Robinson brought the squad to a halt in front of the First Drill. He looked them over carefully and actually smiled. Most of the recruits had sweat running down their faces and one or two were blowing hard, clearly out of breath but trying hard not to show it.

The First Drill spoke slowly and clearly, 'That is one of the best displays of drill I have seen in a long time and I do not say that lightly. I congratulate you and your instructors. Shore leave is granted for this weekend.'

If the squad had not been standing to attention they would have cheered out loud. As it was, they puffed out their chests with a tremendous sense of pride which was the best that they could do!

After 'stand easy' when they had had a chance to recover from earlier exertions, the squad was marched across to the armoury which was to be found in the South Barracks, and also known as the Cavalry Barracks. Here they were issued with their rifles and bayonets, each rifle number carefully recorded in a large ledger by the Storeman.

The squad was then divided into sections of ten men and handed over to the Platoon Weapons Instructors whose task it was to introduce the recruits to the finer points of their weapons. Dacre AJ and Jock found themselves in the same group. Their PWI Corporal took them into a nearby small classroom and told them to sit at ease on the benches. In front of them was a table covered in a grey field blanket on which lay a rifle and a bayonet. To one side stood an easel on which hung a diagram that showed the workings of the said rifle.

'Good morning, gentlemen. I am Corporal Ward your instructor and this is the Lee Enfield No.1 Mk III .303 bolt action rifle.'

He held it up for all to see.

'This rifle is going to become your best friend and may well save your life. It has an internal magazine of ten rounds. The muzzle velocity is 2,441 feet per second. The effective range of this weapon is 550 yards, aimed shot. The maximum range, however, is about 2000 yards but the best you can hope for at that distance, even allowing for wind and elevation, is that it will make the buggers keep their heads down. The weight of this wonderful piece of equipment is just 8lbs 8 oz. It is very reliable and extremely accurate. A good marine can fire twelve rounds per minute. In the butt plate is a small aperture for cleaning materials which is oil, a pull-through and a piece of four by two. However be warned! The firing mechanism is susceptible to dirt and grit. So when you are in the field make sure you cover the barrel with something. I suggest that a certain rubber protective, also known as a 'French letter', is as good as anything. Of course make sure that you take them off before you go on parade.'

Everyone laughed! The corporal then demonstrated how to load and fire the weapon, how to strip it down for cleaning purposes and how to check that the barrel was always kept clean. The latter was easily achieved by simply inserting the thumb into the breach so that the light reflected off the thumbnail. Lastly they were shown how to fix the eighteen inch sword bayonet, a fearsome weapon of stainless steel. Time was then spent practising what they had learnt until Corporal Ward was perfectly satisfied.

As soon as the squad had reassembled, Sergeant Robinson showed them the basics of how to slope arms. Once this was mastered, they were marched back across to the main barracks. It was lunchtime.

In the afternoon the squad began its introduction to drilling with rifles, as per the Royal Marines manual of instructions. By the end of the afternoon most of the recruits felt that their arms were ready to drop off. The rifle may have weighed only eight pounds or so but after three hours of drill it felt as if it weighed more like eighty pounds.

As they staggered back up the stairs to their room, Dacre AJ commented to Jock, 'This is not going to be as easy as I thought!'

'Aye, you're too right there. I have a feeling that this arms drill business is going to be a right bugger!'

That evening in the middle of what had become their ritual of cleaning and pressing uniforms, their barrack room door was thrown open and a head popped in.

'Come on, lads, downstairs! Another squad has got a 'crab' and have been told to get him clean. We are all going down to watch, should be fun!'

Dacre AJ and Jock looked at each other, mystified.

'What the hell is this all about?'

Several other lads were already leaving the room. Jacko stopped to explain.

'A 'crab' or 'crabby' person is someone who is either dirty themselves or cannot keep their kit or uniforms clean. You know how particular the marines are about cleanliness. It's almost like a religion to them. The usual treatment for a crab is a cold bath and a good scrubbing with cleaning powder by his squad mates. That usually does the trick but it can get out of hand if they are over enthusiastic.'

Dacre AJ and Jock decided to tag along, curious to see how this ritual worked. Having gone down the two floors, they made their way to the adjacent shower block.

The unfortunate recruit was already in a bath of full of cold water. His arms were held stoutly by two recruits as he struggled and twisted all over the place. His back and head were covered in the coarse, gritty, white cleaning powder, whilst others, using large floor scrubbers, were ferociously attacking his skin. Most of his back was already a raw pinkish colour and here and there were patches of red where blood was beginning to flow. The recipient of this harsh treatment was screaming his head off and clearly in some distress. The noise in the room was deafening, everyone jeering and shouting at once. No-one was taking any notice of the cries of the poor sod in the bath.

'I don't like the look of this,' shouted Dacre AJ to his friend.

'What? I can't hear you!' replied Jock.

'We need to stop this! Find Jacko and Scouse and the others. Get them to lend a hand!'

With that, he threw himself into the centre of the melee trying to establish some sort of order. Jock and the others, seeing what Dacre AJ was trying to do, dived in to help. Between them they managed to bring things to a halt. One or two punches were thrown and received but nothing too serious. Gradually things began to quieten down when people saw how determined Dacre AJ and his friends were. Several of those who had been doing the scrubbing actually dropped their brushes onto the floor when they recognised Dacre AJ from his evening lessons. They, in turn, began to urge their fellow squaddies to stop. The lad in the bath was carefully lifted out. He was in quite a bad way, shivering and whimpering. His back was a mass of abrasions. A large clean white towel was put around his shoulders, and within seconds blood started to ooze through. Dacre AJ was angry, angrier than he could ever remember. He stood up on a nearby chair.

'This is nothing but bloody bullying!' he shouted, 'If this man was a crab why the hell didn't you help him! That's what real marines do! We fucking well help each other!'

The shower room had gone perfectly quiet. He had everyone's attention. He glared at the upturned faces.

'You two!' he pointed at two recruits standing in front of him, 'Get this man down to the Sick Bay. Now! The rest of you get this shambles cleaned up and I mean marine clean! You make me want to vomit!'

With that Dacre AJ stormed out followed by his companions. Nobody said anything on the way back upstairs. Back in their room the adrenalin rush began to subside. Dacre AJ felt himself begin to shake. Jacko and Scouse came over to his bed space with a mug of hot sweet tea.

'Here, drink this, it will help,' said Jacko.

Dacre AJ looked up, tears were streaming down his face.

'Is it always like this?' he asked quietly.

'No not always, just sometimes. You never really know how you are going to react. Was this the first time you have had to get physical?'

The youngster nodded his head in reply.

'Well you did good! I don't know of many men who would have dived into that lot!'

With that he and Scouse went back to their own bed spaces.

'You okay?' asked Jock, 'Only you look a bit shaken if you know what I mean.'

Dacre AJ looked at his well-meaning friend and smiled. 'I'll be fine. It's just a bit of shock that's all. I'm alright really! Thanks for your help down there by the way, you and the others. I couldn't have managed it on my own.'

'Och, you don't need to thank us. We were only too pleased to lend a hand and to follow you into action, so to speak. You know, AJ, there are a lot of us who would be prepared to follow you if push came to shove. I don't know what it is about you. You just seem to have this natural ability to lead. You're a good kid, AJ, and make no mistakes about that.'

Dacre AJ never heard a thing. He was curled up on his bed, fast asleep.

The following morning after parade, Sergeant Robinson took Dacre AJ to be paraded in front of the Officer Commanding 'R' Company, Captain J. Lawton MC RM. Far from giving him a reprimand, which was half what he had expected, the OC did the exact opposite and congratulated him for his swift action the night before.

'You might like to know that your prompt action saved the lad from serious injury. As it is, he will be confined to the Sick Bay for at least two weeks. But he will, I am assured, make a full recovery.'

Obviously this was good news but Dacre AJ felt that he needed to explain that the situation wasn't just resolved by his efforts alone.

'It wasn't just me, sir! The rest of the lads in my room joined in to help. I really couldn't have done it without them.'

'Yes, well, all very commendable I am sure. But let me tell you that it was the recruits from the other squad that put your name forward as being the one who put a stop to their little shenanigans. So I think that speaks volumes, don't you?'

After Dacre AJ had been dismissed the OC had a quick word with Sergeant Robinson.

'I think you have got a good one there, Sergeant. A possible Kings Badge perhaps?'

'Oh, I couldn't possibly comment, sir, it's far too early to tell. But I have got my eye on him, you can be sure of that!'

Chapter 8

Friday night was going ashore night. This was the squad's first venture into the delights of Walmer and Deal. Rig of the day was 'blues' no. 3 dress, white belts, boots and a blue and red peaked cap. Everyone was freshly showered and shaved and looked immaculate. As they were going out of their barrack room door Jacko reminded them all that they would need to show the Guard Commander the necessary coins for a telephone call, a piece of string and a clean handkerchief.

'What's all that about?' asked Jock in all innocence.

Dacre AJ smiled at his friend and Jacko said, 'Go on AJ you tell him.'

'The coins are so you can call for an ambulance should you need to. The string is for a tourniquet in an emergency and the handkerchief can be used as a bandage. So with these things, plus of course your wallet, you can have a good run ashore and know that you are prepared for anything.'

Fixed to the wall outside the guardroom was a full length mirror. Above it a sign said 'Going Ashore Be Smart'. Automatically they all paused to check themselves before entering the guardroom where they lined up to be inspected. The Guard Commander was extremely thorough: belts, buttons and boots were all given a close and professional examination plus, of course, they had to show the three obligatory items. He looked them all up and down, and then warned them of some of the perils of shore leave.

'Do not forget that your shore leave expires at 2300 hours and not 2301 or 2302. If you are late you will go in the cells for the night. Do not come back either drunk or disorderly. If you do you will go into the cells for the night. Do not get into any fights with the locals. If you do you will go into the cells for the night. I hope that is clear to you all.'

The eight room-mates marched smartly down the street in pairs, laughing and joking. Tonight they felt as if they were 'kings of the world'. Without any hesitation, they made their way to the Admiral Nelson public house on the Strand, the oldest pub in the town. It overlooked the Walmer Green and the beach beyond. This local public house was, they had been told, the place where many recruits gathered to have a beer or two and to possibly find a local girlfriend. They were, of course, at a slight disadvantage since the more senior recruits were well established. However, the local lassies were always on the lookout for 'fresh blood'. After half an hour or so, and a couple of pints of Shepherd Neame bitter, Jock appeared with his arms around two of the prettiest girls that Dacre AJ had ever seen, one was a brunette, the other a redhead.

'This is Joan and this is Dorothy. They have agreed to be our companions for the rest of the evening,' said the Scotsman.

It was quite clear to Dacre AJ that his well-intentioned friend was setting him up with Joan. Looking around the bar he noticed that the remainder of his room-mates were watching him most closely. They raised their glasses in a mock salute whilst giving him a knowing wink. After an hour or so of very pleasant company and small talk, Dacre AJ realised that Joan, the brunette, was a young lady who not only knew a thing or two about life but that she was only too willing to teach him the joys of living. Making their excuses, they made to leave the pub.

At the door Scouse thrust a small round package into his hand.

'You might need this!' he said.

Holding hands, Dacre AJ and Joan walked across the road and headed towards the beach. The youngster noticed two Royal Marines Provosts, distinctive in their blue uniforms and white cross straps, who were patrolling along the pavement, swinging their night sticks as they went. One of them looked in his direction, smiled and waved his night-stick in something akin to a salute to a fellow 'Royal' who had clearly struck lucky.

On the beach at Walmer there were a number of fishing boats pulled up on the steep shingle bank, well above the high tide line. There were also a number of fishermens' huts, mostly used for storing nets and crab pots and the like. It was quiet and dark, with just the sound of the waves breaking gently on the shingle. Joan stopped at one of the huts and, producing a key, opened the door and pulled Dacre AJ inside. Without saying a word, she gently removed his hat and undid his belt. These she laid carefully to one side. The whole place smelt of stale fish, tar and old ropes. Joan sat herself on the edge of a convenient but rickety table and pulling him towards her she unbuttoned his jacket. Putting her arms inside she clasped them behind his back and drew him even closer. They kissed. Her lips were as soft as he had imagined. Her tongue flickered gently against his teeth, parting them with long searching probes. Dacre AJ was fully aroused and he knew that she knew. He was more than a little nervous. He felt clumsy and unsure of himself since this was his first experience with the opposite sex. He need not have worried, Joan had everything under control. Ten, very intimate minutes later it was all over. For a long time they stayed locked together and, as their breathing returned to normal, they made themselves look presentable. Holding hands they retraced their steps to the main road. Dacre AJ offered to walk her home but she told him it wasn't necessary since she lived just around the corner.

Having arranged to meet the following evening, they kissed briefly and went their separate ways.

On his way back to the barracks Dacre AJ supposed that for Joan he had been another conquest but he hoped not just any conquest. For him it had been a momentous event: he was no longer a virgin. Walking through the guardroom gates he imagined that everyone could tell what he had been up to. When he got back to his room everyone was turned in and asleep, except for his friend who was sitting up in bed smoking a cigarette, something most unusual for him to do.

'Go alright did it?' he asked quietly in his broad Scots accent.

'What do you think? Of course it did! I can't begin to describe what it was like.'

'Aye, well don't! I said I would get you sorted and I have, so that is all good then.' There was a very long pause.

'Do you know who she is?'

'No, we didn't talk much.'

'No, I suppose not! Look AJ there is no easy way to say this. She is the First Drill's daughter!'

Dacre AJ felt himself go giddy. He wanted to be sick as the enormity of the situation filtered into his befuddled and love-struck brain.

'Dear Lord almighty! What have I done? And your girl, the other one, Dorothy?'

'She is the daughter of the RSM. Apparently they live here in the barracks in married quarters with their parents. They have quite a reputation, in a nice sort of way, of making new lads feel welcome and wanted.'

'Yes, well they've certainly done that! We've planned to meet up again tomorrow night. You?'

'Oh Aye, I think so. You don't look a gift horse in the mouth, do you?'

'We shall have to be careful, bloody careful. If their fathers ever find out they will probably kill us!'

'Too right, AJ. Still it's turning out to be good fun, this being a Royal Marine. I'll wish you a good night then and sweet dreams!'

Chapter 9

No.10 Downing Street, London. Winston Churchill sat in one of the anterooms. He was waiting. The wireless set was switched on and he was listening to the British Broadcasting Corporation's Home Service. By his elbow on a small reception table stood a cup of tea which had gone cold and half a glass of his favourite brandy. He had just lit his first cigar of the day. It was Sunday the third of September. The time was nearly 11.15 a.m. Churchill was waiting to hear the Prime Minister's speech to the nation. The Home Service programme was interrupted and a dull, monotonous voice entered the room.

'I am speaking to you from the Cabinet Room at 10 Downing Street. This morning the British Ambassador in Berlin handed the German Government a final note stating that unless we heard from them by eleven o'clock that they were prepared to withdraw their troops from Poland, a state of war would exist between us. I have to tell you now that no such undertaking has been received, and that consequently this country is at war with Germany.'

Churchill got up from his seat and switched off the wireless set. He had heard enough. He drained the last of his brandy and began pacing up and down the room, deep in thought. Twenty minutes later the door opened and Mr Chamberlain's Assistant Private Secretary, John Colville, entered.

'Mr Churchill, the Prime minister will see you now, sir.'

In the Cabinet Room Neville Chamberlain stood up to greet his guest. They shook hands.

'Thank you for coming to see me, Winston. You were listening to the broadcast? How do you think it went?'

'Yes I was listening Prime Minister and I believe that I could not have done any better myself.'

Chamberlain looked steadily at Churchill trying to ascertain if this was just flattery. He decided it was not.

'Praise from Caesar I believe.'

'No, Prime Minister, honesty. I believe now is the time for nothing but honesty.'

'Yes, quite. I take your point. Look, Winston, it is well known that you and I haven't always seen eye to eye over certain issues such as appeasement. However, I want to put that all behind us, because the reason I have asked you here is to offer you the post of First Lord of the Admiralty. I consider that you are the right man for the job and I urge you to accept the appointment.'

Churchill paused briefly before answering, a real sparkle lit up his eyes.

'It would be my honour to serve in your War Cabinet, Prime Minister,' he answered.

'Good! Thank you, Winston. I knew that I could count on your co-operation. I have also appointed Lord Hankay as Minister without Portfolio. I hope the two of you will give the cabinet a little more balance. Do you know the other members?'

'One or two, Prime Minister, are known to me personally, the others only by reputation.'

'I see. Well there will be a meeting here this evening at 6.00 p.m. so I shall be able to introduce you to everyone. I have also asked the three service chiefs to attend and the Commander in Chief of the BEF.

'Thank you. I will most certainly be there.'

***

Top Priority Signal

Dated: 03.09.39.

Time: 1400hrs.

Origin: Admiralty Building

To: All HM Ships, Shore Bases and RM establishments.

Signal reads: 'Winston is back!'

End of message.

***

At precisely 6.00 p.m. Neville Chamberlain called to order his first real war-time meeting. He looked around the long table in the Cabinet Room and as he did so he realised that the men gathered here were going to have high expectations of his leadership. Recently he had had some nagging doubts about his own abilities which were exasperated by his constant tiredness and the feeling of being unwell. He pushed these thoughts to one side – time to get on with the business of the meeting.

Very quickly he went around the table and introduced all those present. To his right was Sir Samuel Hoare the Lord Privy Seal. Next to him was the Chancellor of the Exchequer, Sir John Simon. Then came Lord Halifax, the Foreign Secretary, followed by the Secretary of State for

War, Leslie Hore-Belisha. After him came Churchill and finally Lord Hankey. The Cabinet members greeted each other cordially enough which was clearly what the Prime Minister had wanted. Next, Chamberlain welcomed the three service chiefs: Air Chief Marshall, Sir Cyril Newall, then the Admiral of the Fleet, Sir Dudley Pound, followed by General Sir Edmund Ironside. His final introduction was to be the key man for the moment, the Commander in Chief of the British Expeditionary Force to France, Lord Gort.

The discussions of the War Cabinet went on long into the night. Their main preoccupation was, of course, focussed on the movement of the BEF across the Channel, which was due to start the following day. Lord Gort went into considerable detail to explain how difficult it was going to be to move over four hundred thousand men plus their equipment and vehicles over that narrow stretch of water. However, he was confident that if everyone pulled their weight the transfer could be achieved eventually. Nevertheless, he hesitated to give a specific end date and would not be drawn on the subject. He did, however, emphasise that in his opinion the key to success lay in detailed planning. Consequently, a considerable amount of time was spent thrashing out the logistics and time tables for the movement of troops. In addition, Lord Gort also pointed out that he had serious reservations about the Allied Forces being put under the command of the French and, in particular, General Weygand whom he felt was not up to the task. Unfortunately this left very little time to discuss and plan other important decisions to be made such as a proposed leaflet raid on Germany by the RAF, the issue of gas masks to all adults (children already had theirs) or the evacuation of children and pets from likely target areas such as London, the Midlands and the coastal cities and towns. Neither did they have time to consider the issue of identity cards or the construction of air raid shelters. The list of things to do seemed to be endless: so much to do and so little time to do it in.

Winston felt a certain sense of disappointment with how the meeting had progressed. Many of his Cabinet colleagues had ventured opinions on military matters of which they clearly had little knowledge. On the other hand the chiefs of staff had not confined their comments to purely military matters as they should have done. It was, Churchill felt, all rather frustrating. If, in the future, he had anything to do with the organisation of such meetings, things would have to change, and change quickly if they were to win the war.

Chapter 10

The fact that England was once again at war with Germany spread like wildfire around the barracks. Those men who had been in the NAAFI or the wet canteen had heard the broadcast on the wireless directly, as had those living at home or in the Sergeants' or Officers' Mess. However, for the majority the news had come by word of mouth.

'It will all be over by Christmas' was a comment circulating on the grapevine.

'What do think AJ?' asked Jock when they heard the news.

'I very much doubt it. Didn't they say that about the last one, you know, the war to end all wars? And look what happened there!'

'Aye, I suppose you're right. Well at least we'll get a chance to have ago at the Hun as soon as we finish our training.'

'I agree. But just remember the main priority for the Marines at the moment is to service the fleets from the three divisions of Chatham, Portsmouth and Plymouth. So, unless things change, any fighting we do is likely to be on ships of the Royal Navy.'

'Not really what I had in mind, but I suppose beggars can't be choosers!'

News that the SS *Athena*, a ship bound for Canada with eleven hundred passengers many of whom were women and children, had been sunk by a German submarine only served to make the occupants of the barracks feel as if they had been personally violated. Tempers were running high amongst instructors and recruits alike, so much so that hardly anyone had noticed that of the one hundred and eighteen dead most of the deaths had actually been caused by one of the rescue vessels. If that wasn't enough, London had received its first air raid of the war. German bombers had flown across the North Sea and followed the River Thames up to the designated targets. These had been the Woolwich Arsenal and the surrounding docks. However, many of the bombs had missed their target and had fallen on the overcrowded housing of the east end of London.

Despite the distressing news from the outside world, things were still not going well for the squad. For some unaccountable reason the transition from marching drill, at which they had originally excelled, to arms drill was proving to be a disaster. The next three weeks turned out to be almost like a living hell. Initially, their two drill instructors had been patient. They had tried through a variety of means to cajole the squad into getting the complicated rifle drills correct. All the countless precision movements required unbelievable manual dexterity from each recruit. The squad had managed some of the basics, mostly those done at the halt such as saluting, presenting arms and reversing on your arms. Even fixing bayonets at the halt went reasonably well. True, one or two men dropped their bayonets onto the parade ground because they weren't properly fixed but compared to how they performed, or rather didn't perform when they were marching, it was a whole different story. Changing arms on the march and moving from the slope arms to the trail they managed to achieve with constant practice. However, when fixing bayonets on the march, something the Royal Marines specialised in, it ended up looking like a war zone with bayonets scattered all over the place. If that wasn't enough, several members of the squad were actually stabbed by the person behind them, thankfully not too seriously. One day when drilling with white gloves on, two of the squad actually managed to hook their gloves onto the ends of their bayonets. They remained there like pennants, flapping in the wind until the manoeuvre was completed.

By now the squad instructors' patience had run out and they began to apply the more traditional punishments. At first it was an hour's extra drill for everyone. Individual transgressors were sent doubling around the edge of the parade ground with their rifles held high above their heads. When that didn't seem to work, the whole squad was assembled in battledress with greatcoats and full battle order equipment. Packs and ammunition pouches were filled with sand and bricks. An hour or more of such drilling began to sort the men from the boys. It was almost unbearable. Several of the squad collapsed on the parade ground, only to be dragged back onto their feet by some of the others, their highly polished boots becoming seriously damaged. During one such session they were even ordered to put on their gas masks. The agony of drilling dressed like that was totally unbelievable. There was not one person in the squad who felt that he could take much more. They were getting dangerously close to the edge of despair. Their iron willpower and sense of discipline was being tested to the full. One morning, just for a variation in their punishment, the squad was doubled down to the shingle beach on the waterfront. Here, they were drilled for two hours, up and down the beach, in and out of the sea, their heavy studded boots sinking into the shingle. Then, dripping wet, they would drag each other back onto their feet in order to try to keep going. It was totally exhausting and by far the worst punishment they had ever received.

That evening, as they were cleaning their kit, Dacre AJ and his room-mates had a discussion about the situation.

'I don't know about you chaps but I am pretty close to the end of my tether with all this punishment. I think we need to do something about it and soon,' he said.

Everyone agreed.

'Have you got any ideas?' asked Scouse.

'Not really, except to say that we are collectively at fault with the exception perhaps of you and Jacko. You two have some experience whereas the rest of us are hopeless.

Jacko interrupted. 'No you're not hopeless! Your ordinary drill is fine, even better than fine, it is good. The First Drill said so and he should know. What seems to be happening is that you just can't put the two things together. It's as if you all need personal tuition.'

Everyone lapsed into a silence. Suddenly Jock's face lit up with an idea.

'Here's a suggestion, then. You all know how AJ gave extra lessons in the evenings. So, why don't Jacko and Scouse give us extra arms drill, here in our room. We can clear the tables and chairs out of the way. That should give us enough space.'

'That's a great idea,' said Dacre AJ. 'What do you think Jacko? Scouse?'

'It could work,' they both agreed.

AJ looked around the room trying to gauge the level of enthusiasm. They were all grinning like school children at the start of a holiday.

'So let's call a meeting of the whole squad and put the proposition to them. It will, of course, need a hundred per cent participation, but I suppose anything will be better than that bloody shingle again!'

'You never know, we might be able to make use of the drill shed on a Sunday,' replied Jacko.

'Now wouldn't that be something? A squad doing extra drill voluntarily,' said Jock with a huge grin on his face.

The squad's ability to absorb punishment had become something of a talking point amongst the other recruit squads and even amongst the cadre of instructors. However, the following morning they were told to parade outside the gymnasium in shorts and plimsolls for a completely different form of punishing exercise. They were immediately paired off with whoever was standing next to them. No account was taken of height or weight. Dacre AJ was paired with a lad from another room who was considerably taller, heavier and older than he was.

'Do you know what this is all about?' whispered Jacko.

Dacre AJ shook his head.

'It's a form of boxing known as 'windmilling,' he explained. You just get in the ring and hammer away at each other for about three minutes. The instructors and the officers will be assessing each of us as to our level of aggression. So when it's your turn, give it all you've got.'

It was Dacre AJ's turn in the ring. As the ten ounce gloves were fitted by the PTI, he noticed all the instructors and officers sitting ringside. The bell went. Dacre AJ actually ran towards his opponent who was a little slow out of his corner on the opposite side of the ring. His stance suggested that he had boxed before. The youngster never gave him a chance. Arms flailing like a machine, he smashed his fists into his opponent's head and body. Surprised by the ferocity of the attack, the other recruit backed off and tried to defend himself as best he could. One or two of his punches did get through. Dacre AJ was given a bloody nose and a cut lip. His eyes were watering so much that he could barely see the other man. Undaunted, he chased his opponent around the ring and continued to bombard him with all his might. Eventually it proved to be too much for the other recruit who went down onto one knee. He had had enough! The PTI stopped the fight and ushered both men to their respective corners. The round had lasted just two minutes and thirty seconds. The other lad was brought across to shake hands, as was the tradition, since the match was nothing personal.

'Bloody hell, AJ! Remind me never to upset you when we go ashore. You nearly half killed me. Anyway, well done!'

Bloodied but victorious, Dacre AJ went and rejoined the rest of his room-mates who all congratulated him on his success.

Jacko was the next in the ring. He amazed everyone – recruits, instructors and officers alike – by giving a first class exhibition of how to box correctly, even against someone who was windmilling. His opponent never even landed a single blow. At the end of just two minutes the fight was stopped. The other man had taken enough punishment.

When Jacko returned to his companions the Scotsman said in his broad accent, 'Aye so you can box a wee bit then?'

Jacko nodded and replied modestly, 'Just a little!'

At that moment the PTI came across to the group.

'Alright Jackson! It is clear to everyone that you are no novice in the ring. So what is your background in the noble art?'

'I was the Army Middleweight Champion in the Middle East, Colour Sergeant,' he replied.

'I thought it must have been something like that. You're good, very good. How do you feel about boxing for the Depot in the next Corps Championship?'

'I'd like that,' Jacko replied. 'Can I bring my supporters with me?'

The PTI looked the small group over. 'Well I can't promise anything but I'll see what I can do.'

Then he looked at Dacre AJ.

'We might be able to do something with you as well. No style, no experience but, by heck lad, you've got some aggression in you. You could well be our novice entry.'

With that he turned and left.

Chapter 11

It was a Wednesday. This was the day each week that the Adjutant oversaw the main parade. Captain G.D. Thompson RM sat quietly on his horse, some sixteen hands high and beautifully groomed. He surveyed the squads of marines that were lined up in front of him. It had never ceased to amaze him that the tried and tested method of training a more or less hapless civilian, or should that have been a hopeless civilian, into a disciplined marine of the highest order worked so well. What he saw before him was, he felt, a testimony to that process and to the Corps, his Corps.

He had decided to inspect the recruit squad that many of the instructors were talking about because of its ability to absorb so much punishment. He wanted to see for himself what had made it so special. Leaving the RSM to organise the rest of the parade, he rode his horse slowly across the parade ground to where Sergeant Robinson had already put the squad at extended open order. The extra distance was necessary in order to allow the officer and his horse to move between the three ranks. Dacre AJ and most of his room-mates were in the centre rank so had a good view of what was going on. As the Adjutant and his horse approached the front rank the animal became skittish and began siding dangerously towards the recruits. Not wishing to be stepped on or to be bumped by the large rear end of the horse, the line of men began to inch themselves backwards out of the way. They rather resembled reeds, swaying gently in a wind.

Captain Thompson, seeing this, became extremely cross and shouted in a high pitched voice, 'You there, stand fast! Don't you dare move! My horse won't hurt you!' Then, as an afterthought added, 'Sergeant Robinson, take the name of any man who dares to move.'

The horse and its rider moved into the second rank. The horse was calmer now and stood patiently whilst the Adjutant closely examined the recruits in front of him, looking them up and down. Suddenly he stood up in his stirrups. The horse began to relieve itself, first urine and then dung falling to the ground, splashing over the boots and trousers of Dacre AJ and his friends. Nobody moved a muscle. They stood like statues, eyes firmly fixed to the front, not even a blink of the eye.

Captain Thompson was impressed and congratulated them.

'Well done men! That is what I like to see, real discipline! Thank you Sergeant Robinson, I have seen enough, you have a good squad here. Carry on please!'

With that he rode back to the centre of the parade. The recruits sighed with relief. The smell was pretty grim.

A comedian in the rear rank said out loud, 'We thank you kindly, sir, for your approval and for your shit!'

Sergeant Robinson chose to ignore the comment although those that could see him swore he had a smile on his face.

This was also the day for the monthly march through the town. With the Band of the Royal Marines in the front playing A Life on the Ocean Wave, the parade moved off in columns of three with the Adjutant at the head of the procession. It was a fine and stirring sight: four hundred men marching in step as one.

The band then struck up a different tune, the well-known Blaze Away. Sergeant Robinson happened to be marching alongside Dacre AJ, his pace stick held firmly under his right arm. The sergeant was clearly enjoying himself. As they marched along, the youngster could hear the SNCO singing quietly to himself perfectly in time with the music, 'Aint it a pity she's only one titty to feed the baby on'. It was all Dacre AJ could do not to burst out laughing. Sergeant Robinson looked at him out of the corner of his eye.

'Don't you bloody dare!' he whispered in an aside. It was a shared moment and one that the youngster would always remember.

An hour later the squad were back on the parade ground pounding up and down with yet more arms drill. When it came to fixing bayonets on the march both Sergeant Robinson and Corporal Varley were pleasantly surprised. Only one bayonet was dropped onto the ground and no-one was stabbed in the back. When the manoeuvre was repeated for a second and then a third time, there were no bayonets left lying behind. The sergeant brought the squad to a halt. He spoke to them in an almost avuncular manner.

'Well I must say this is a most pleasant surprise. Well done! I have to say that we didn't think you were going to make it, did we, Corporal Varley?'

'No, Sergeant! They have clearly proved us wrong. As fine a piece of arms drill that I have ever seen.'

'I'm not going to ask you how you achieved this amazing transformation, that's your business. It's sufficient to say that I am proud of you all!'

Every man in the squad felt really chuffed. The extra hours of arms drill in their rooms had clearly paid off.

Dacre AJ and his room-mates were, as usual, hard at work cleaning and polishing their boots and equipment. It was 2015 hours when suddenly the barrack room door was thrown open and in walked Sergeant Robinson accompanied by the PTI Colour Sergeant. Everyone leapt to a position of attention, cleaning cloths and tins of polish went scattering across the highly polished deck. The two SNCOs stood still for a moment impressed by the response of the recruits.

'At ease,' said the Sergeant. 'Colour Sergeant Hughes here wants to talk to you all. George?'

'Right then, lads. You, Recruit Jackson, and you, Recruit Dacre, have been selected to box for the Depot RM next weekend in the Corps Tournament. This will take place down in Eastney Barracks at Portsmouth. The rest of this room will be allowed to travel with you. I have arranged for everyone to have a weekend pass. Your squad instructor has agreed that you two may be excused your afternoon activities next week in order to join my fitness training programme. So, starting on Monday next, you two will report to the gymnasium at 1400 hours. Next Saturday forenoon, early, we will all travel down to Eastney by vehicle. The tournament starts in the afternoon with the finals in the evening. We will stay overnight and return on the Sunday. Each of you will bring an overnight bag with your essentials. Because we're going to Eastney Barracks, the home of sea-going marines, dress of the day will be blues no.3 with white belts and peaked caps. Make sure you are clean and smartly turned out. Any questions?'

Dacre AJ put up his hand. 'How many will there be in the boxing team, Colour Sergeant?' he asked.

'Six! There is one other recruit from a more senior squad plus one trained soldier and two corporals. You will all be training together for the week. Anything else?'

No-one answered.

'Right then, we'll let you get on with your cleaning,' said Sergeant Robinson.

Both SNCOs did a smart about turn and marched out of the room. Just as everyone breathed a sigh of relief, the door was reopened and the sergeant stuck his head back in.

'Oh, and in case you are wondering, I do not expect any of my high standards to slip from any of you, but especially not you Jackson or you Dacre – is that quite clear!'

With that he was gone.

'Well!' said Jock, 'I was going to say that they almost sounded human but now I'm not so sure. You two have really got your work cut out, make no mistakes about that! Still, a weekend off sounds pretty good to me. No bull and no church parade. What more could a recruit ask for?'

Chapter 12

The following week the squad spent their time preparing for the 'in the field' part of their training. This entailed weapon handling and training in the forenoons and route marches in the afternoons. In addition, there was the drawing of additional equipment and supplies for their extended absence from the barracks which all had to be checked and cleaned.

It was Monday afternoon. Dacre AJ and Jacko reported to the gymnasium as instructed. They were both wearing their rugby shirts and shorts. The two of them were briefly introduced to the other four members of the boxing team. Then, under the watchful eye of senior PTI Colour Sergeant Hughes, the team was put through its paces by half a dozen overenthusiastic corporal instructors. Their method of training was to shout loudly and to demand an even greater effort. Rank had no privileges. Each member of the team was put through the same hell. The exercises in the main consisted of running, jumping, skipping and lifting weights. These sessions were interrupted with bouts in the ring where sparring and guidance in the manly art were the order of the day. Everyone except Dacre AJ did time in the ring. As he was going to be the novice and had to rely just on his ability to 'windmill', it was felt by the instructors that he should not be taught any of the actual skills that a real boxer was required to develop. Instead they focussed on his strength and stamina. Consequently, he spent a large amount of time pummelling an old kit-bag full of sand until he felt that his arms would fall off.

By the end of the first day it was all the team members could do to drag themselves back to their rooms for a well-deserved shower and change of clothing and then go for the evening meal. The team were required to sit and eat together at a table reserved for them. Their meals were specially prepared by the chief cook. The Depot RM was taking this tournament very seriously. Despite this special treatment the two recruits missed the companionship of their room-mates. By the time they got back to their room both of them were fit for nothing. They collapsed onto their beds and fell fast asleep. The others in the room tip-toed around as carefully as they could lest they wake their sleeping comrades. But truth be told, nothing short of an earth-quake would have stirred them.

Tuesday and Wednesday came and went. Thankfully the forenoons were not too demanding. However, the afternoons seemed to get longer and more strenuous for the whole team. By comparison the squad were having it easy. They only had to contend with the occasional route march albeit five or six miles in full battle kit. Nevertheless, by Thursday there was light at the end of the tunnel. Both Dacre AJ and Jacko had turned the corner, so to speak. Yes, they were tired but not with the exhaustion that they had experienced earlier in the week. They both looked and felt extremely fit. It seemed that what at first they had thought as a harsh training regime had in fact paid off. On the Friday morning Colour Sergeant Hughes announced that he was very pleased with the way things had gone that week. So after the morning session and some last minute instructions the team was given a 'make and mend' for the rest of the afternoon. What a joy that was, an almost unheard of privilege.

It was 0530 hours on Saturday and it was raining, that steady drizzle that seems to find its way into whatever clothes a person is wearing. There was a strong smell of the sea in the air. Those travelling to Portsmouth were all assembled at the guardroom. They were wearing their waterproof capes over their blue uniforms. An old covered charabanc with transverse seats from the East Kent Road Car Company in its distinctive cream and maroon livery pulled up at the curb side. Everyone looked the old bus over.

The dour Scotsman said what everyone was thinking, 'Do you think this old crate will make it?'

Several of the group gave a half-hearted laugh.

Colour Sergeant Hughes opened the door of the bus from the inside and called them in, checking off their names on his clip-board as they entered.

'Make yourselves comfortable; belts and hats off,' he said. 'This is going to be a long trip.'

The marines relaxed, buttons and collars were undone, several had brought along newspapers to read. The recruits all sat together busy discussing their forthcoming training 'in the field'.

It was, by and large, an uneventful trip. The driver took the back road from Deal to Canterbury, then from there to Ashford and onto Hastings. At that point he followed the coast through to Bexhill, Eastbourne and Newhaven. When they reached Brighton they stopped for a welcome cup of tea taken in an old fashioned restaurant that overlooked the East Pier. The sea was rough and there were white horses as far as the eye could see. Huge waves were breaking heavily onto the shingle beach with a tremendous roar. Inside the restaurant it was warm and cosy. The marines, in their smart uniforms, caused a bit of a stir amongst the other customers. Many of the locals didn't even know which regiment they were. Royal Marines didn't usually come this way.

From Brighton they motored on through Worthing and Chichester until they came to Portsmouth. Taking care to avoid the town centre and the docks, the driver, a former 'Royal', took a side road which led them directly to the seafront at Southsea and the Royal Marines Barracks at Eastney. He had clearly done this trip before.

The main entrance to RMB Eastney was through a massive Victorian brick built arch. On either side of the vehicle access there were smaller gates for pedestrians. The bus was stopped by a provost corporal. Colour Sergeant Hughes got off and entered the guardroom to sign the group in. He was seen shaking hands with the Provost Sergeant. They were laughing and joking, clearly old friends. He returned to the bus.

'Right, lads, smarten yourselves up. Bring your bags and fall in outside on the pavement in two ranks.'

The group quickly did as he had ordered. It had stopped raining. Standing to attention, he turned them to their right and marched them up the road to the marine barracks. To gain access to their accommodation they had to march into a massive drill shed that covered the area between the barracks and a row of buildings that were opposite. The sound of their boots echoed off the walls. At the far end of the drill shed they could see that a boxing ring had been set up and that chairs and benches were being placed around it by a working party.

'Their gymnasium is too small to take all the spectators,' explained the Colour Sergeant, 'So in their wisdom, the powers that be have decided to use this space instead. Your barrack room is here in 'A' Block on the ground floor.'

With that he led the group into a small hallway and then into a large and airy room on the right hand side.

There were twenty beds all made up with crisp white sheets, pillows and blankets, plus the ubiquitous blue naval coverlets.

'You may have to share with some of the marines from the other divisions. It's only for one night so be on your best behaviour. Your heads and showers are across the hallway. The midday meal is at 1230 hours and the first bout starts at 1400. So, for those of you who are boxing, I suggest a light meal. I'll leave you to settle in but I shall be back to collect you at 1345 hours, so make sure you are ready.'

The team, having chosen their beds, unpacked their overnight bags. Dacre AJ was looking out of the window towards the beach and the sea. The parade ground immediately to his front was enormous. He let a long and almost silent whistle.

Turning to his friend Jock, who had come up to see what he was looking at, he said, 'That parade ground is even bigger than the one at the Depot.'

'Aye, you're right there, my young friend. Too bloody big, if you ask me. Imagine doubling around that with your rifle over your head! Now I wonder what that big white building is at the far end?'

They both craned their necks to get a better look. The stunning building was of white Portland stone. It had double sweeping steps up to the main entrance which was beneath an elegant portico. One of the corporals in the team who was on his way to the heads stopped by.

'It's the officers' mess. It may look grand but rumour has it that the building is so cold the officers have to wear their greatcoats to dinner. The parade ground is over a quarter of a mile long and the sea in front of you is the Solent. To our far right and beyond Southsea is Portsmouth Harbour and the Naval Base. On our left and beyond the officers' mess is Fort Cumberland where they do the gunnery training. Now that really is old: it was built, I believe, during the time of Napoleon Bonaparte.'

'How do you know so much about this place?' asked the young marine.

'This is where I did my ship's detachment training back in 1936. I was here for nearly two months.'

At that moment a bugle sounded the call for the midday meal.

At precisely 1345 hours, Colour Sergeant Hughes stuck his head around the door.

'Right, you lot, follow me. There are some seats reserved for all of us.'

Those who were going to box had changed into their PE kit. The colour sergeant was wearing his PE rig: a white pullover and dark blue serge trousers. He was carrying a tin bucket half full of cold water and on the top was floating a large sponge. They made their way across the drill shed to their seats. Here he explained how the tournament was going to work.

'There are four teams taking part, one from each division, that is Plymouth, Chatham, Portsmouth and us from the Depot RM. Each team is made up of six men, four of whom will box, the other two are reserves. This afternoon, each of the teams will box a preliminary bout so that by this evening we will have a final in each of the four weights – novice, light, middle and heavy. Each match will consist of three, three minute rounds. The name of each team will be put into a hat and drawn out. That decides who you will fight. Each win earns five points. If you lose you are out. At the end of the evening the team with the most points is declared this year's Corps Champions. It's all quite simple really.'

Dacre AJ put his hand up to ask a question.

'Have I got this right? We don't actually box all the other teams, just the one team we are drawn against?'

The Colour Sergeant looked at him carefully before replying.

'Yes that's correct!'

The youngster just nodded.

'That's the way it has been done for years. I know what you are thinking. What about the other two teams? Wouldn't it be fairer if all teams boxed each other? Well I suppose it would. However, time is the big constraint. This whole tournament has to fit into a weekend and that includes travelling time.' Then, not unkindly, he added, 'Some things, my young Royal, are difficult to change in this man's army.'

About half the seats and benches were occupied for the afternoon's contests. Most of these spectators were from the barracks since it was Portsmouth's turn to host the event. The working party was still setting out yet more and more chairs.

Dacre AJ was the first to enter the ring. Colour Sergeant Hughes was in his corner acting as his second. The rest of the group were sitting nearby waiting to cheer him on. The Depot RM had drawn the team from Plymouth. The young marine was receiving some last minute instructions whilst his ten ounce boxing gloves were put on.

'Go in fast and hammer him. Don't give him a chance. Use your natural aggression and put him on the deck as fast as you can,' said the Colour Sergeant.

The referee called both men to the centre of the ring; he checked their gloves in turn and briefly explained the rules. Dacre AJ studied his opponent carefully. He was a good couple of inches shorter but appeared to be a lot heavier, perhaps as much as sixteen stone, much of which seemed to be fat. He would, in all likelihood, be slower moving around the ring but his body may well have the capacity to absorb the youngster's punches. He would also have to be careful not to be caught by one of his opponent's fists. With all that weight behind a wild swing, things could get out of control.

The bell went for the first round. The young marine literally ran from his corner across to the other side and proceeded to deliver a fearsome barrage of powerful blows onto his opponent's head and upper body. The Plymouth marine tried to defend himself as best as he could. He tried ducking out of the way but Dacre AJ forced him into a neutral corner and continued to deliver a ferocious array of lethal punches. Outside the ring, his team mates were shouting themselves hoarse in their support for him. The rest of the spectators had gone quiet as they witnessed the trained soldier being given a sound thrashing by a recruit. Back in the ring, the Plymouth marine had gone down on one knee. He was bleeding from a nasty cut on his right cheek. The referee checked him over and then decided to stop the fight. Dacre AJ had won his first contest in just one minute and forty seconds.

He rejoined his companions to receive their congratulations with many slaps on the back. The Colour Sergeant cut through all the jubilation and urged him to watch the next fight which was between Chatham and Portsmouth because he would be boxing the winner that evening. The Portsmouth marine was enormous. He was, perhaps, six foot, four inches tall and weighed about fourteen stone. He looked all muscle. He had very long arms. The bell went. He walked across the ring, his large hands hanging loosely by his side. As he approached his opponent he swung his right arm back as far as it would go and unleashed a most devastating punch. With the full force of his height and weight, the punch crashed through the other man's defence, such as it was, and landed on the point of his jaw. It was a knock-out blow! The Chatham marine collapsed onto the canvas, unconscious. There was an unbelievable thirty-five seconds on the clock. Colour Sergeant Hughes was shocked to say the least. He tried to put on a brave face to be encouraging.

'Don't you worry, young Dacre, you will be alright.' The youngster wasn't convinced, neither were his team mates and friends.

With Novice bouts over, it was the turn of the lightweights. First up it was Chatham versus Plymouth. Chatham won comfortably. Next, it was Portsmouth against the Depot RM. Their trained soldier, a quiet lad who went by the name of 'Buster Brown', went the three rounds but narrowly lost on points. It was a close run thing but even he admitted that the better man had won.

Then it was the turn of the middleweights. The Depot RM was boxing against Chatham. Jacko was in fine form and simply danced and boxed his way expertly to a points win. Even the partisan spectators showed their appreciation for what was obviously a class performance. In the second bout Plymouth soundly beat Portsmouth, to gain a place in the evening's final.

That just left the heavyweights. Corporal Kelly was boxing for the Depot RM against Plymouth. He won his bout easily when the referee stopped the fight half-way through the second round. As it turned out, his opponent in the final was going to be last year's champion who just happened to be from the Portsmouth Division.

By the end of the afternoon, Colour Sergeant Hughes declared himself to be well pleased with the way things had gone. They were in three of the four finals that evening which was far better than he had expected. The points scored so far were five to Chatham and Plymouth, whilst the Depot RM and Portsmouth both had fifteen. Clearly the latter two were going to be the main focus of the evening's entertainment. The team retired to their room for a rest. Supper was at 1800 hours, the first bout of the evening began at 1930hrs.

Dacre AJ and Jacko were on their way for a shower. Walking across the hallway they opened the shower room door to be confronted by four of the biggest marines you wouldn't want to meet on a dark night, especially when all you have on is a towel around your waist. They both hesitated, only to be pushed into the room by two more burly men who had come up behind them. The near naked pair found themselves backed into a corner. The youngster was the first to find his voice.

'Six against two isn't very fair,' he said.

'We're not here to be bloody fair. Our job is to discourage you from winning your bout this evening,' the ringleader growled as he pointed at Jacko. 'We're not worried about you, youngster, our man will sort you out on his own!'

'Well it will take more than six of you,' said Jacko.

With that he promptly stepped forward and knocked the nearest man to the floor with a perfect right hook. Then all hell broke loose as fists and boots started to fly. Although the two recruits gave a good account of themselves, they were clearly outnumbered and it was beginning to tell. Suddenly the door was thrown open and in piled the rest of the Depot's boxing team along with their squad mates. The shower room was jammed tight with heaving, sweaty bodies. It would have been more difficult to swing a cat yet alone a punch. Gradually the melee turned into a rout.

As the last Eastney marine made his escape, Corporal Kelly looked at his team mates.

'Are you two alright?' he asked, concern etched across his craggy face.

Apart from a few minor cuts and bruises, they were fine, they both assured him.

'What the hell was that all about?' he asked. 'That's a hell of a way to warm up before the big event.'

The two recruits looked at each other.

'Oh nothing much,' replied Jacko, 'Just a little disagreement over tonight's bouts.'

The corporal didn't believe them, but he decided to let it pass.

'In that case I suggest we all get cleaned up and then go for some supper. It might be better if we don't mention this little incident to anyone, especially the Colour Sergeant. He's likely to get very upset if he was ever to find out that somebody here in the barracks had tried to nobble the pair of you.'

Chapter 13

By the time the Depot team took their place in the drill shed, there was not a spare seat to be had. The whole place was alive with a buzz of conversation, excitement and anticipation. The four teams that were competing were all in an area that had been roped off. The small group of recruits didn't, of course, know anyone else and because of this they felt more than a little isolated, even intimidated, by the vast assembly in front of them. By contrast, the other team members seemed to be comfortable with the whole thing and were heard exchanging some ribald, yet good natured remarks, with certain members of the other teams whom they clearly knew. The seats in the front row had all been especially reserved for the officers and the SNCOs and their guests. Suddenly a single note from a bugle was sounded. All talking stopped as everyone stood to attention. The Commanding Officer and the Regimental Sergeant Major entered, each leading their own party. All the officers were in formal mess dress whilst the SNCOs were wearing their best no.1 dress uniforms. The RSM climbed into the ring, then after ordering everyone to 'sit at ease' introduced the evening.

The first bout of the evening was the heavyweight fight between the Depot RM and the Portsmouth Division, much to the delight of the spectators. Corporal Kelly boxed well and gave a good account of himself. However, at the end of the third round his opponent won by a difference of just one point. Disappointed, he returned to his team mates and their commiserations. Portsmouth was ahead by five points. Next, it was Jacko's turn to box in the middleweight final. This bout was against Plymouth.

The noise in the drill shed from all the shouting was deafening, since the majority of marines were from the barracks. Jacko boxed exceptionally well and was hardly touched by his opponent. He was clearly in a class of his own but having been an army champion it was to be expected. He won easily on points, thus bringing the Depot RM and the Portsmouth Division to a score of twenty points each.

The third match of the evening turned out to be a real scrap between the two lightweights from Chatham and Portsmouth. They went at each other like hammer and tongs. It finished at the beginning of the third round with a knockout and Chatham taking the five points.

The final bout of the evening, the Novices, was clearly going to be the deciding event. Everyone in the drill shed could see the importance of this last fight. Those marines from Portsmouth in the audience who were, of course, the majority, could smell victory in the air. The final bout was just going to be a formality. The trophy was as good as theirs.

Dacre AJ stepped into the ring. The noise from the spectators was unbelievable. Colour Sergeant Hughes was in the youngster's corner trying to reassure him that all would be well. The referee called both men to the centre of the ring for the usual brief instructions and inspection of the gloves. The Portsmouth marine towered over the youngster. They returned to their corners; then the bell went for the first round. Dacre AJ literally ran across the ring to his opponent and began to rain down as many blows as he could. The big marine, somewhat surprised, stood his ground and took the onslaught from the younger man. Slightly winded, Dacre AJ backed off a little. His opponent just shook his head, he was completely unhurt. The older marine feinted left, then stood his ground watching the youngster carefully. He stepped forward and swung a massive right hand punch. He was fast. The youngster saw it coming, sidestepped and ducked under the swinging arm, then delivered an almighty punch to the man's kidneys. It had no apparent effect. The big marine simply bounced off the ropes and came straight back into the attack. Dacre AJ dodged out of the way again. He felt the breeze from his opponent's fist as it narrowly missed his chin. The big man backed off a bit, the youngster saw that he was breathing quite heavily. This was a man who, because of his physique, was used to winning after the first punch. The sheer size of him was very intimidating. Could he be tired out, the youngster wondered. The big marine came back into the fight like a tank. Dacre AJ tried to dodge to his left but received a right hand blow to his face which knocked him sideways. He went down onto one knee and took a count of five. He staggered back to his feet just in time to jump backwards as another massive fist just missed his stomach. The bell went for the end of the first round.

Back in his corner, the Colour Sergeant was giving him all the encouragement that he could, not that there was much he could say. The bell went for round two. This time it was the big marine who was the first to be in the centre of the ring. He was smiling and clearly enjoying himself. He just knew that he was going to win. Dacre AJ approached cautiously. He had to keep out of the way of those big hands, which wasn't going to be easy. The big marine swung a huge left hook, the momentum of which took him past the youngster. Dacre AJ lashed out with all his strength onto his opponent's unprotected head which he followed up with a series of 'windmill' blows to the body. There was a small cut over the big marine's left eye. He swiftly recovered and began moving easily around the ring sizing up the youngster. A small drop of blood fell onto his cheek.

Moving lightly for such a big man, he danced in and landed a seriously heavy blow on the youngster's chest. Dacre AJ went down onto the canvas and took another count of eight. All he could hear was the blood pounding in his ears. Back on his feet, he avoided a ferocious right hand smash. His chest hurt badly and he found it difficult to breath. He struggled to bring his breathing under control. The youngster managed to land a lucky punch onto his opponent's nose. It started to bleed. A small victory but, in the great scheme of things, it meant nothing. The big man came in again and delivered a huge punch to Dacre AJ's kidneys and another to his right shoulder. He felt his arm go numb. This was followed by a backhanded slap to the jaw. The youngster went down for a third time and took another count of eight when he managed to stagger back to his feet. He felt sick and dizzy. He was hurting. Luckily for him, the bell rang for the end of the round.

Back in his corner Dacre AJ spat out some blood from his mouth. Some of his teeth felt loose. Colour Sergeant Hughes got to work with his 'magic' sponge. Outside the ring, the spectators were howling for blood – his!

'Keep going, lad, you can do this. Go for the cut over his eye, it's your only chance,' said the Colour Sergeant.

'I can't do that, it wouldn't be fair,' replied the youngster.

'Fuck fairness! He's going to slaughter you if you don't stop him.'

The bell went for the final round. The Portsmouth marine came charging across the ring determined to finish the fight with one mighty punch. Dacre AJ stood his ground. He dodged onside as a heavy blow went flying past his head. The big man was off balance, leaving his head unprotected. The youngster saw his chance. He literally jumped up off the floor, perhaps no more than ten inches (although those watching would have sworn it was at least two feet) and struck his opponent right on the cut above his eye as hard as he could. Under such pressure, the skin bunched up and tore off leaving a gaping wound. Blood spurted everywhere. The big marine cried out in real agony and fell to his knees, holding his head in his hands. The referee took one look at the injury and ushered the youngster to a neutral corner. The drill shed was hushed for the first time that evening. The Medical Officer was sent for and, following his assessment, the fight was stopped. Against all the odds, Dacre AJ had won. That also meant, of course, that with his five points the Depot RM were the champions, beating Portsmouth Division by the narrowest of margins.

Dacre AJ was the hero of the hour, at least to his teammates and friends, although it must be said that a good number of those present in the drill shed begrudgingly admitted that the young recruit from Deal had actually fought very well. Some of them even came up to him to shake his hand and to wish him well.

Chapter 14

London: The Cabinet Room. Neville Chamberlain, the Prime Minister, brought the meeting to order.

'Gentlemen, good morning. There are a number of issues for us to discuss today as you will see from the agenda, a copy of which is in front of you. With your agreement may I suggest that we leave the SS *Athena* affair and the so-called peace plan put forward by Herr Hitler until later. I am sure you will agree with me that our primary task is to consider the sinking of HMS *Royal Oak*. So, with your indulgence, I shall ask the First Lord of the Admiralty to make his report. Winston?'

'Thank you, Prime Minister.

'On the fourteenth of October the Royal Oak was anchored at Scapa Flow in Orkney, Scotland. In the early hours of the morning she was torpedoed by the German submarine U-47. Of the ship's complement of one thousand, two hundred and thirty four men and boys, eight hundred and thirty three were killed that night or later died of their wounds.

'At 0058 hours, the submarine fired three torpedoes of which only one struck, hitting the bow and shearing off the anchor chain. It shook the ship and awoke the crew. However, little damage was observed and after routine checks many of the crew returned to their hammocks. It would seem that no-one appreciated that they were actually under attack. At 0116 the Germans fired three more torpedoes all of which struck the ship in quick succession. The explosions blew a hole in the armoured deck and destroyed the stokers', boys' and Royal Marines' mess-decks. At 0129 hours the ship sank. It had taken just nineteen minutes to founder.

'I have to report to you that amongst the dead were Rear Admiral Henry Blagrove, Commander of the Second Battleship Division, over one hundred boy seamen not yet eighteen years old and almost the entire detachment of Royal Marines.

'I propose to make a statement to Parliament on the seventeenth of October. However, whilst I mourn the loss of so many lives, I have to say to you that although the raid was a remarkable exploit of professional skill and daring by the U-Boat commander, the loss of the Royal Oak will not materially affect the naval balance of power. This was an old ship and was no longer suited to front line duty.'

The cabinet members sat in a stunned silence.

The Prime Minister spoke. 'Winston, I know that I speak for all of us when I say to you that this is the most awful news to receive at the beginning of the war. It will, I fear, have a devastating effect on the morale of the people of this country. How did it happen? Why were there so many boy sailors serving on board? How are you going to proceed?'

Churchill looked around the table at his fellow members of the war-cabinet. He consulted some handwritten notes in front of him.

'Well, Prime Minister, Gentlemen. Scapa Flow is a near-ideal anchorage. It is situated at the centre of the Orkney Islands, off the north coast of Scotland. The natural harbour was large enough to contain the entire Grand Fleet during the last war. It is surrounded by a ring of islands, separated by shallow channels. The threat from enemy U-

Boats has however been long recognised, so a series of counter measures were installed in 1915. Despite all these extensive measures, it was considered just possible, but highly unlikely, that a daring captain could attempt to enter. Indeed, several did try during the last war but were either captured or sunk.

'As to the Royal Navy's tradition of sending boys to sea, it has always been so and I defend their right should they wish to continue. Our navy is run on tradition and that is what makes it the finest in the world. However, the Admiralty may wish to reconsider this practice in the light of this disaster. If that is so, I shall not stand in their way.

'How to proceed? I shall immediately order the Board of the Admiralty to carry out a full and comprehensive investigation. You can be assured that no effort will be spared in searching out any possible negligence and, where appropriate, apportioning responsibility. Should that come to pass, then those involved will be certainly called to account.

'I shall of course make the findings known to you, Prime Minister, and to this cabinet and, of course, to Parliament.'

'Thank you, Winston, for that very clear and concise report. If there are no questions for the First Sea Lord, I suggest we move on.

Chamberlain continued. 'On the home front, here in London, you need to be aware of the current situation. We have evacuated over one million children and approximately two hundred thousand women to safer parts of the country.'

Winston Churchill put up his hand to interrupt.

'Yes Winston, you have a question?'

'Am I correct in my understanding that some of these evacuees have been moved down to the south coast to places like Dover?'

There was an embarrassing silence from those present.

'I believe so,' Chamberlain replied tersely.

'If, in fact, it is as you say Prime Minister, then I doubt the wisdom of those in charge who have sent our children to what I believe is known as 'Hell Fire Corner', perhaps the most dangerous place in all of England at this present time.'

The Prime Minster stared at Churchill intently. Was the man being deliberately difficult he wondered?

'I take your point, Winston. I am, however, given to understand that the children you are referring to have been moved to other places of safety.'

Churchill growled a noncommittal reply.

'Now, if I may continue? Many of the London hospitals have been cleared, ready for expected casualties. We have laid in large supplies of quicklime for mass burials and we have stockpiled papier-maché coffins in local swimming pools which, to all intents and purpose, are closed for repairs. Next, the bombing of London has increased dramatically. On one night alone over one hundred and eighty Luftwaffe bombers dropped over three hundred tons of high explosive bombs and thirteen hundred incendiaries, killing and wounding hundreds of civilians, as well as destroying warehouses, shipping and blocks of flats. The East End and the docks have been particularly badly hit. Our emergency services and the Royal Air Force are stretched to their very limits. I do not know how much longer we can hold out.'

Chamberlin paused and looked around the table at his cabinet colleagues. Their faces were tired and drawn with an obvious lack of sleep.

He continued. 'Now let us consider the last two items on our agenda, the sinking of the SS *Athena* and then Hitler's so called peace plan for Europe.'

Winston Churchill stifled a yawn behind his hand. He really did dislike these meetings; they went on for hours and hours. Of course most of what they discussed was necessary and vital to the war effort but surely there must be an alternative way of communicating such information. Now if he were in charge things would be different. As the Prime Minister droned on, Churchill drifted off into his own world of thoughts.

Chapter 15

It was early in the morning. Reveille had yet to be sounded. Despite this, the squad was busily loading blankets, bedding and kitbags into the backs of waiting trucks. There was a sense of excitement in the air. For the next ten weeks the parade ground would be forgotten. There would be no 'spit and polish' or square bashing. Instead, there would be a different kind of discipline: one that would be fully enforced, one that could possibly save their lives in the future. The only cleaning would be the cleaning of weapons, and heaven help anyone who failed that test as the punishment would be most severe. The recruits were dressed in fatigues, full battle order webbing with steel helmets and gas masks. Their Lee Enfield rifles were slung over their shoulders and long bayonets dangled from their waist belts. Everybody was looking forward to the weeks of real soldiering in the field, including the PWIs. After all, this was the real reason they had joined up.

After a hurried breakfast, the recruits climbed aboard the trucks and were driven across to the armoury in South Barracks. Here, they loaded up with the necessary platoon weapons and ammunition: two Vickers machine guns, six Bren guns, four two inch mortars and two three inch mortars, several PIATs, six .38 Webley pistols and several boxes of Mills and smoke grenades. As soon as everything was loaded and made secure, they said goodbye to their drill instructors and the barracks, and were driven out of Walmer along the coastal road to the historic port of Dover.

Passing the famous Norman castle that dominated the port, the vehicles descended a steep winding hill into the town. Sitting in the back of their truck, Dacre AJ and his friends listened intently to PWI Corporal Ward, who explained that for this part of their training they would normally have been under canvas. However, since it was late in the year, they would, instead, be billeted at the Western Heights, here in Dover.

Owing to the huge movement of troops across to France as part of the BEF, both the barracks at nearby Folkestone and the Grand Shaft Barracks on the Western Heights were full. Fortunately some space had been found for them in the old Napoleonic fort, The Drop Redoubt. Originally built in about 1804, it was later extended after 1859 and would then have housed some two hundred troops. With the onset of the current hostilities, it was now being used mainly for anti-aircraft guns and their crews. There was also an aircraft observation post up on the rooftop.

The trucks wound their way up a very steep road, at one point finding it necessary to change down into first gear. Then, passing through an imposing red brick gateway, they crossed a wooden drawbridge over a dry moat. The small convoy of vehicles eventually arrived at its destination, the Drop Redoubt. Alighting from their vehicles, the recruits began to unload all their equipment with the exception of the weapons and ammunition. These were to stay in the vehicles overnight and be guarded by the recruits in pairs, taking it in turns. The entrance to the Redoubt was via a large swing bridge which was barely wide enough for two people at a time. The bridge spanned another dry moat which was massive and could, in an emergency, be swung closed thus completely isolating the fort. Crossing the bridge, the recruits had to be extremely careful because, although there were safety barriers on each side, the drop down into the moat below meant serious injury or even death. Entering the fort through enormously thick walls, Dacre AJ and the remainder of the squad, heavily laden, passed the guardroom on the left and the officers' quarters on the right. A set of cast iron railings prevented them from going any further, so they had to ascend a short but steep set of worn stone steps to a small parade ground at the top. All around them there were a number of old fortifications, now modified and updated to take the more modern weapons. The place was a hive of activity: soldiers, mostly artillerymen, busying themselves with their guns and equipment. It all looked very professional. The squad assembled on the small parade ground in three ranks. Behind them were five bomb-proof casements, parabolic in shape. The fronts of these had been bricked up to form a wall, and each had a wooden porch and doorway. These were used as dormitories. There was no mess hall: the soldiers had to eat their meals in their barrack rooms. In front of the squad were the latrines and showers, and next to them the accommodation for the NCOs. Just beyond was a small but functional kitchen. The whole place was militarily clean and well kept, with considerable evidence of white paint everywhere. To the marines it seemed to be very much an army barracks.

The whole squad was detailed to one of the casements. On entering they found rows of triple-tiered bunks against the walls and large iron pegs on which to hang their equipment. At each end of the room were the ubiquitous black iron stoves and in the centre of the room were a number of wooden benches and tables. The recruits looked around in total disbelief. It was cold and the whole place smelt of damp.

'We have to eat and sleep in here?' said Jock incredulously.

Jacko, who was listening in to the conversation, replied, 'This is how it used to be everywhere, including back at the Depot. Before they built our new dining hall, all meals were eaten in barrack rooms. The senior marine would be in charge and he would send the youngest marine down to the galley to collect the cooked food for the entire room, and woe betide him if the food was cold when he brought it back.'

Dacre AJ just smiled, then added, 'We'll get used to it. Remember it's only for ten weeks. We could be a lot worse off, you know!'

'Oh aye, and how is that then?'

'We could be under canvas. Then you really would have something to moan about!' replied Dacre AJ.

At that moment one of the PWIs stuck his head around the door and told them that they had just five minutes to be on parade with full webbing and rifles. There was a mad rush to claim a bunk before everyone piled outside.

Back in their trucks they were soon on the road and heading for the training ground which was located at Lydden Spout Battery Range. This was about half way between Dover and nearby Folkestone. It extended for nearly three miles along the shoreline above Abbot's Cliff. There was a fine view out to the East Wear Bay and on a clear day you could easily see across the English Channel to France.

On arrival at the range, the squad was once again divided into their ten man sections, each with their own PWI. In addition to the five corporals, there were two sergeants and a sergeant major. The recruits were impressed. Clearly this was going to be a time of very intensive training.

Each section was led away by its instructor and their initiation began. First it was the simple matter of lying down in the prescribed position – body flat on the ground, legs splayed out in a 'V' formation, head up and to the front, arms and elbows supporting the rifle. Then they were given the order to 'advance'. They stood up and moved forward in an extended line until the order 'down' was given, which they carried out as quickly as they could. There followed countless hours of this drill, each time the instructor trying to find a wetter and muddier part of the ground, whilst at the same time demanding that they were quicker both in getting up and in getting down. There was no let up!

Eventually satisfied, Corporal Ward moved the group to the one hundred yard firing point. It was time to learn how to shoot their rifles. Many of the section were covered in mud and were wet through. More importantly, their hands were caked in a thick brown mud. Since there was no water available to wash, many took five minutes to piss on their hands to clean them as best they could.

Dacre AJ and his comrades listened intently to the instructions they were given by their corporal.

'Left hand underneath at the point of balance and hold it tight. Right hand firmly round the small of the butt, grip it hard and pull the rifle firmly into the shoulder. Brace your legs and body. Place your trigger finger on the trigger guard. Keep your weapon in an upright position. Get the tip of the foresight in line and level with the backsight. Line up everything on the centre of the target and, holding the rifle firmly, gently squeeze the trigger.'

At one hundred yards it was difficult not to miss. Many of the group, including Dacre AJ and Jock were rewarded with a bull's eye. The men in the butts raised their triangular indication markers and, waving them across the face of each of the targets, placed them where the bullets had entered. The group was then moved back to the five hundred yards point to repeat the exercise. At this distance the target was little bigger than a postage stamp. Their corporal briefed them about windage and elevation in firing from such a distance. This time a number of the group either missed completely or had an 'outer'. This was signified by a rotating marker, creating a black and white effect. Those with a complete miss felt the wrath of Corporal Ward, who would strike their steel helmets with his walking stick.

Dacre AJ was enjoying himself. He had managed to achieve a bull's eye every time he fired, which was no mean achievement. His friend, Jock, wasn't quite so successful but nevertheless was still doing well, as was Jacko and Scouse the qualified sniper.

Lunch, when it arrived, was a hot meal delivered in large green hay boxes. Swiftly eaten, mess tins and utensils cleaned, the men were soon back on the range putting into practice what they had learnt that morning. By the end of the day, shoulders and cheek bones were bruised from the incessant recoil of the rifles and bodies ached from the constant pounding they had taken.

The Drop Redoubt was a very welcome sight when they returned to Dover. The two stoves in the room were quickly lit which cheered the place a little. The men spent time cleaning their weapons, then showered, ate a hearty meal and turned in for an early night. For the most part, they were happy in the day's achievements but utterly exhausted.

The following day the recruits were scheduled to take their range tests. This meant using their rifles from each of the firing points, starting with one hundred yards, then moving on to the two hundred and so on, right back to the one thousand yard marker. It was an unusually warm, sunny day and there was a slightly more relaxed atmosphere. However, whilst the whole of these tests were vital, if a recruit failed any part then he would be back squadded for several months. All the instructors wanted their trainees to do as well as they could and to pass with flying colours, since to fail would be a reflection of their own ability.

They were on the three hundred yard point. Dacre AJ was one of the dozen men who were lying in the prone position. They had just been given the order to load. Magazines were clipped into place and bolts pulled back, then pushed forward so that a round was fed smoothly into the chamber. Backsights were adjusted for the correct distance. Next, came the order to watch and shoot. Everybody on the firing line tensed up in anticipation. The sergeant in charge checked with his binoculars that the red flag was flying which indicated that live firing was in progress. He gave a slight nod to the corporal who was manning the field telephone, who then cranked the handle, lifted the receiver and said, 'Now!' Immediately, as if by magic, the targets appeared in the butts at the end of the range. Each recruit in his own time fired several measured shots with great care. Suddenly, there were whistles blowing and instructors screaming out 'Cease fire, cease fire!' It was as if all hell had been let loose. Then came the order to unload and to relax. Completely mystified, the recruits did as they were told. Both the sergeant and the corporal were staring into the distance to the left of the targets. The recruits sat up so that they could see what was going on. There, unbelievably, walking across the grass towards the targets were two women and half a dozen children.

'What the fuck are they doing here?' shouted the sergeant. His face had gone an interesting shade of purple. 'Didn't they see the sodding flag? Oh my gawd they could have all been killed!'

He looked down at the line of recruits.

'Now then, I need a volunteer. You, Dacre, you'll do. Get your arse over there as quick as you can. Give them ladies my compliments, explain to them that there is a war on and then escort them off my fucking range pronto like.'

The young marine leapt to his feet.

'One other thing, you had best be polite, we don't want any complaints do we?'

Fifteen minutes later Dacre AJ returned. The range was now clear and firing could recommence.

'Well, lad, what did they say?'

'They were very apologetic, Sergeant. They hadn't seen the flag, and they thought the firing was fireworks, so they brought the children to see them.'

The sergeant just shook his head and went away muttering something about indulgent mothers who should know better.

For the remainder of the week, the recruits learnt how to fire their rifles from a variety of positions: kneeling, standing, from the hip, from a trench, from a window or doorway, even lying on their backs and firing over their heads. It was remarkable how accurate they had all become. Many of the squad, including Dacre AJ, had qualified as marksmen. This was duly entered on their company record and, more importantly, were paid an extra three pence a day and could wear the coveted crossed rifles on the sleeve of their uniforms.

One evening, they went back to the range for a night firing exercise. Instead of the normal red flag flying, to warn people that live firing was taking place, a red lamp was hoisted up the flag pole. The instructors made it abundantly clear that if anyone was caught firing at the light instead of the target they would be in very serious trouble, not so much for shooting at the light but for disobeying an order which, in the Marines, was tantamount to treason! At two hundred yards the red light was an extremely small target. When the targets in the butts appeared and the order to open fire was given, nearly everyone fired two shots at their own target and one at the light. It took five minutes for the light to shatter. The instructors went mad running around trying to find the culprit but without success. Later, back in the Redoubt, nearly a dozen of the squad claimed the victory. Dacre AJ just smiled to himself. He had fired only one shot at the light which had gone out immediately. He just knew that his had been the winning shot.

Over the next couple of weeks the squad was introduced to a variety of platoon weapons and allowed to fire them. Both of the mortars proved simple to operate, whether you were using HE or smoke, as long as you kept your head out of the way. Likewise the PIAT, although here you had to ensure that no-one was behind you, lest they got caught in the back-flash. The Webley pistol was useful as a hand-gun but really only effective at close range. The Vickers machine gun was an impressive weapon: belt fed and water cooled, it laid down a murderous barrage of firepower. On the downside, it was heavy to carry and therefore not really suitable as a platoon weapon.

Throwing the Mills grenade was fairly straightforward as long as you kept your nerve. One recruit panicked at the last moment. Having drawn the pin and released the lever, he dropped the grenade onto the floor. The sergeant in charge reacted with lightning speed. He pushed the recruit into a recess in the trench, specially designed for just such an event, whilst diving into another himself. Luckily, neither was hurt. The recruit, although somewhat shaken, was immediately made to throw again, this time successfully.

The weapon that everyone loved to fire was the BREN Light Machine Gun Mk III. Introduced only the year before, it replaced the old Lewis gun. It was an inspired choice of weapon. Using .303 ammunition, the same calibre as the Lee Enfield rifle, it could fire up to five hundred rounds per minute. It had an external magazine of thirty rounds that was spring and gravity fed, although it was usually loaded with only twenty-eight to avoid over-stressing the spring in the magazine. It was light – just twenty-one pounds – very portable and could even be fired from the hip. It was an ideal section weapon and could also be used in a defensive role. Every second round was often a 'tracer' so that the fall of shot could be easily spotted.

One afternoon when live firing was taking place, a small fishing boat had strayed into the restricted zone in the bay below the cliffs. The range lookout reported seeing tracer rounds bouncing off the boat's deck as the fishermen dived over the side into the sea in an effort to escape. Luckily no-one was hurt. It was estimated that the boat was nearly a mile away from the actual firing point.

One evening on returning to Dover, the vehicles stopped on Snargate Street on the sea front, instead of going up to the Redoubt. Dismounting from the trucks, the squad was led up a brick lined tunnel to the foot of a staircase.

The Sergeant Major explained, 'This is the Grand Shaft. It was built in about 1805. It is twenty six feet wide and one hundred and forty feet deep. It has two brick lined shafts, one inside the other. The inner shaft acts as a light well, with windows cut into the outer wall to illuminate the staircases, as you can see. In the outer shaft there is a triple staircase. It was built in order to get troops quickly from the barracks and the forts down to the harbour. When you get to the top of the staircase, continue on up the road past the barrack blocks until you reach the Redoubt. Of course some of you may be wondering why you are using this staircase. It is to maintain your levels of fitness. From now on this is how you will leave and return to the Redoubt. If that doesn't keep you fit, nothing will!'

'Dear Lord Almighty!' said Jock. 'It never rains but it pours! Just what we need at the end of a hard day – I don't think!'

Many of those around him whilst agreeing with the sentiment, gave a hollow laugh.

'Save your breath,' replied Dacre AJ. 'I think you are going to need it!'

The days and weeks sped by as the squad moved into the 'field exercise' part of their training. Section and platoon attacks, the art of camouflage, how to make good use of the natural terrain and the ability to dig a variety of trenches all became second nature to them.

How to use the bayonet proved to be one of the most demanding parts of their training. At first it was just running, screaming and stabbing a stuffed dummy. Then they progressed to one-on-one combat. They formed up in two lines facing each other. Bayonets were fixed but scabbards were on. Then came the command to thrust, parry and attack. The noise from the shouting men echoed across the range. Then the order to remove scabbards was given. There was a natural reluctance from the squad to set about each other with these lethal weapons. One of the SNCOs, not satisfied with the level of aggression being shown, took someone's rifle and began to attack the recruit nearest to him. Taken completely by surprise, the recruit did his best to defend himself. He tried to deflect the assault but the sergeant was too quick for him. Knocking the rifle to one side, those watching were horrified to see him plunge the bayonet into the recruit's stomach. He fell to the ground, blood gushing everywhere. Mortified, the sergeant did his best to staunch the flow of blood whilst an ambulance was sent for. The remainder of the squad was put back to training as if nothing had happened. Later they were to learn that by some miracle all the lad's vital organs had been missed and, although the bayonet had gone all the way through and out through his back, he would eventually recover and finish his training with, of course, two neat scars. They never heard if the sergeant was ever censored or whether there was even an enquiry.

The final week saw them putting into practice everything they had learned. The weather had by now changed and it rained almost every day. The squad was continually wet, as were the instructors. Despite this, mock attacks with live ammunition went ahead. Night attacks, living and sleeping in a trench half full of water, the use of smoke grenades and thunder flashes all gave the squad the nearest experience of warfare that it could have under reasonably safe and controlled conditions. They had all learnt a lot that week!

Saying goodbye to the Redoubt and the friends they had made there, the squad returned to the Depot RM at Deal. As soon as they had disembarked from the trucks their Drill Instructors were there, reminding them in no uncertain way that they were back where it really mattered, on the 'holy of holies'. The following morning everyone was on parade, shining like new pins. It was as if they had never been away. There followed ten days' revision of square bashing before the squad, along with most of the rest of the barracks, went on two weeks' Christmas leave.

'Are you going home, Jock?' Dacre AJ asked his friend.

'Aye, I am that, home to Glasgow! It's a long way I know but I need to be there especially for Hogmanay. What are you doing?'

'Oh, I shall go to my place over near Whitstable. I've some good friends there who I haven't seen for a while.'

'You are more than welcome to come home with me if you like.'

'Thanks. That's very good of you but I shall be fine.'

There was a long pause in the conversation as they both continued to pack their bags.

'You know, AJ, that when we come back in January we shall be the King's Squad!'

'I hadn't given that much thought. Where has the time gone? King's Squad! Then gunnery training at Plymouth. Who would have thought it possible!'

'Aye! It's a bloody miracle, that's what it is, a bloody miracle!'

Chapter 16

With Christmas leave behind them, the recruits returned to the Depot and as the most senior squad in the Corps they were now known as the 'King's Squad'. As a result they were entitled to wear the most coveted second chin strap on their peaked caps and the white lanyard on their left shoulder.

This was now the time for practising their ceremonial drill. The main difference between this and any other type of drill was that no orders were given by the Drill Instructors. Every movement had to be memorised to perfection, there could be no mistakes. And so it went on, day after day, until everyone felt that they could do it in their sleep which they probably could.

At the end of another long and hard day, the recruits staggered back up to their rooms. Dacre AJ couldn't help but notice that his friend Jock seemed to be in a particularly good mood which was most unusual for him. If anyone would be moaning, it would be him. The rest in the room were absolutely knackered. Their feet hurt, their legs ached and their undergarments and shirts were damp from the sweat generated from beneath their heavy serge uniforms. But not the Scotsman, no! For once he was light on his feet and whistling a tune that might possibly have been a Scottish ballad. It was difficult to tell since Jock always whistled out of tune.

'You seem very pleased with yourself,' said Dacre AJ.

'Aye, you're right there, pal,' Jock replied.

'We're all bloody shattered and here you are prancing about like some young gazelle.'

'Aye, you're right again,' the Scotsman replied with a broad grin on his face.

'Well, come on, give? What's the big secret?'

By this time the other marines in the room had forgotten their tiredness and were beginning to take an interest in the conversation. Their curiosity had been aroused; they were also waiting for the answer. Jock looked around the room at all the expectant faces. He was barely able to contain his enjoyment.

'Och, alright then. It's ma fucking birthday!'

You could have heard a pin drop in the room. Mouths dropped open, such was their surprise.

'Your birthday?" said Dacre AJ incredulously.

'Aye too right, ma bloody birthday to be sure.'

Everyone present burst into laughter as they tumbled off their beds to shake the Scotsman's hand and to wish him well.

'You kept that damn quiet,' said the young marine.

'Aye, well you know me, it's no' a big deal.'

Jacko called out from across the room, 'I think this calls for a pint or two in the NAFFI tonight. Okay?"

'Aye cheers, lads, that would be just great.'

Scouse looked around the room then added, 'How about we have a special run ashore on Saturday to really celebrate.'

'Do you have anywhere in mind?' asked Dave.

'No, I'm not sure yet. I need to look into it a bit. I'll ask around the other squads, somebody will know of a good place to go. I'll let you all know later.'

The following evening after supper, Scouse got everybody together.

'Right then! The general opinion seems to be that for a really good run ashore we need to get out of Deal. It has been suggested that we take the train along to either Ramsgate, Broadstairs or Margate. Most 'Royals' seem to head for Margate. It has a lot of seaside attractions, pubs and so on and, of course, Dreamland.

'What's that then?' asked one of the others.

'It's a gigantic fun fair that covers several acres. It's right in the centre of the town just off the sea front. There's also a scenic railway, a ballroom, a skating rink and a cinema.'

'Sounds pretty good to me,' said Dave, 'Bound to be plenty of girls there.'

Scouse looked around the room before continuing, 'The only problem is that a lot of Londoners and day trippers go there, so it has a bit of a reputation of being something of a rough house.'

Dacre AJ interrupted, 'That's not your only problem. Dreamland is about to be requisitioned by the Government due to the war. It is, or shortly will be in the next few days, closed to the general public.'

'Oh aye and how do you know that then?' said Jock crossly.

'It was in last week's Kent Messenger newspaper, that's how I know," replied the young marine.

'So that means it's Broadstairs or Ramsgate,' said Jacko stating the obvious. 'What's the word on those two?'

'Broadstairs seems to be the place to go. It's quieter, has some good pubs and fewer Londoners, and as a bonus very few marines go there,' replied Scouse.

'Right then, Broadstairs it is, this Saturday. You okay with that Jock?' said Dacre AJ.

'Aye! Suits me just fine, I canna wait.'

Saturday arrived all too soon. The early part of the forenoon was spent cleaning their part of the barrack block as was usual. The heads, bath block and their room all had to be 'marine clean' in order to pass muster. It was a routine that they were well used too. Later, their no. 1 uniforms were pressed and brushed, boots cleaned so that you could see your face in the toecaps, white belts blancoed and brasses polished until they gleamed. At 1400 hours the small group of friends presented themselves at the guardroom for the going ashore ritual.

A swift march, all of them in step of course, to the railway station at Walmer, and they were just in time to catch the Southern Railways steam hauled passenger train at 1420 hrs.

As soon as they were seated in a compartment Jock, looking somewhat bewildered, said, 'I don't understand why we are going on shore leave so early. It's not as if the pubs will be open when we get there.'

The others all looked at him in mock surprise.

'You tell him AJ, he'll listen to you,' said Jacko with a smile on his face.

'It's like this, Jock. As soon as it becomes dark everyone has to abide by the blackout regulations. That means there will be no lights anywhere, even the street lights are switched off, so it will be pitch black everywhere. They've painted some of the curbs white and put white lines down the middle of some of the main roads. All vehicles now have their headlamps covered and their bumpers are also white, and to make matters worse you can't smoke a cigarette in the street. Even the trains and stations are blacked out which has caused some real problems. All of this of course is to prevent any German aeroplanes from seeing a light and dropping their bombs on us.'

'Aye, I understand all that well enough. I'm no daft you know. But you have not answered my question, why are we going out so early?'

'Because, my friend, with it being winter, it will be getting dark by about 1530 hours. So if we want to see anything of the town we need to be there in daylight.'

'Right enough then. Why didn't you just tell me that in the first place instead of blathering on?'

An uneasy silence followed for the rest of the journey. Thirty minutes later they arrived at Broadstairs.

'Where to then?' asked Jock looking around the rather dismal railway station. He was naturally anxious to begin celebrating.

'Down through the town to the sea,' replied Scouse. 'I thought we might start with a walk around the harbour and along the sea front. Then, perhaps, we can find somewhere for a cup of tea and a sandwich or two before the pubs open. We don't want to be drinking on an empty stomach, now do we?'

As it turned out there wasn't that much to see. The small harbour had a dozen or more fishing boats either tied up or bobbing at anchor. There were two Royal Navy minesweepers alongside the main jetty. The marines exchanged some good natured banter with a couple of matelots who were busy chipping and painting part of the deck. The Viking Bay sands were also disappointing. All the beach huts had been taken down and the golden sands had been criss-crossed with rolls of barbed wire. There were even signs up warning of landmines. Along the promenade there were machine gun emplacements made from sandbags and manned by the Local Defence Force. The marines were made welcome by the soldiers and were invited to look through the binoculars and telescopes at the sea that stretched out before them. Scouse had got into a quiet but intense conversation with one of the sergeants.

Afternoon tea was taken in the only teashop on the seafront that was open. The marines were the only customers. It was a clean and tidy establishment, and despite the rationing that had just been introduced the sandwiches and cakes, all homemade, were excellent.

'Well,' said Jock, halfway through his second mug of tea, 'Where shall we start, which pub then?'

Scouse wiped some crumbs from his mouth before answering, 'That sergeant I was talking to said The Dolphin down by the harbour is good, as is The Tartar Frigate up by the old lifeboat station. The Charles Dickens is also quite good but The Albion Hotel is, in his words, a bit posh. For his money The Nelson is the place to go. It has the best beer and the landlord is a former sailor.'

'I like the sound of that,' said 'Jock'. 'What are we waiting for? Let's get going.'

And so it was. The local Shepherd Neame beer was exceptionally good, each pint slipping down easily with a wonderful taste of brewed hops. The recruits were made very welcome both by the landlord and the locals. Royal Marines rarely came to this town, the old sailor told them. One or two of the town's younger customers asked about life in HM Forces, more out of curiosity than anything else. Later several of the fishermen challenged the bootnecks to an arm wrestling competition which the marines easily won, only to be soundly thrashed in the several games of darts that followed. It was an enjoyable evening that everyone appreciated. Towards closing time, which because of the war was now 9.30 p.m., the marines said their goodbyes and made their way to a nearby fish and chip shop which they had difficulty finding because of the blackout. So that no light escaped, they had to knock on the door to be let in. Once inside, it was warm and snug and they had a right good slap up meal of fresh, locally caught fish. Several of the lads had begun flirting with the two very attractive waitresses who cast the marines some admiring glances with more than a hint of what might be available for 'dessert'. Jacko, older and wiser than the others, had spotted all the danger signs.

'Leave it, lads,' he urgently whispered. 'The girls are bound to have gentleman friends and we don't want any trouble do we? Besides, we might like to come back here again.'

Reluctantly they took his advice and backed off, much to the disappointment of the two young women.

Having paid their bill, they made their way cautiously up the darkened streets to the railway station where a completely blacked-out train was waiting at the platform. There were one or two other passengers being shepherded aboard by station staff using dimmed torches held down towards the ground. The smoke and steam from the old engine billowed across the platform, lending an unreal feel to the whole situation. As soon as the group of friends had settled themselves into a compartment and had pulled down the blackout blinds, Jock produced a small silver hip flask from his pocket and, rather like a conjurer, held it up with a flourish for all to see.

'Where did you get that from?' asked Dacre AJ.

'Och, it's a wee present from my grandpa. It arrived earlier this week.'

The flask was clearly very old and there was a large dent on one side.

'See that,' he said, pointing with his finger to the damage, 'That's where a Jerry bullet hit my grandpa when he was on the Somme in the last war. Saved his life it did. Now he has given it to me, perhaps it might save mine, who knows?"

The others were impressed, and in the gloom of the single blue ceiling light squinted to get a good look. Jock unscrewed the top and took a long hard sniff.

'Ah, nectar of the gods! Just a small sample of Scotland's finest whisky.'

He took a small nip and passed the much prized Scotch to the person next to him. After they had all whet their whistles, the group broke into a spontaneous burst of Happy Birthday which up until now they had forgotten to do.

Dave interrupted the celebrations by announcing that he needed to relieve himself. None too politely he was told to hold his water until they got back to Walmer station. He crossed his legs but looked distinctly uncomfortable. Five minutes later he interrupted again.

'It's no good, lads. I'm breaking my bloody neck here. I've really got to go.'

As there was no corridor on the train, there was no lavatory available. Jacko looked on sympathetically.

'Well, piss out of the window then if it's so urgent,' he said.

The stricken marine stood up, then turned to face his friends with a look of panic written all over his face.

'That's no bloody good; the sodding window is too high.'

Dacre AJ realised quickly that there was only one thing to do.

'Okay,' he said, 'We'll open the carriage door. You can brace yourself as best as you can and one of us will hold onto your belt so that you don't fall out.'

No sooner was this said than it was done. Fortunately the train was only moving at a walking pace so there was little real danger. As quickly as he finished, the others all realised that they needed to go. Within seconds an orderly queue had formed, each marine taking it in turn to hold the man in front whilst he took a well-needed piss.

By this time the train had passed Durlock Junction where the line divides into east for the coast and west for Canterbury and beyond, and had picked up some considerable speed. It was only then did they realise that because of the increased slipstream from the train it was now impossible to close the door. Several of the marines actually leant out to try but had to give up, it was too dangerous. Jock then stood up and holding onto the door frame looked up and down the outside of the moving train. He had just had a brilliant idea.

'How far do you think you could go by holding onto the rain gutter and using the running board?" he asked.

'What?' they all chorused at once.

'Och it's a simple enough question. Do you think you could walk on the outside of the train by hanging on?'

'Are you mad?' said Jacko. 'One slip and you'll be dead. Failing that, if you are seen and reported that will be the end of your career as a 'Royal'. You'll be booted out of the Corps for conduct unbecoming. Is that what you want?'

The Scotsman took another nip of his whisky then passed the flask around again.

'Aye, well that might be, but I still think we should give it a go - a sort of test of courage if you like.'

He stood up and took off his white belt and cap which he threw carelessly onto the nearby seat. Without another

135

word he went to the open carriage door and, with great care, pulled himself out and onto the side of the train. There was a collective sharp intake of breath from everyone.

Dacre AJ stood up and with a mock salute to the others said, 'Right then, one for all and all for one,' and with that he swung himself out onto the side of the train.

Somewhat reluctantly the rest began to follow. Within several minutes all the marines were on the outside of the train, their fingers gripping vice-like to the overhead rain gutter as they edged their way cautiously along the train. The first compartment they passed had the blackout blinds shut tightly. The second contained an elderly couple who had not bothered to close the blinds. The old man was trying to read his newspaper in the dim blue light of the carriage; the elderly lady was knitting. Just then she happened to look up as the last two marines slid past, faces pressed tightly against the glass. One of the marines gave her a conspiratorial wink and a smile. She stared, hardly believing what she had just seen. Carefully she put her knitting down and went to the window to make sure she had not been imagining things but it was dark outside and the dark uniforms of the recruits hid them from her gaze. She returned to her seat, shook her head in disbelief and resumed her knitting.

'I must have a word with the Station Master when we get to Deal', she thought.

As Jock and Dacre AJ arrived at the third compartment they found that the blind was only partially closed. They were amazed to see a corporal of Marines in a very heavy clinch with an attractive young blonde. Although the JNCO had his back to them, they recognised his bull-neck at once. The King's badge on his left arm confirmed it. There was no doubt. It was Corporal Varley their Assistant Squad Instructor and he was very involved with a young woman. Her blouse was unbuttoned down to her waist and his head was buried between her generous breasts. Her skirt was pulled up high, revealing a glimpse of white thigh above her stockings. His left hand was clearly busy beneath her undergarments. But she saw them with their grinning faces and gave a little start and a squeak of disbelief as each marine passed by. The Corporal thinking that her level of passion had at last matched his, continued with his endeavours in complete ignorance of what was happening outside the carriage.

Arriving at the last compartment, Jock and Dacre AJ managed to open the carriage door and swung themselves effortlessly inside, much to the consternation of two young sisters who were wearing Salvation Army uniforms. They had been to a regional parade that day in Ramsgate.

'It's all right, ladies,' said AJ as quick as a flash. 'Don't be alarmed, this is all part of an initiative test that we marines have to undertake.'

The two girls nodded their heads as if understanding. Gradually the others began to arrive, glad to be safe and sound, and with a real sense of achievement. Jock passed the remains of the whisky around, not that there was much left. The two young women graciously declined; they were not allowed to drink alcohol. Everyone managed to find a seat. The two 'Sally Army' girls sat happily on the laps of two of the handsomest young men they could ever wish to meet although, as they both agreed later, they must not tell their parents, both of whom were senior officers in General Booth's 'Army'.

All the marines broke into gales of laughter not only because they were safe but also because of catching their Corporal out. Out of respect for the two girls they kept their comments as clean as they could. However, it was Dacre AJ who eventually pointed out that they would never be able to reveal what they had witnessed. To do so would only identify their own recklessness. Although everyone was disappointed, they all agreed that AJ was right. Perhaps it would be for the best if they just put it down to an interesting experience and then forget that it had ever happened.

Thirty five minutes later they arrived at Walmer and having said goodbye to the two girls who were going on to Dover, they alighted onto a darkened platform. Three of the group quickly sprinted down the platform to their original compartment to recover their caps and belts. Once properly dressed, the group made their way back to barracks arriving at the guardroom at precisely 2359 hours, happy in the knowledge that they had had a very memorable run ashore and that Jock had celebrated his birthday in real style.

It was about a week later that a small item was to be found tucked away in a corner of the Kent Messenger newspaper. Briefly, it commented on the fact that it been reported that a 'large' group of Royal Marines had been seen walking along the outside of a 'fast' moving train, defying certain death and breaking all the known rules of the Southern Region Railway Company. Despite extensive enquiries and the offer of a reward for information, none of the culprits had as yet been identified. When interviewed by officers of the Kent Constabulary, the Commanding Officer commented that he had hundreds of very fit young men under his command who were full of high spirits. However, he assured them, that if it had been any of his men he would see to it that it would never happen again.

Chapter 17

After what seemed an age, the great day arrived. The squad was up early, making their last minute adjustments to their equipment and brushing each other's blue Number One uniforms down so that not a speck of dust showed anywhere. Rifles and bayonets were as clean as they could be; white belts, rifle slings and pith helmets were immaculate and all the brasses glistened in the early morning sun. Despite being the beginning of February, the morning was crisp and bright. At 0950 hours, the squad began to assemble in the drill shed. Sergeant Robinson and Corporal Varley, both immaculate and straight as ramrods, carried out a final inspection. There was nothing they could improve on. Everyone was nervous, yet at the same time eager to give as fine a performance as they could.

From the parade ground came the sound of the bugler calling the officers. Then it was the call for the band which assembled behind the squad in the drill shed. The musicians marched off to take their place on the parade ground. At last there was silence. The assembled officers, guests, families and friends were arranged on three sides of a square. The Adjutant General of the Royal Marines, General Sir R. F. C. Foster RM would be taking the salute but the special guest of honour was the First Sea Lord, the Right Honourable Winston Churchill MP. He had always had a soft spot for the Marines and had asked to be allowed to attend today's passing out parade. Who could have refused him?

Sergeant Robinson brought the squad to attention.

'In one minute from now you will be parading in front of your Commanding General. Remember, you are the best that there is. Now go out there and show them!'

He then gave the order to move to the right in threes, 'Right turn! Quick march!'

With that, fifty nine left heels hit the stone floor as one as they marched onto the parade ground to the band playing the Corp's Regimental March, A Life on the Ocean Wave. The squad was greeted by a tremendous applause from the whole assembly. It was a most thrilling moment for the recruits. The next hour was automatic but with total concentration. The squad faultlessly went through its well-rehearsed routine: changing direction, changing formation, arms drill at the halt, fixing bayonets on the march and advancing in review order. Then, at the halt in front of the dais came the moment when the King's Badge was to be awarded. Normally this was undertaken by the Adjutant General. However, this morning on the spur of the moment he deferred to the guest of honour, Winston Churchill. Together, they left the dais and walked the short distance to the squad. The RSM, standing close by, announced the citation.

'The King's Badge, instigated at the command of His Majesty King George V in 1918, is awarded to the best all-round recruit of the squad. Step forward Ch/X 06821 Marine Dacre AJ.'

There was a tremendous round of applause from all the spectators. The marine took a step forward, his heart beating so fast that he felt it might burst. Winston Churchill stood in front of him. He was a small, round man with slightly hunched shoulders. He barely came up to the marine's chest. There was a strong pervading smell of cigars and maybe something else, possibly brandy. Since they were unable to shake hands, Churchill patted the youngster on the cheek in an avuncular manner.

Then, in his deep gravelly voice said, 'Well done, my boy! You are a great credit to your squad and to the Royal Marines. This country of ours is going to need men like you and your fellow marines if we are to defeat the Nazi menace.'

Churchill then pinned the badge onto Dacre AJ's left sleeve. The squad re-formed and, marching in column, gave the final salute before they disappeared back into the darkness of the drill shed. Here they were congratulated by their two instructors.

It was all over! They were given a short pep talk and then dismissed for the rest of the day. Nearly all the squad wanted to congratulate Dacre AJ on winning the King's Badge. He was slightly embarrassed by all the attention since in his own mind there were others who were more qualified than he was. However, his good friend put it all rather well.

'AJ, you're by far the best man in this squad and you rightfully deserve the prize. There isn't a man here who would disagree with me. I know you, so dispel any doubts you may have and enjoy the rewards that you've earned. Well done, my friend, the best man won!'

Many of the squad, including Dacre AJ, Jock and the rest of the room, made their way down to the town for the last time to pre-arranged appointments with their girlfriends. It was time to say goodbye. Joan was naturally upset like many of the girls and there were floods of tears. However, Dacre AJ assumed that by now she was used to the routine of saying farewell, no doubt practice made perfect. He knew that by the end of the week her heart would be in one piece again and that she and her friend Dorothy would be all set for new conquests.

Two days later the squad was posted to Plymouth, the chosen place for its naval gunnery training. The journey by train was uneventful, although at Paddington Station in London, dressed in their best 'blues' and white helmets, they attracted some admiring glances.

One inquisitive youngster came up and asked Dacre AJ, 'Excuse me, sir, what is your uniform?'

'Why, young man, it is the uniform of His Majesty's Royal Marines,' he replied.

The young boy looked up at these two enormous men in total bewilderment.

'Please, sir, what does a marine do?' the young boy managed to ask, blushing deeply.

The Scotsman leant forward so that he could look the lad kindly in the face, 'Well now, ma wee laddie, we are the Royal Navy's sea soldiers. We are trained to fight both on board ships and on the land.'

Satisfied, the boy simply nodded and then skipped away to join his parents who had been watching from a short distance away. Dacre AJ and Jock looked each other up and down, then both burst out laughing realising that they really were Royal Marines.

Chapter 18

It was late in the afternoon when the squad arrived at one of the oldest barracks in the country. The headquarters of His Majesty's Royal Marines, Plymouth Division, was to be found at Stonehouse Barracks near Millbay Harbour. The sentry on duty, standing in the middle of Durnford Street, halted the traffic so that the squad could march in under the impressive brick and stone nineteenth century archway. The sound of their boots echoed in the entrance tunnel as they marched onto the parade ground. They halted in front of the Officers' Mess. Dacre AJ noticed a huge clock high up on a wall. It was 1815 hours.

Colour Sergeant Kelly introduced himself as their gunnery instructor. He was well over six foot tall and had a chin that resembled the prow of a battleship.

'When I dismiss you',' he roared, 'the duty orderly will show you to your quarters. Get changed and make your way to the dining hall. I shall see that there is a hot meal for you in thirty minutes. One last thing! This is not the Depot. You are now fully trained marines so you will be treated as such!'

That evening the squad settled into its new accommodation. Before turning in, Dacre AJ, Jock and several of the others had a wander around in order to get the lie of the land, particularly making a mental note of the where the NAAFI and the wet canteen were to be found.

The following morning the squad was divided up into four sections. Dacre AJ and his friends found themselves once again in the same group. Their instructor introduced himself as Sergeant Wilkes.

Without any preamble, he informed them that, 'Gunnery is a serious business and it is going to be discipline and training and yet more discipline, for without it a catastrophe may be just around the corner. The first hour of every day will be spent at 'Cleaning Quarters'. Every inch of every gun mounting is to be cleaned to perfection. These will be inspected by your instructors who are the experts. The slightest smear will be frowned upon and you will be required to start all over again.'

Their training began with the smaller four inch anti-aircraft gun. Then they progressed to the six inch breech-loading secondary armament and finally the massive fifteen inch turrets. The marines were taught the drill for each member of the gun crew because at some time in the future it might be necessary to carry out their duty with only half of the gun crew left standing.

There were, of course, the odd punishments such as standing to attention, cradling a six inch projectile in their arms for an hour or more. That certainly helped to focus the mind on the importance of listening to the instructor. The marines were also taught about the different types of shells that they might have to deal with: the timed fuse for aircraft, the armour piercing for enemy ships and the high explosive for enemy troops ashore. In addition they had to learn the rudiments of fire control and range finding. They were also taught the important difference between 'bearing' and 'inclination': the bearing being the angle formed between your own fore and aft line and your line of sight, measured in degrees, red or green (port or starboard), whereas inclination was the angle formed between the enemies fore and aft line and your line of sight, again measured in degrees, left or right. Several of the marines had some difficulty in remembering the colours for port and starboard and which was left and which was right. Dacre AJ remembered a simple phrase that someone had taught him when he first started sailing years ago: there is no red port left in the bottle. After that, things became a lot easier and mistakes were few.

Good training was essential to the safety of any ship. To emphasise this, the instructors would constantly remind everyone of the story of HMS *Devonshire* which took place in the 1920s. During a live firing exercise, the gun captain had opened the breech after a misfire which led to the cordite charge exploding, killing the entire marine gun crew comprising an officer and sixteen other ranks. The sergeant was never found; he was missing presumed drowned.

Once they had finished their gunnery training, the four groups moved onto general seamanship. Here they were taught how to 'pull' a whaler, semaphore and Morse code, plus a variety of nautical knots such as running bowlines, reef knots and sheepshanks. Then they were taught about fire-fighting and damage control.

However, by far the most demanding was the rigging of 'sheer legs', a tripod lifting device. Each group was required to compete against each other. They were given three huge rounded beams of timber, each one maybe fifteen feet long and about six inches in diameter, some rope and a block and tackle. The object of the task was to rig the poles into a tepee shape by lashing them together at one end and spreading the other end into the shape of a triangle. From the top was hung the block and tackle which could then be used as a crane for lifting a gun barrel. The whole structure was erected by simply using brute force. After several days, Dacre AJ and his team became so proficient that none of the other groups could out-perform them.

One morning Colour Sergeant Kelly informed them that he had arranged another little test. Out of the back of a parked Royal Navy truck jumped a dozen huge sailors and their Petty Officer. They all looked amazingly fit. The Colour Sergeant informed the marines that these matelots were part of the Plymouth Gun Team, who regularly competed with sailors from Portsmouth and Chatham in the famous gun race at the Royal Tournament.

Both teams squared up and prepared themselves for the competition. A whistle blast started the race and the two teams flew into action, muscles straining, hearts beating extra fast as they struggled to get the sheer legs up and into position. To make things more difficult, a gun barrel actually had to be lifted off the ground. By sheer effort and determination the marines just managed to be first but it had been a close run thing. Then the order to dismantle the structure was given. The Navy were very fast and managed to finish several seconds ahead of the marines. Both teams were blowing hard from their exertions. The competition was judged to be a draw. The two teams gave each other 'three cheers' and they all shook hands.

One of the sailors commented to Dacre AJ, 'Bloody hell Royal! We do this for six months of the year. You lot have only just learnt. Promise me you won't ever think about entering the Tournament, we wouldn't stand a chance!'

It had not been all work and no play. At the weekends many of the marines were to be found in nearby Union Street, in the public houses, amusement arcades or dance halls. One particular evening Dacre AJ and his friend Jock met a lovely young girl named Violet. Being gentlemen, they tossed a coin to see who would have the good fortune to take her home. Jock won. Smiling happily, he put his arm around his prize as they disappeared into the night.

Being a Royal Marine alone in Plymouth did not last for very long. Dacre AJ soon found himself talking to an equally lovely young woman named Maria. She was Italian and just eighteen years old. He felt that he was 'well in' there and they spent most of the evening conversing in Italian. Maria explained that she was the companion to an elderly lady who liked to be in bed by nine o'clock each evening. If he felt so inclined, he might knock gently on the front door after nine thirty, in which case he might be lucky enough to get some refreshments on his way back to barracks. At the appointed time Dacre AJ knocked on the door. As Maria opened it he could see that she was stark naked. Taking his hand she gently led him into the front room and onto a large settee in front of a roaring coal fire. She was a young lady who believed in taking her time and experimenting. Her lips and hands were everywhere. She was also patient and knew exactly when to pause and hold off. It was clearly not her intention to see all of her hard work pass by in one mad moment of passion.

Much later, on his way back to barracks, he recalled some of the educational lessons given at the Depot which they all had to attend. Their teacher was a young lieutenant in the Royal Navy. His lessons were on the effects of carnal pleasures, in particular the consequences of not taking any precautions when in foreign ports. The illustrations were too lurid and awful to ignore. Dacre AJ could not remember if the officer said anything about British ports. Nevertheless, he did make it very clear that whether on a ship or in barracks, there was always a free supply of 'French Letters' to be had from the Sick Bay and no questions were ever asked.

The girls that frequented the bars near the barracks were renowned for their generosity. Those that had earned the reputation as an 'easy lay' were more or less ignored by the bulk of the vigilant marines. However, there were always a few who were caught out. They would end up in front of the Medical Officer because they were either 'squeezing up', 'pissing broken glass' or, in the worst cases, both! The treatment, he had been told, was equally painful and didn't bear thinking about. Anything was better than getting a dose of the clap.

Dacre AJ then realised that he hadn't actually had anything to eat. He was famished. No matter, he thought. Food had been the last thing on his mind that evening. Anyway, there was bound to be some bread, cheese and pickles available in the dining hall when he got back.

For the next few days everyone watched the noticeboard for their postings because, as fully trained Royal Marines, the members of the squad were expected to take their place wherever the Corps required them to go. Eventually the notice was put up. Since they already had their Divisional numbers, they found themselves being split up between Chatham, Portsmouth and Plymouth. Each of the three ports had certain units of the fleet attached to them. In all probability this would mean that they might never see two thirds of their squad mates again. This was how the Corp worked and you just had to accept it. Dacre AJ had already said goodbye to his Italian temptress, so that night he and his squad mates had a last get together in the barrack's wet canteen.

The following morning they all paraded for embarkation but this time not as a squad but as three separate groups. It was hard to do since they had been together for well over six months, through hell and back some might say. However, it had always been expected, and at the end of the day they were prepared for the separation. So it was that Dacre AJ and twenty other marines said farewell to Plymouth as they boarded their train and hello to Chatham.

PART TWO

Per Mare – By Sea

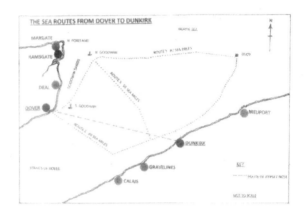

THE SEA ROUTES FROM DOVER TO DUNKIRK

Chapter 19

The War Rooms, London. Deep beneath the bowels of Whitehall a cabinet meeting was taking place. The Prime Minister felt it was safer down there since London had already experienced a number of German air raids. Winston Churchill sat watching Neville Chamberlain very carefully. He was clearly not a well man. He looked pale and exhausted and his hands were shaking, albeit slightly. Churchill also knew that the PM was beginning to lose much of his political support, both in the House and in his own party. Things did not look good. The other members of the cabinet were making their reports. Churchill was only half listening as he reflected on the current situation.

The war with Germany was not going well. It was true that His Majesty had visited the forward areas of the British troops in France in order to see the situation for himself. This had, of course, been a great morale booster for the men but had actually achieved little else. On the home front, rationing was well underway as the country began to tighten its belt. Already the idea of 'digging for victory' was being used to encourage more people to grow their own food, and not just in the countryside. There was even talk of digging up Lord's Cricket Ground and planting vegetables. On the plus side, the Air Minister, Sir Archibald Sinclair, had reported that aircraft production had risen dramatically and had at last outstripped the Germans. However, tactically things were deteriorating.

True the BEF was now fully in place, bolstering the French and supporting the Belgians. Numerically the allies were strong. But Churchill knew that the Maginot Line would not hold. He had seen for himself when he had visited the region. Anthony Eden had been correct in his assessment. Unfortunately the French just couldn't see it themselves. The Germans would simply go around the so-called impregnable defences. The French were living in a fool's paradise if they thought for one minute that that archaic defence system would keep the might of the Nazi war machine at bay. The enemy were moving swiftly and efficiently across Europe. Nothing and no-one seemed to be able to stop them.

It was at this point that the Prime Minister interrupted Churchill's reverie.

'Would the First Sea Lord like to make his report now?'

Immediately Churchill was back in the present, all his private thoughts pushed to back of his mind.

'Thank you Prime Minister. As you know, on the morning of the ninth of April the Germans invaded Denmark and Norway. Denmark, totally unprepared, surrendered by lunchtime. The Norwegians fought back with spirit, although simultaneous enemy landings at six different places pushed their limited forces to near breaking point. Both we and the French sent troops to Norway in an effort to assist them. These landed at Namsos, Andalsnes, Trondheim and at Narvik in the north. The first ashore were the Royal Marines detachments from the two cruisers, HMS *Sheffield* and HMS *Glasgow*. Their task was to secure the harbour and railhead at Namsos until the main force, under Major General Carton de Wiart, arrived which it did two days later. As soon as the main force had landed, the marines re-joined their ships and returned to the UK. A few days later another force made up of Royal Marines from HMS *Nelson*, *Hood* and *Barham*, at present refitting in the

UK, landed from four sloops. Their task was to hold the landing place and railhead at Andalsnes. I have to tell you that whether on ship or ashore, our troops were subjected to continual air attacks since the Germans had seized the key air fields and had therefore quickly gained air superiority. Our troops, who were neither trained nor equipped for winter warfare, were easy targets for air attacks. Although they fought well, as one would expect of them, they were out-classed by the German Mountain Division. In less than ten days the allied forces were pushed back and had to be evacuated through Namsos and Andalsnes. Incidentally, the Royal Marines were the last to leave in both ports.'

'Thank you, Winston, for your concise report,' said Chamberlain.

Those gathered around the table murmured their agreement.

'There is one other thing, Prime Minister.'

Chamberlain looked up sharply. Now what, he thought? He indicated with his hand that Churchill should continue.

'As you know, the Military Co-ordination Committee which consists of the three Service Ministers and their Service Chiefs was set up under the chairmanship of Lord Hatfield. Its role was to advise the War Cabinet on strategic proposals. Unfortunately the group seemed to lack the authority to override a Minister when he was fighting his corner. I was as guilty as the next man. You asked me to take over the chairmanship but I fear I may have done more harm than good, particularly when we were discussing Norway. You may wish to review the arrangements for this committee.'

'Thank you, Winston, for your appraisal. I am sure that we all appreciate your honesty. I will give some serious thought to how the Committee should function and I will come back to you with my ideas.

'Gentlemen, to finish our business of the day, you will be pleased to know that the first Commonwealth troops will start to arrive tomorrow. The Canadians will dock at Liverpool and the Australians and New Zealanders will land at Southampton. Arrangements for their stay and training are well in hand. Finally, I would just like to say that we do not know what the next few days or weeks will bring. We must, therefore, be prepared for all eventualities.'

Chapter 20

Dacre AJ and his fellow marines arrived at the Chatham Barracks on a very cold, wet and miserable Monday. After being dismissed from the parade by the Regimental Sergeant Major, they were allocated to their various companies. The rest of the day was theirs to settle in. Once again there was some shuffling around of billets in order to ensure that friends were as near as possible. Dacre AJ knew that he would miss his friend Jock and, of course, all the others. However, he did have a standing invitation to visit his Scottish friend in Glasgow at any time. In the Royal Marines friends are always moving on, it happens all the time. You just hope that sometime in the future you meet up again.

Dacre AJ found that making new friends was quite easy. When he had first joined up, everyone was as different as chalk from cheese but after the hardships of training, so necessary in order to create the finished article, it was as if they had all come from the same mould. They were now members of one of the strongest families in existence: they were a brotherhood that would remain united both in war and in peace, the elite of the armed forces. Men were encouraged, indeed expected, to give that extra five per cent above and beyond what was required. This was achieved by instilling into every marine a pride in his unit, his Corps and a belief in oneself.

Once the marines had settled in, each man had his own responsibilities. The daily grind of barrack life inevitably rolled on. Keeping a close eye on the company noticeboard was essential for things like guard duty, fire piquet and the like. Morning parades became routine, interrupted with sessions of drill and the occasional ceremony for a visiting admiral or other dignitary. The news that the Prime Minister had resigned and that King George VI had asked Winston Churchill to lead a coalition government was greeted enthusiastically by the marines at all levels. However, the fact that Germany had invaded Holland, Belgium and Luxembourg dampened their spirits. Just to underline the seriousness of the situation, the government cancelled the Whitsun holiday and the King's official birthday in early June.

One morning, Dacre AJ and his company were ordered to parade in full fighting order and rifles. They were told that there was to be an extended period of further infantry training, pending deployment either as a ship's detachment or as a landing force. Whichever of these it was going to be, it meant that they were going abroad and were likely to see some action. However, to Dacre AJ's surprise he was told to 'fall out' and report to the CSM's office at the double. On arrival he was marched straight in to see the Company Commander, Major A. Perrett RM.

'Stand at ease!'

The marine naturally obeyed the command, completely mystified as to what was going on.

'Now look, old chap, I'm afraid I have some rather bad news for you. I know you are itching to get at Jerry, aren't we all, but I can't let you go. According to our records you are underage. You will not be eighteen until the first of August. I'm sorry but there it is. Rules is rules. You are confined to barracks until further notice.'

The youngster was shocked. He couldn't believe what he had just heard. After all that training he had to stay behind. Once outside in the coolness of the morning air he suddenly became angry: angry with himself for being under eighteen and angry with the Corps which he felt had let him down. Taking off his equipment and rifle he threw them down on the ground in complete frustration. He felt the tears begin to well up, he couldn't help it, such was his disappointment. Unknown to the marine, the CSM had been watching him. He came up to the youngster and spoke in a quiet, fatherly manner, full of understanding yet with authority.

'Now then, young Dacre, that will not do. Someone might see this as an act of insubordination. I suggest that you pick up your kit and follow me, there's a good Royal Marine.'

The youngster did as he was bid, discipline taking over, and followed the Sergeant Major into his office.

'Sit yourself down, lad. Now I know you are disappointed but as that officer of marines has said, rules is rules. You can't buck the system I'm afraid. It's there for a purpose and we have to abide by them whether we like it or not.'

Dacre AJ just sat and looked at him. Much of his anger had gone by now. He was just left with a feeling of total hopelessness. He knew the CSM was right but that didn't make his situation any easier.

The CSM continued, 'You know a bit about small boats don't you?'

Dacre AJ nodded his head.

'How serious are you about doing something worthwhile, you know, getting involved?'

'I am very serious, Sergeant Major. If the Corps won't let me fight then by hook or by crook I'll do something else, something that will let me help the war effort.

Anything is better than being stuck in barracks as 'rear party'.'

The CSM studied the youngster carefully. He liked what he saw. The lad had a good nautical background and was clearly very competent. His King's Badge was evidence of that. He had made up his mind.

'Okay, son, here's the situation. The Admiralty has ordered all small boat owners to register their boats within fourteen days. We have not been told why this information is needed but I can make an educated guess. If what I suspect comes to pass in the next couple of weeks, some of those small boats are going to need crews. Are you up for this?'

Dacre AJ didn't need long to think about this opportunity. Like the CSM, he could see immediately where this was going.

'Yes, Sergeant Major I am!' then added, 'Do you think it will come to this?'

'I do, lad, I'm afraid to say. I can't see it ending any other way. Hold yourself ready. Just take an overnight bag and, of course, no uniform. I'll square it with the Company Commander, so you won't have to worry about that. Just don't say anything about this to anybody else. Let's keep this just between the two of us.'

Chapter 21

The War Rooms, London. Winston Churchill sat looking at his War Cabinet colleagues. Neville Chamberlain had agreed to stay on as Lord President of the Council. He was joined by Clement Atlee as Lord Privy Seal, together with the Foreign Secretary, Lord Halifax, and Arthur Greenwood, Minister without Portfolio. Churchill believed in keeping the War Cabinet to a relatively small number of people, he felt that it allowed for a more efficient war effort. Today they were joined by the three service Ministers and their Chiefs of Staff and the Minister for War and Anthony Eden as well as the Chief of the General Staff, Lord Ironside. Also present were numerous aides and secretaries. As a result the room was overcrowded and the air was thick with cigarette and cigar smoke. There was an animated buzz of conversation. On a table covered in green baize lay a large scaled map of Northern France and Belgium. Churchill brought the meeting to order, the room went very quiet.

'Gentlemen, I am going to ask General Ironside to give us an overview on the current situation in France with particular regard to the BEF.'

'Thank you, Prime Minister. As you know, on the tenth of May the Germans attacked France and the Low Countries. The German Panzer Divisions and their mobile infantry columns have moved more quickly than we anticipated.'

Picking up an old billiard cue, he pointed to the map on the table. The positions of the Germans were shown in black and the Allies were in red.

'This is our front line. To the left of the line and in the north, we have the Belgians and the French 1st and 7th Armies, together with the BEF. They are facing German Army Group B. To the right of the line and to the south are the French 2nd and 9th Armies. They are facing the German Army Group A. The Germans have managed to punch a breach nearly sixty miles wide between the Allies and their troops are flooding through here.' He pointed to the relevant position. 'The French 2nd and 9th Armies are collapsing. General Gamelin, the French Commander, has been blamed for this and has been replaced by General Weygrand as Commander in Chief of all French Forces. The situation to the left of the line is also becoming critical. At our previous meeting we discussed Lord Gort's plans: either to fall back to the Channel Ports or to retreat to the River Somme. You will recall that I advised against these. I felt that a retreat south was a better plan and, on your orders, I went to France to tell him. On arrival, I was horrified to find that the Germans had advanced much further and faster than we could have ever imagined. If the BEF had gone south, as I had suggested, they would have run headlong into Panzer Divisions and in all likelihood they would have been decimated. I must tell you that I have learnt a valuable lesson from that experience: there is no substitute for 'eyes on the ground'.

'I then went to see the French High Command only to find that they had lost their nerve and didn't really know what was going on. As far as they were concerned, France was collapsing around their ears. After some effort, I did manage to persuade them to counter attack northwards, as Gort and the BEF pushed south, hopefully cutting the

German line of communications. However, the French were not able to counter attack as Gort had requested and, without any air support, the attack failed, thus ending any hope of a break through.'

General Ironside paused to take a sip of water from his glass.

The Prime Minister interjected, 'I should like to confirm that I flew to Paris with Lord Ismay in his capacity as the Head of the Military Wing of the War Cabinet Secretariat, to talk to General Weygrand. Although I am given to understand that he has never actually commanded troops in the field, he did impress me with his appraisal of the situation and his plan to counter attack northwards. At that time I was so convinced that his plan would work that I sent a telegram to Gort telling him as much and wishing him well in the coming battle. However, at that time I was not aware that there actually wasn't a French army to move northwards. I subsequently sent a telegram to Weygrand, emphasising that his plan would only work if the French took the initiative. I have to tell you that they did not!'

General Ironside then continued, 'With the collapse of the French counter attack, Lord Gort became convinced that it was no longer possible to stand against the Germans. His forces have insufficient supplies and ammunition. His men have already gone onto half rations. He has received no battle orders from the French High Command.'

At that moment the Secretary of State for War, Anthony Eden, chose to interrupt.

'I received a telegram from Lord Gort voicing his misgivings about the whole situation. I gave this a good deal of thought before replying: that if all else failed, arrangements would be made to withdraw the BEF and Allies from the north coast.'

General Ironside nodded his head in agreement and then continued.

'As we now know, in order to avoid encirclement, Lord Gort has ordered a withdrawal from Arras, back to the coastal ports of Boulogne, Dunkirk and Calais. In his view the only way to save the BEF is to evacuate the army, and this time I agree with him.'

Complete silence descended on the room, each person trying to come to terms with the implications of the General's report. The Prime Minister was the first to speak.

'Thank you General. I am sure we all appreciate your illuminating and frank report. Well, gentlemen! How are we to progress from here if we are to save the BEF?'

Anthony Eden spoke next. 'Clearly, Prime Minister, we must evacuate our troops as soon as possible!'

There was a general consensus of agreement from around the table. Churchill fixed him with a steely gaze.

'I am aware of that, Anthony. What I want to know is how! How are we going to get these thousands of troops home?'

The Naval Chief of Staff decided to take the bull by the horns.

'Prime Minister, I propose that we appoint Vice-Admiral Bertram Ramsey as Operational Planning Flag Officer Commanding to see this through. He can operate from Dover; perhaps make use of the underground bunkers at the castle. He is a good man and a brilliant organiser. If anyone can do this, he can. However, I'm afraid he doesn't have a great number of ships at his disposal, some destroyers and personnel craft, but not enough to move an army.'

Churchill sat pondering the suggestion. The more he thought about it the more he liked the idea. After all, he had been the one who, as First Sea Lord, had encouraged Ramsey out of retirement. He couldn't think of a better man.

'Agreed,' he said. 'Make the order and inform all those who need to know. I will speak to the Vice-Admiral personally. I do not think he will need much persuasion.'

One of the naval aides raised his hand.

'Yes!' growled the Prime Minister.

'Sir, about the transport. There is the register of small boats.'

'What?' he snapped back.

Undeterred, the aide managed to continue, 'All the owners of boats between thirty and one hundred feet long were requested to register their boats with the Admiralty.

'And who originated this order?'

There was an embarrassing silence. You could have heard a pin drop.

'Well? I am waiting for an answer.'

'We don't know, sir.'

'Don't know, don't know! You sit there and tell me that you don't know. The man deserves a medal and you don't know!'

Churchill raised his eyes towards the ceiling in utter desperation.

'Well there's part of your answer. I suggest that the Admiralty should assemble as large a number of these small vessels in readiness to proceed to France as soon as possible. Anything else?'

'There is one other thing, sir. Although Boulogne and Calais are still in Allied hands, it would seem that Dunkirk has the better port facilities and would, therefore, lend itself more readily to a planned evacuation.'

'So be it!' said the Prime Minister. 'Now, I suggest that we alert the railways so that they can get themselves organised, especially the Southern Region. They will have to bear the brunt of transporting the troops once they have landed at Dover. Also, notify all hospitals and medical facilities in the south east of England to expect casualties. No, on second thoughts change that to include the Midlands. You had better include all military establishments and barracks, make sure that they have the necessary clothing and equipment just in case it is needed. Oh, and do not forget the bus companies. They will have just as an important role to play. Finally, let us not delay in planning this venture so that, if and when the time comes to make the final decision, we have everything in place to save what we can of the BEF.'

Chapter 22

Dacre AJ sat at the back of the single decker bus as it made its way between Chatham and Maidstone. He was deep in thought, going over the events of the last few days. Some of his company had gone to Boulogne to cover the naval demolitions team that had been sent to destroy the docks. They had embarked on a destroyer at very short notice and had returned the following day, safe and sound. Two days later, a larger force of marines had mustered at the Chatham Barracks under Captain Courtice RM and had landed at Calais where the fighting was reported to be heavy and desperate.

The CSM and the Company Commander had decided to send Dacre AJ on two weeks' compassionate leave. It was explained to him that what he did on leave was his business and had nothing to do with the Royal Marines. This was not strictly true, of course, but it was a neat and simple solution, thought Dacre AJ. It gets him out of the way and free to get involved as a boat's crew.

The trip to Maidstone was uneventful to say the least, except for the elderly passenger sitting next to him who started telling ghost stories about the steep hill they were descending on the last phase of the journey. Apparently Blue Bell Hill was renowned for someone, often a young woman, who would cadge a lift with an unsuspecting traveller, only to have disappeared by the time they had got to the bottom of the hill. This was not the first time he had heard such stories. Generally, he chose to ignore them.

The bus meandered down off the North Downs and into Maidstone, the county town of Kent. In the town centre the marine got off the bus and took a couple of minutes to get his bearings. The High Street was very wide and clearly still used as a market place. It sloped gently down towards the River Medway and the bridge that crossed it. Both sides of the High Street were lined with shops, inns and hotels. It looked a fairly prosperous place. He checked the street signs. Week Street intersected with King Street and Gabriel's Hill. At the crossroads there was a large and imposing statue of Queen Victoria, celebrating her Diamond Jubilee. Nearly all the buildings had their windows taped up as a precaution against bombing and several of the banks had sandbagged entrances. Despite this, the place was busy, people trying to go about their normal business almost as if the country wasn't at war.

Dacre AJ hefted his grip and began to walk down towards the river. His Sergeant Major had given him the name of a boat and its owner who, he said, would be pleased with some help. How the CSM had come by this information the youngster thought it better not to ask. When he arrived at the quayside it was bedlam. A Naval party, under the command of a Chief Petty Officer, was 'liberating' as many boats as they could, simply by cutting the mooring lines and attaching them to a steam pinnace at anchor, midstream. A number of the owners were remonstrating with the CPO but he was very firm.

'Either you crew your own boat or we take it – simple choice!'

Dacre AJ found what he was looking for, a thirty-five foot long sleek cabin cruiser. The boat had a dark blue hull whilst the superstructure was made of beautiful varnished

166

mahogany. The name *Gypsy Rose* was on its stern. The owner, Mr Leslie Thomas, was standing in the wheelhouse. He was a tall, thin man with dark receding hair, greying at the temples. He looked up as the marine approached the quayside. He had a friendly face.

'Are you Dacre AJ?' he asked.

'Yes, sir!'

'Come aboard, you're most welcome. Stow your gear in the forward cabin. Oh, and by the way, you can cut out that 'sir' nonsense. You can call me Tim or, if you prefer, Mr Thomas, I don't mind which. What do you answer to?'

'AJ is fine, sir, I mean, Mr Thomas.'

They both laughed.

'Right then, let us get away from this mad house; we have a long way to go.'

As soon as the marine had cast off the bow and stern line, Mr Thomas expertly helmed the boat into mid river, and gently opened the throttles to a quarter speed as they slipped quietly downstream.

'Do you fancy a cup of tea?' asked the owner.

'Thank you. That would be good.'

Dacre AJ hadn't realised how hungry and thirsty he was.

'Take the helm then. I'll go below and brew up. I expect you would like a sandwich or two!'

The marine took the wheel. What a joy this was, he thought, steering such a fine boat on a warm sunny day. Overhead in the clear blue sky there were one or two vapour trails of fighter planes, Spitfires maybe. These were the only sign that the country was at war. Mr Thomas came back into the wheelhouse with two large mugs of tea and a pile of doorstop sandwiches.

'Do you know this part of the river?' asked Mr Thomas.

The marine shook his head since he had a mouthful of sandwich.

'Well Maidstone is a small but busy inland port. It serves the commercial and agricultural hinterland for this part of Kent. Of course it is less busy since the railways came, but, nevertheless, it is still well used. Between here and the lock, which is about three miles downstream, there are some paper mills and warehouses to our right, whilst on our left it is mainly open countryside and orchards with the exception of Allington Castle which is twelfth century, I believe. It was restored in 1905 by a certain Sir Martin Conway. The lock up ahead is very large, so that in the old days it could take the massive Thames barges that needed to get up to the town. Below the lock the river is tidal.'

He checked his wrist watch.

'The tide should just about be on the turn. That should help, perhaps, give us an extra couple of knots of speed. We are heading for Whitstable to refuel and take on supplies. The Admiralty has arranged all this.'

They were fast approaching the lock. Mr Thomas took the helm. Fortunately the lock gates were open so they were able to motor straight in and tie up. Since they were the only boat, the lock keeper closed up and began to let the water out. Fifteen minutes later they were on their way. The going was good, maybe ten or twelve knots with the tide, the bow wave striking the river bank as they passed.

The trip down to the Rochester Basin and beyond to Chatham Reach passed quickly. The two men spent time getting to know each other, pausing occasionally to look at the massive paper mills or the lime and cement works that lined the river bank. Dacre AJ told Mr Thomas about his grandfather, then about his training as a Royal Marine and why he couldn't go abroad. In return, Mr Thomas explained that he was classified as an 'essential war worker' because he was in the film processing business. Of course films, particularly war information and propaganda films, were of vital importance to the war effort, so he had to stay at home. He was married, his wife's name was Amy but there were no children as yet. He had owned the boat for about three years and had bought it at a knock-down price from someone who had gone bankrupt. He and his young nephew, John, used the boat at weekends or during the summer holidays and had often gone across the Channel to France.

At Rochester they slowed down as they entered the basin. Even so, Even so, the wake from their boat managed to set several of Short's sea planes rocking at their anchorage. About a dozen other boats, either similar in size or slightly larger, were by now going in the same direction, all heading out to sea. The crews waved to each other and shouted greetings that were mostly lost on the wind. Nevertheless, it was comforting to know that they were not alone in this great adventure.

Chatham Harbour came and went. It was a hive of activity! Numerous warships had steam up and were clearly getting ready to put to sea. A whole host of other smaller boats such as tugs, drifters and small coasters were also getting ready. Dacre AJ even saw a couple of ferry boats; goodness knows where they had come from. On the starboard side he could see the dockyards and beyond that the Naval Base and his Marine Barracks.

Once in the more open water, Mr Thomas opened the throttles to full power. The boat leapt forward as they entered Gillingham Reach. Mr Thomas shouted above the wind and the sound of the powerful twin engines.

'We have to follow the marked way. It is really for the warships so that they can come and go at will. Although we are a shallow craft, we only draw about eighteen inches.

The salt marshes and sand flats are so treacherous that it pays to follow the buoys.'

They motored on, following the meandering route and taking great care to avoid the numerous islands that choked the entrance to the River Medway. Mr Thomas stared at all the warships, mostly cruisers and destroyers with the occasional frigate. He was impressed by their sheer size and robustness. Dacre AJ decided to show off his little bit of naval knowledge.

'Did you know that the really big battleships, like HMS *Royal Sovereign* or HMS *Revenge*, can't get into Chatham, it's too shallow for them. The nearest they can berth is Sheerness on the Isle of Sheppey. So the Admiralty, in their wisdom, has them dock down at Plymouth which is a deep water harbour. This means that marine detachments and ship's crew from here have to travel all the way down to there in order to join their ships. It never makes any real sense to us but I suppose it does to someone somewhere in the Admiralty!'

They motored on, passing East Hoo Creek on the port side and Burntwick Island on the starboard. The open sea beckoned. As they passed Queenborough they could just see that the harbour was packed tight with ships and boats of all shapes and sizes. As they rounded Garrison Point at Sheerness, it was the same story again.

'It's as if the whole of the Merchant Marine is on the move,' said Dacre AJ.

'Well I expect they are, certainly from the east and south coast. Who knows, maybe from even further away.'

Once clear of the town, Mr Thomas set a course east south east for Warden Point, about seven miles following the shoreline. On reaching the Point, Mr Thomas took a compass bearing for Whitstable Harbour. Crossing the mouth of the River Swale and then Whitstable Bay, the sea was as calm as a mill pond, no wind, just the sunlight reflecting off the water.

Entering the harbour was difficult because it was choc-a-block with boats. Many of these were either the local fishing boats or oyster dredgers. Whitstable was famous for its oysters. There were also a dozen or more small craft like themselves, clearly en-route for Ramsgate and beyond. On the quayside there were two small steam trains which served as shunters for dockside duties, as well as making the twice daily trip for passengers and freight to nearby Canterbury on what was known locally as the 'Winkle Line'.

Eventually they managed to tie up alongside two other boats. A young naval lieutenant had to climb across both boats to reach them. Checking his clipboard, he noted their names and that of the boat. He then issued them a chitty for fuel and supplies.

Dacre AJ elected to go for the supplies whilst Mr Thomas went to collect several five gallon cans of fuel. The marine found that there was a long queue. As he waited patiently, he was surprised to learn that many of the boat owners had come from as far as the Norfolk Broads. Indeed, some of the owners and their crew had never actually been to sea before! When he arrived at the head of the queue, he was handed eight large white loaves direct from the back of a delivery van. He couldn't help but notice that on the side of the van it said 'Dilnot's Bakeries'. He had been at school with a boy named David Dilnot and wondered if there was a family connection. No more time to think about that. He was promptly given a hessian sand bag containing six tins of sardines, four tins of bully beef, two packets of loose tea and four tins of condensed milk. He asked politely if there was any sugar.

'Sugar! You want to know if we've got any bleeding sugar! No there bleeding well ain't. Don't you know there's

171

a bleeding war on? Well I don't know! Whatever bleeding next!'

Feeling somewhat chastised and embarrassed, Dacre AJ made his way back to the *Gypsy Rose*. Back on the boat, the supplies were stowed away in the cabin and the fuel tanks were topped up. There were two fuel cans left over which they lashed tightly to the bulkhead of the cockpit for use later on.

'We'll be moving on the high tide which will be about 2.00 p.m. I suppose that is 0200 hours to you. I suggest we go ashore and get something to eat, then a couple of hours' sleep. Tomorrow is going to be a very long day,' said Mr Thomas.

'I know Whitstable quite well,' replied Dacre AJ. 'I have a small house on the seafront in nearby Tankerton. There's quite a good fish and chip shop just down the road from here in Harbour Street. We can eat there.'

An hour or so later, their appetites fully satisfied, the two of them were back on the boat wrapped up in a couple of blankets apiece. They were soon sound asleep.

At precisely 2.00 a.m., whistles and shouts awoke everyone in the harbour. There was nothing subtle about this send-off. Wiping sleep from their eyes, they began to get into their clothes, with some difficulty.

'I don't think I'll bother to undress again,' said Dacre AJ. 'It's too much like hard work!'

'I agree', said Mr Thomas. 'Now where the hell is my other boot?'

The boats left the harbour almost immediately, single line astern, their navigation and steerage lights seeming to wink in the darkness. Once outside the harbour, it was up to each boat to set its own speed. Mr Thomas powered the twin engines onto full throttle, the boat leapt forward. Soon they were passing Tankerton, then Swalecliffe and Herne Bay. Since these towns were observing blackout regulations it was quite difficult to know precisely where they were. However, the occasional light from the shore did help. It was a long, cold trip. The wind had got up during the night and a cool northerly was trying to push the boat in towards the shore. The helm needed to be constantly adjusted in order to prevent the boat from being driven onto the beach.

Dacre AJ was studying the chart down in the cabin. By his calculations it was a good thirty miles to the Foreness Point which was at the very easterly end of the Isle of Thanet. After that it was a further five miles or so to their first port of destination, Ramsgate. Mr Thomas had to reduce their speed because the wind had veered to a more easterly direction. The *Gypsy Rose* was barely making ten miles per hour. Eventually they passed Margate on the starboard side. It was at this point that Mr Thomas changed the boat's direction to due south, passing the North Foreland Point and the town of Broadstairs on the port side. Away to the east they could just make out the flashing light of the North Foreland lightship. As they arrived at the entrance to Ramsgate harbour, a signal light from the breakwater began to blink.

'AJ, do you read Morse code?' asked Mr Thomas.

'Yes I do,' the marine replied.

He picked up a pair of binoculars and began to study the signal.

'Message reads, 'Do not enter harbour. Anchor offshore and await further instructions. You may use your riding light.'

'Well, that's a fine welcome I must say! Still, I suppose we had better move a bit further out. Better to be safe than sorry. We don't want to be run down by some other boat, do we?'

Chapter 23

The War Rooms, London. General Sir John Dill, the new CIGS, sat idly tapping his fountain pen on the top of the table. He was a patient man and used to waiting. His predecessor, General Ironside, had warned him of the Prime Minister's penchant for one to one briefings. He felt that he was as well briefed as possible. However, he had been warned that Churchill had a nasty habit of asking the unexpected question and wanted an immediate answer. Prevarication was not a word that the Prime Minister recognised or tolerated.

The full War Cabinet was due to meet later that morning at 9.00 a.m. The Service Ministers and their Chiefs of Staff had been in conference, virtually throughout the night, thrashing out the problems that a full-scale evacuation of the BEF from Dunkirk would entail and how, more to the point, they could resolve them.

Winston Churchill entered the small room that served as his office. He was freshly shaven and in a clean shirt. He looked amazingly alert for someone of his years, especially at 7.00 a.m. in the morning. There were no preliminaries or pleasantries.

'Tell me the worst, General, and do not spare me any of the details.'

'Yes sir. Firstly, if I may, I'd like to give you an overview of the whole situation. The French High

174

Command does not seem to be able to find any answer to stop the German advance, even when it enjoys superior numbers. It would seem to me that their army is nothing more than a vast inefficient tool, incapable of taking the offensive. Where speed, massed strength and drive are needed in an attack, they make contact with the enemy only piecemeal. It is as if they are only concerned with self-defence. Their attacks are badly mounted and do not, I suggest, take into account the speed at which the Germans are advancing.

'Now, to Boulogne. The Germans have encircled the town, having already cut the French forces to pieces. The town is subject to heavy bombing and ground attack. Douglas Brownrigg moved his headquarters to a safer location in order to avoid further casualties. In the north, the Germans have broken through the Belgians who, it is believed, are likely to surrender at any time. This movement of the German army is threatening to cut off the BEF from the coast. Brownrigg was desperate for more fighting troops. He sent an urgent plea to the War Department. As a result some Royal Marines were despatched from Chatham as a stopgap, whilst the 20th Guards Brigade were sent to help defend the port. But it was too late! The Germans had already cut the road to Calais where there is still fierce fighting. The British positions in Boulogne were under heavy and constant attack, and although they managed to hold the line for a while, they were forced right back to the harbour. They were fighting German tanks with nothing but rifles and Bren guns. Some troops are fighting a rear guard action by holding the Gare Maritime railway station. They will remain there until their food and ammunition runs out. Their sacrifice has allowed us to withdraw a good number of the troops who have been evacuated by the Royal Navy, whose ships are under constant air attack. They have done a wonderful job of work under the most difficult conditions. I have nothing but the highest praise for them.

'Our intelligence tells us that the Germans did not see the capture of Calais as a priority. It would appear that Dunkirk was more important to them. Everything they had was focused there – troops, weapons, armour, supplies – all ready to support the final push to take that port. Then out of the blue comes, 'Haltbefehl'. The order to halt is believed to have come direct from Herr Hitler. Why, we do not know. There is some suggestion that their tanks may have run out of fuel but we are only guessing.'

The Prime Minister interrupted the General.

'Well, whatever the reason, they have left an open gap that we must exploit. It would seem to be a heaven-sent opportunity that may allow us to get the BEF away.'

The general nodded in agreement then continued.

'With the pressure off Dunkirk, the Germans then decided to refocus their efforts onto Calais. The 10th Panzers were tasked with taking the port. However, the town is well fortified and surrounded by marshland and dykes. Brigadier Nicholson is in command there. He set up his headquarters in the old citadel which was garrisoned by two hundred French troops, supported by a detachment of Royal Marines. You will recall that I recently sent Major General McNaughton over there in order to appraise both Calais and Dunkirk. His task was to assess, in principle, which of the two ports to use in the event of an evacuation. He informed me that in his opinion Dunkirk was the better choice but he felt that it was a question of organisation rather than re-enforcements if it were to be successful as a place of evacuation. Calais, he felt would not be able to hold out. As he predicted the situation in Calais worsened. They were being shelled and bombed continuously; our troops were facing an all-out attack. Gradually, they were forced back to the harbour. The Citadel became isolated, then overwhelmed. Nicholson was forced to surrender in order to save lives, although almost two hundred French and British troops did manage to escape. The Germans took twenty thousand prisoners of whom three thousand, five hundred were British. Calais managed to hold out for three days under tremendous pressure and in doing so gave the 10th Panzer's 2nd Infantry Regiment a very bloody nose. They took huge losses. The British and French forces are now pulling back to Dunkirk where, together with what remains of the BEF, they will form a bridgehead which will be held with no thought of retreat.'

Churchill interrupted again.

'I have always felt that Calais must be held for as long as possible. The longer we hold out, the more the Germans will try to take it, thus taking some of the pressure off the attack on Dunkirk. I have also thought that if we managed to hold the port, it would provide a useful 'sally-port' home, but I suppose one must be grateful for small mercies.'

There was a knock at the door and a young WRNS officer, slim and smart in her dark blue uniform, entered. She handed a signal paper to the General. He read it quickly and then passed it to the Prime Minister. It read:

'King Leopold of the Belgians has finally surrendered – unconditionally. In Lille, the French IVth and Vth Corps have also had to surrender. That just leaves the BEF and what is left of the French 1st Army.'

Churchill studied the signal for a good few minutes without saying anything, deep in thought.

Finally he said, 'I suppose that at the War Cabinet this morning we only need to make the decision to evacuate formal. We must save what we can of the BEF and of our Allies. I don't believe any one will object, do you General?'

'No sir. I don't see that there is any alternative.'

Silence filled the room as the enormity of what was going to happen came upon them. After a short while General Dill spoke quietly.

'I wonder what history will make of this retreat, sir, perhaps the worst that our country has ever suffered.'

Churchill thought for a moment or two, his mind racing and calculating as he considered possible ways forward.

Then he replied, 'History will make of it what we make of it! How we present this disaster to the people of Britain and to Parliament will largely depend on whether we are going to be pessimistic or optimistic. Personally, I have always tried to remain optimistic. The Battle for Flanders has ended, the Battle for Britain is about to begin. Somehow we must find a triumph in this defeat. Perhaps, if we are lucky, this extraordinary evacuation that we about to undertake, of so many men from beneath the German guns, might lend itself as a rallying cry.'

Both men sat quietly, reflecting on what the future might hold. The General thought about what the Prime Minister had said. It gradually dawned on him that Winston Churchill clearly had an iron resolve. It was no wonder that he had been asked by the King to steer the country through these dark and dangerous times.

'Come along, General, time for some breakfast. I am told that they do some very good eggs and bacon down here. Just what we need, I think.'

Chapter 24

The gentle rocking of the boat due to a slight swell awoke Dacre AJ. Dawn was just breaking, daylight was creeping up over the eastern horizon. The sea was still quite calm although there was a cool northerly wind blowing. Mr Thomas was already up. He had made a brew of tea and had cut some sandwiches. Entering the small wheelhouse, the marine saw that they were surrounded by about thirty or more other boats of all shapes and sizes. They were, like themselves, at anchor and had clearly been there all night. The signal light from the Ramsgate breakwater began to 'chatter' again.

'What is he saying?' asked Mr Thomas.

The marine studied the flashing light carefully, then said, 'Proceed to Dover with all speed. Report to the Harbour Master on arrival.'

A man from one of the nearby boats called across to them, asking what the message was since he didn't understand Morse code. Dacre AJ shouted across the message and then heard it being passed on to other boats. He hoped that they had all understood and that it hadn't got mixed up in the passing on. He remembered as a child playing a game known as Chinese Whispers, where a group of children would sit in a circle and a message was whispered from on to another, only to end up as something completely different. It was great fun he seemed to recall.

On the *Gypsy Rose* they winched up the anchor and set off. The marine decided to check the chart. The course was fairly straight forward, due south for the most part, following the coastline. The distance to Dover was about seventeen miles which, with the present weather conditions, they should manage in a couple of hours. They would cross Pegwell Bay, followed by Sandwich Bay and then onto the Small Downs. Although the Downs were a popular anchorage for inshore coastal vessels, nearby were the Goodwin Sands, a notorious graveyard for generations of ships, many of them still lurking just beneath the surface of the water. Of course their boat had a shallow draft which helped but, as Mr Thomas explained, the Goodwin Sands had a nasty habit of shifting so that maps and charts were often out of date or, at the very least, unreliable. Many an experienced sailor had been caught out. After that they would pass Deal and Walmer, then continue south past Saint Margaret's at Cliffe. At the South Foreland lightship they would alter course to south west and enter Dover Harbour.

Dacre AJ studied the sea with interest. Then he reached for a pair of binoculars. About a mile away to the east he thought he could just make out the tip of a masthead of some long forgotten sailing vessel, poking up above the water. Then he wondered if he might have been mistaken since it seemed to have disappeared.

'I have heard that people play cricket on the sands,' he said.

'Yes, that's right. I actually played there on one occasion. There needs to be a very low tide. They come out by boat usually from Ramsgate or Broadstairs. All being well, you can get a couple of hours' of play before the tide comes in. It can get pretty wet and the sand is soft, not ideal, but it is good fun. Some parts of the sands have pockets of quicksand so you have to watch out. More than one person has had to be pulled out with a good strong rope.'

They were making good time. Strung out behind them were twenty to thirty other boats all heading in the same direction.

As they passed Deal and Walmer, Mr Thomas called out, 'Your Alma Mater AJ?'

The marine looked at the long, low buildings on the shoreline. Memories came flooding back: the bull, the discipline, the parade ground, the shingle, the runs ashore, his girl Joan and, best of all, his friends, Jock and all the others. It all seemed so long ago and yet he still wasn't eighteen years old.

They entered Dover Harbour through the east entrance of the breakwater and headed towards the Harbour Master's quay to tie up. The activity in the harbour was frantic. Naval warships, mostly destroyers, were everywhere. Civilian boats were moored wherever they could. The whole place was alive with activity.

Dacre AJ noticed that the railway which ran onto the west pier was lined up with carriage after carriage of Southern Region trains. The roads leading to the harbour were full of buses, in a variety of garish colours, all waiting expectantly.

Mr Thomas went to check at the Harbour Master's office, whilst the marine went in search of supplies and some more fuel. They met up again an hour later. Mr Thomas explained that there was to be a briefing for all civilians by a Royal Naval officer at 11.00 a.m. in a nearby warehouse which they should attend.

At the appointed time, they arrived to find nearly a hundred men crammed into a small space not much larger than a double garage. At the far end was a stage and on it there was a large blackboard and easel which was covered with a grey blanket. A Royal Naval officer entered and took the stage. The gathered assembly went very quiet.

'Good morning. My name is Lieutenant Commander Copping of His Majesty's Royal Navy. Thank you for coming. You are all very welcome. Firstly, I have to explain to you that as civilian volunteers you will be subject to naval orders but not naval discipline! Having said that, you are free at any time to leave and return to your homes. Of course we hope that you will stay with us in order to see this emergency through.'

He continued, 'Following the collapse and surrender of our allied forces across the Channel, together we are going to evacuate as many of the British Expeditionary Force as we can that have been forced to retreat to Dunkirk. Your job will be to get into the beaches and to ferry out as many of the troops as you can to the larger vessels and warships waiting offshore.'

The officer paused and unveiled a large map that was pinned to the blackboard. It clearly showed the three routes from Dover across to Dunkirk. Taking a pointer he indicated the routes.

'You will all be given a copy of this map and a set of instructions. These are the three routes that you will be using. To the north is Route Y. This is the longest route at eighty-seven sea miles. It goes north to the Goodwin Light Ship, then across to the Kwinte Whistle Buoy and then down to Dunkirk. Route X is fifty-five sea miles. This also goes up to the North Goodwin Light Ship but then cuts diagonally down to Dunkirk. Route Z is the shortest route at just thirty-nine sea miles. However, this route is really only safe to use at night because the Germans have captured the coastal guns at Gravelines and they are shelling all boats during daylight hours. These three routes are being kept clear of mines. Should you wish to take a more direct route take great care because there are mines everywhere, both ours and the German's. I have to tell you that this will not be a 'walk in the park'. The port and beaches are under heavy fire from German artillery and infantry. The BEF and its allies are fighting a strong rearguard action but are gradually being pushed back. The whole area is also subject to aerial bombardment by the Luftwaffe. It is a very dangerous place. Let me emphasise that no-one will think any the worse of you if, in the end, you decide not to go. Please hold yourselves in readiness for the command to sail. One last thing. I would like to see the owners or skippers of the following boats right after this meeting.'

He then read out six names of which one was the *Gypsy Rose*. As the meeting broke up, Mr Thomas and Dacre AJ pushed their way to the front where they were joined by a dozen or so other men. Lieutenant Commander Copping gathered them around him.

'It has come to our attention that there may still be some survivors at Calais who were unable to get away. In particular, there is an army colonel who, if he is still alive, we are anxious to bring home. Last night nearly two hundred soldiers and marines were rescued by two of our small naval boats from right under the noses of the Germans. We have confirmation that there are others who are still hoping to be rescued. We are asking you to undertake this mission because your boats are fast, very manoeuvrable and have the great advantage of a shallow draft. I cannot order you to go; all I can do is to ask you to consider it. It will be extremely dangerous. You may be sunk or bombed. If, by chance, you are captured you will, in all likelihood, be shot as spies.'

Not one of the men said a word.

'Thank you. Now, to business. Most of your boats are too bright and shiny. Go to the paint store where each of you must collect a five gallon tin of dark grey undercoat. Use this to paint your boats from stem to stern, especially the bright work. Tonight, wear dark clothing and blacken your faces and hands. I will see to it that each boat is sent two marines to accompany you. They will be armed with light machine guns. I am afraid it is the best we can do at such short notice. I shall be in the lead boat, acting as navigator, so that we do not get lost. Good luck to you all and thank you once again.'

By mid-afternoon the *Gypsy Rose* was almost unrecognisable, lost under several coats of dark grey paint.

'It's a crying shame doing this to such a lovely boat but needs must I suppose!' said Dacre AJ.

Mr Thomas shook his head sadly. Was that a tear in his eye or was it caused by the wind which had suddenly sprung up, Dacre AJ wondered.

'Never mind,' the owner replied quietly, 'I am sure it will all come off with a bit of elbow grease. In any case, it will give me something to do when this lot is all over.

At that moment the two marines arrived as promised. One was carrying a Bren gun as if it were a toy. The other marine, who was considerably smaller, had two boxes of magazines.

Dacre AJ didn't recognise either of them and assumed that they had come from a ship's marine detachment, here, in the harbour. He had decided not to say anything about being a 'Royal' himself. He reasoned that it kept everything simpler and, of course, avoided any awkward questions. Mr Thomas had agreed to go along with this. He wasn't too happy about having weapons on board but had recognised the need. The two marines deposited their gear then disappeared back to the dockside. They returned fifteen minutes later, each of them carrying two full sand bags apiece. The big marine introduced himself as 'Timber' Woods and his oppo was 'Nobby' Clarke. Once on board, they busied themselves setting up a small gun emplacement on the forward deck; for the rest of the afternoon they kept themselves very much to themselves.

Sitting in the cabin, having a mug of tea, Dacre AJ decided to share a concern with Mr Thomas that had been nagging away at him since the briefing earlier that day.

'Does anything strike you as odd about this whole business?'

The older man thought for a second or two.

'Can't say that it does, AJ,' he replied.

'Look, the navy are using civilian boats and crew, now armed, to mount a rescue of a few men left behind in Calais.'

'Well that's true. But don't forget the colonel. The naval officer did say that he hoped he would be there.'

'Yes, that's just what I mean! Most colonels are either a commanding officer of a regiment or are something at Brigade or Division level, a staff officer perhaps. I admit I don't know much about what senior officers do but this whole thing seems to me to be all very odd.'

'You may well be right, AJ, I wouldn't know anything about how the military mind works but rest assured time will tell, it always does!'

Chapter 25

At precisely 2100 hours that evening, the small convoy slipped quietly out of Dover Harbour and headed across the English Channel towards France. The speed of the boats was much reduced in an effort to keep the sound of the powerful engines as quiet as they possibly could. They were barely making any headway. Without any navigation lights it was difficult to see the other boats. On leaving the harbour, Mr Thomas had taken the precaution of working out a compass bearing that would take them to Calais. He was not a novice at crossing the Channel and had, before the war, made over a dozen trips across this narrow strip of water.

The sea was amazingly calm. The half-moon was hiding behind some large clouds. After about thirty minutes they ran into a bank of sea mist. It was so dense that they could barely see their hands in front of their faces. Mr Thomas shut off the engines and they drifted silently, everyone on board listening for the sounds of the other boats. Nothing! He restarted the engines and, coming back onto his bearing, slowly moved forward. Suddenly from somewhere up ahead came several bright flashes accompanied by the sound of heavy gunfire. Mr Thomas immediately swung the boat through a ninety degree angle to port and gave the engines full throttle for a minute, before shutting everything down. They drifted silently, waiting.

'What do you think AJ?' whispered the older man.

'I'm not sure. If I had to guess I would say that one or two of the other boats have run into a German patrol boat. From the sound of it, I suspect that they may even have been sunk.'

'I agree. I'll come back onto our course and the try to 'box' our position.'

The marine knew exactly what Mr Thomas was trying to do. He had used this method during his training in map reading when trying to find his way around an obstacle, such as a wood or a quarry. It was a clever, but simple, idea. Assuming you were on a compass bearing, you turned either to your right or left at ninety degrees and counted the paces until you were well clear of the obstacle. Then you resumed your original bearing, until you were once again well past the obstacle. At that point you took a back bearing and, counting the exact number of paces, returned to a position that allowed you to pick up the original bearing. In theory it was all very simple but the marine knew that it could all go fearfully wrong.

About fifteen minutes later they emerged from the sea mist. Visibility was quite good and they could just make out the dark outline of the French coast ahead. There was no sign of any of the other boats. In the distance, directly in front of them, maybe four or five miles away, was Calais. The smell of burning was on the wind. Flames from the destruction of the port and the town could be easily seen through the binoculars. Further to the right and down the coast, a similar situation was apparent.

'That must be Boulogne over there,' whispered Dacre AJ.

'Yes, and over to our left, that must be Dunkirk!'

They both listened intently. The sound of the bombardment and explosions, together with flashes of light, came rolling towards them carried on the offshore breeze.

'Bloody hell!' said Mr Thomas. 'Those poor buggers are taking a real pounding and no mistakes. I wouldn't want to be in their shoes for all the tea in China.' They watched and listened for a few more minutes. 'Well, we had better try to get into Calais harbour. Will you tell those two up front what we are doing and ask them to keep a sharp lookout?'

Slowly the boat edged forward until they were well inside the harbour entrance. A number of ships had been sunk thus preventing any large rescue vessels from entering. Mr Thomas switched off the engines and, using some oars that Dacre AJ had liberated back in Dover, the four of them paddled their way between the obstacles. The occasional dead body was gently pushed out of the way as they nosed their way towards a wooden pier. Flames from the dockside buildings gave an unholy glow to the whole situation. The smell was appalling. German troops and vehicles could be seen some distance away moving freely about their business. Gently the boat touched a couple of the pier's wooden pillars. The two marines held the boat steady.

'There's no-one down here,' said Dacre AJ. 'I'm going to take a look up on top.'

'For goodness sake be careful, AJ!' said Mr Thomas in a stage whisper.

With that, the young marine scrambled up the side of the pier. When he reached the top, he threw himself flat onto the deck boards. Checking that all was clear and that he wasn't going to stumble into a German sentry, he snaked his way as quickly as he could towards what looked like a pile of fishing nets and old tarpaulins. He paused beside them to survey the situation in front of him. Suddenly an arm reached out and grabbed him around the throat. He felt himself being pulled under the nets.

A voice growled in his ear, 'Make a sound and I'll slit your bloody throat!'

Dacre AJ relaxed completely and offered no resistance.

The voice spoke again. 'Who the hell are you and what the fuck are you doing here?'

The arm around his neck eased slightly, allowing him to speak.

'I've come from Dover! We're here to rescue you!'

There was a shocked silence. The arm was removed. The youngster looked around the cramped hidey hole. There were six men crowded into a tiny cave-like sanctuary that had been burrowed deep beneath the nets and the tarpaulin. The owner of the arm was a Royal Marines corporal who introduced himself as 'Scouse' Lloyd. Four of the other men were soldiers. The fifth man was clearly an officer. He had been seriously wounded and just lay drifting in and out of consciousness. They were all dirty and dishevelled. Not one of them had a weapon. The corporal spoke for all of them.

'This 'ere officer is nearly done for. We did what we could for 'im, not that it was much. See that satchel he's clasping, he won't let it go for love nor money. 'Ere, watch. See for yourself.'

The corporal leant over and gave the satchel a tug. Immediately the officer awoke and hoarsely cried out a strangled 'No!'

The corporal looked around at the others then asked, 'Can you get us out of here then?'

'I think so but we need to go now and you have got to bring the officer with you, I think he may be important!'

Checking that all was clear Dacre AJ led the way back across the pier and down onto the boat. It proved to be difficult to get the wounded man down, so they had to rig a bowline and lower him as carefully as they could.

As soon as everyone was on board they cast off. Mr Thomas had decided that full throttle was the best strategy for getting them away as quickly as possible and to hell with the noise. The harsh boom of the twin engines echoed off the harbour walls. They were just leaving the entrance when German searchlights picked them out. This was immediately followed by the rattle of enemy machine guns. Mr Thomas began to steer the boat from side to side in an effort to avoid the deadly hail of bullets. Corporal Scouse Lloyd crawled forward to assist his fellow comrades. Together they returned fire and actually managed to put out the searchlight, which was a remarkable achievement considering what Mr Thomas was doing at that time with the boat.

By now, dawn was rising in the east. Tea and sandwiches were made for the soldiers which was the first food they had had in nearly three days. The officer, whose badges of rank indicated that he was a colonel, was sound asleep. His wounds had been re-dressed and he had been given some tablets to help ease the pain.

Just as everyone was settling down for the trip home, one of the marines shouted out 'Enemy planes!' Everyone looked up into the grey sky. They could hear them but not yet see them. Sure enough, two Stukas screamed low overhead. They banked sharply and came around for a second run. The marines on deck swung into action, bringing the Bren gun to bear and opening fire. But they were just a fraction too late. The bullets from the leading plane could be seen kicking up the water as they ploughed a deadly furrow towards the boat. The two marines, Nobby and Timber, took the full impact of the onslaught. The force of the enemy bullets flung them over the side. They were both dead before they hit the water. The corporal was slightly luckier. Although hit in several places, he collapsed on the deck with blood seeping from his wounds. Dacre AJ scrambled as fast as he could to the front of the boat. He picked up the weapon and clipped in a fresh magazine then waited for the planes to come around again.

'More planes!' someone shouted.

The young marine waited, holding the Bren gun on his hip. 'They're ours' he shouted, as two Spitfires streaked overhead, waggling their wings.

The Germans had had enough and were happy to head for home.

They searched for the two dead marines but without success, the sea had just swallowed them up. The wounded corporal was dragged below where they did the best they could to patch him up. Dacre AJ thought he would live since his injuries didn't seem to be life threatening, although the same couldn't be said for the colonel who appeared to have taken a turn for the worst. As the youngster was tying up the last bandage on the corporal's arm, the veteran looked him squarely in the eye.

'You're no civilian! You handled that Bren like a professional. Just who the hell are you?'

The youngster thought about this for a second or two then decided to come clean.

'I'm a 'Royal' like you! I'm underage and I'm supposed to be on compassionate leave.'

The JNCO looked at him and just smiled.

'I knew it! I can always spot a bootneck. Don't you worry, lad, I'll say nought! You and your mate have just saved our lives. Your secret is safe with me. Good luck to you!'

Eventually, on reaching the safety of Dover Harbour they tied up the *Gypsy Rose* and unloaded the wounded and the soldiers. Dacre AJ took the satchel from the unconscious officer and climbed up onto the quayside. To his surprise, walking towards him was Lieutenant Commander Copping.

'So you made it back! How did you get on?' he asked.

'We managed to save six men, including your colonel and his satchel, but we lost the two marines when we were attacked by enemy planes. How about you, how did you get on?'

'We ran into a German patrol boat just as we emerged from that sea mist. They surprised us, just seemed to come from out of nowhere. We lost four dead and two boats were sunk. The rest of us were so badly damaged that, what with casualties, we had to give up and return to Dover. We only managed that by slipping back into that bank of mist and hiding from the Germans. We were very lucky.'

'This was an expensive trip then: six dead and two boats lost!'

The officer shook his head slowly.

'It all depends on how you look at it. Do you know what is in that satchel that you're still holding?' The marine shook his head. 'It's the German's battle plans for the taking of Dunkirk. It contains all the information that you could possibly want, such as troop positions, regiments, numbers of men, status, supplies, ammunition and fuel. The whole bally lot! Apparently the colonel came across a crashed enemy staff car in a ditch outside Calais. Both the driver and his passenger were dead and had been for some time. He found the satchel and checked the contents. He knew immediately the value of the documents and was desperate to get them back to England. He managed to send us a signal before getting himself wounded.'

The marine handed over the satchel.

'In that case you had better take this to their 'lordships'. I just hope it was worth it. But you had also better tell them that from what we saw last night through

192

our binoculars, I suspect this information is far too late. Dunkirk is about to fall to the Germans.'

Chapter 26

As soon as it was dark, the fleet of small boats left Dover Harbour. They were to rendezvous off Dunkirk at midnight. Other groups of boats were also coming from Ramsgate and Folkestone. Together, they formed a small armada. They all had to keep to the three agreed routes which the Royal Navy was constantly sweeping clear of mines. Operation Dynamo had begun. There were so many craft of all shapes and sizes going across the Channel that it was impossible to get lost. The sea was flat calm and visibility good. The sky was clear, the bright moon lending an eerie feeling to the whole proceedings.

Dacre AJ and Mr Thomas had spent much of the day carrying out some basic repairs to the *Gypsy Rose*, particularly to the forward section of the boat where cannon fire from the German Stukas had ripped open some of the decking. Nobody had come to claim the Bren gun so, with the owner's permission, the marine stowed it away in the hold, out of sight yet easy to access. He had thought that the weapon and its boxes of ammunition might come in handy and it was as well to be prepared.

On their way across the Channel, the two men had tried to identify as many of the boats and ships as they could. It was no easy task, particularly since they had to rely on the moonlight, and the sea seemed to be covered in all manner of small and medium sized craft. However, they did manage to spot several barges, a car and a passenger ferry, a few motor launches, a couple of tugs, several lifeboats, a wherry, some eel boats and three picket boats. There were also a number of yachts and pleasure craft of all kinds, some obviously expensive, others more modest in design. There were Thames River excursion launches, a Thames River fireboat and even a Woolwich Ferry. It was a truly amazing sight. Had the weather not been so good, many of these craft would not have been able to make the crossing.

Dunkirk was the third largest port in France. It had seven deep water basins, four dry docks and five miles of quays. It was surrounded by flat marshland which, in an emergency, could be flooded. Like Calais, Dunkirk had a series of old fortifications facing both to the sea and inland. Bastion 32 commanded the dock area. The beaches to the east of the town stretched for nearly sixteen miles beyond Nieuport to the mouth of the River Yser. These were remarkable for their uniform appearance, gently sloping down to the sea. Little wonder that before the war they had been popular with holiday-makers. Malo les Bains to the east of Dunkirk had even been famous for its casino and fun fair. Indeed, Mr Thomas had visited this area in his boat on numerous occasions and knew the area quite well.

Just after midnight, the *Gypsy Rose* arrived off the beaches of East Dunkirk. As Mr Thomas steered them carefully in towards the shore, Dacre AJ spotted a number of wooden piers extending out into the sea.

'We can moor up on one of those,' he said.

Mr Thomas looked ahead carefully.

'That's funny, I don't remember those piers being there before the war,' he replied.

As they got closer the marine picked up the binoculars and scanned the beach.

'Bloody hell! Those aren't piers, they are men standing in the water waiting to be rescued!'

As soon as the boat was near enough to the beach and didn't risk grounding, they managed to take on board some twenty soldiers. In many cases Dacre AJ had to drag them up onto the boat with some difficulty. They were all exhausted and wet right through. Most of them had discarded their weapons and equipment; several were wounded. With a full load, Mr Thomas backed off into deeper water.

As they were leaving, Dacre AJ shouted out to the desperate men left behind, 'We'll be back as soon as we can!'

As they turned and headed out towards the nearest large boat, a trawler or a ferry and other small craft took their place at the 'jetty'. The evacuation had begun. By the time dawn had arrived the *Gypsy Rose* had made five trips to the beaches. For the most part the troops were amazingly well disciplined and waited patiently for their turn. The only upset was a group of French soldiers who, fed up with waiting, jumped the queue and rushed the boat. Dacre AJ and Mr Thomas had to beat them off with the oars lest they capsize the *Gypsy Rose*. With great difficulty they managed to persuade them to return to the beach and wait their turn like everyone else. The soldiers who were queuing patiently in the sea were either too exhausted or too indifferent to help resolve the situation.

As dawn broke, the full horror of the situation on the beach could be seen. There were literally thousands of men waiting to be rescued. Many of them were in the nearby sand dunes, some sitting in small groups whilst others queued. To the crew on the *Gypsy Rose* it all seemed to be total chaos. As soon as the sun was up, the German Luftwaffe took to the air and began bombing the town, the port, the beaches and the rescue vessels. Ships and boats were being hit and sunk, some almost as soon as they had taken troops on board. Dacre AJ saw a destroyer alongside the eastern mole take a direct hit and start to sink immediately. There were hundreds of troops on the decks, many of whom were killed outright. All around the town and the harbour fires were blazing, a heavy pall of smoke hanging over the whole area. Offshore, British warships could be seen bombarding the German positions inland or were trying to shoot down the diving Stukas. Many of the men on the beaches and in the sand dunes had dug themselves shell scrapes, so that as soon as they were bombed or strafed the beach appeared to be empty, everyone having dived into the nearest hole. Those soldiers lining up in the shallow sea just had to stand and take the punishment.

In the early morning light, Dacre AJ and Mr Thomas could see long queues of men stretching back into the dunes, perhaps a quarter of a mile away. At the head of each queue was a naval officer with several ratings trying to keep the men organised and disciplined, which, for the most part, they were. There must have been ten or twelve of these lines.

Just as the *Gypsy Rose* was taking on another group of soldiers, the bombing started again. One man ran out of his place to the head of the queue. As he waded up to the boat, the marine could see the look of desperation and panic in his face. A naval officer who was supervising the queue turned towards him, raised his pistol and fired a shot over the soldier's head. Dacre AJ clearly heard him say loudly so that everyone could hear, 'Go back to the place you have come from or I will shoot you dead!' The soldier slunk back to his previous position, ignored by the rest of the queue. Everybody had learned a valuable lesson: never argue with a man who has a gun!

The tide had begun to recede. Men who had been standing in the water up to their necks, now found themselves in water lapping at their knees. The *Gypsy Rose* gently rested on the sandy sea bed. They had been caught out. There was no way that they were going to re-float her. They would have to wait for the incoming tide to lift her clear.

'There is no point in sitting here,' said the marine. 'We might as well go ashore, it will hopefully be a little bit safer amongst the sand dunes.'

'I agree!' replied the older man. 'Also we need some more water and fuel, we are dangerously low on both. In fact we haven't enough fuel to get us back to Dover.'

Having made the boat as secure as they could and seeing that it was well anchored, the two men waded through the shallow water and up onto the chaotic beach.

Chapter 26

The beach at Dunkirk was littered with bodies and discarded equipment. A dead officer lay in a small pool of sea water. Dacre AJ bent down and removed a revolver from the officer's holster. It was a standard issue Webley Mk VI .455 calibre and it held six rounds. That would do he thought. He also picked up a steel helmet that was lying nearby. It had a nasty dent on one side but other than that appeared to be quite serviceable. He passed the helmet to Mr Thomas and, after removing the lanyard from the revolver, he put the weapon into one of his pockets.

'Better safe than sorry!' he said with a grim smile on his face.

Dunkirk was all noise and confusion. Black smoke was blowing over the whole place whilst enemy planes continued to fly overhead, bombing and strafing at will. Everything seemed to be on fire. Vehicles, men and bodies were being blown to smithereens. Huge crowds of soldiers were moving along the already choked roads towards the docks whilst others, thousands of them, just sat amongst the sand dunes and waited. The beach was black with men. Naval officers could be seen desperately trying to organise and marshal the troops into certain areas without, Dacre AJ thought, much success. Despite this, a group of enterprising soldiers, on the orders of their senior officer, had begun to build several makeshift piers by driving lorries into the sea to form a line. These were placed head to tail and two abreast and stretched right out into the water. On top of these they placed wooden duck boards and lengths of timber to form a walkway. Almost immediately, small boats began to line up alongside them and started to take on troops who could be seen scrambling and crawling as fast as they could along this heaven-sent lifeline.

The two men decided to split up in their search for water and fuel. They agreed to meet back on the beach in no more than four hours' time. By then the tide would have turned and would be coming back in, so that the *Gypsy Rose* would hopefully be afloat again. They had both agreed that they did not want to be any later in case someone else decided to commandeer their boat. Mr Thomas suggested that he should check the beach area and nearby roads. In that way he could also keep an eye both on the tide and the *Gypsy Rose*. Dacre AJ said that he would work his way towards the town and the port. Wishing each other good luck, they parted company.

There were so many soldiers moving towards the docks, many of them drunk on local wines which they had looted, that Dacre AJ quickly realised that if he was going to be successful in his search for fuel then he would have to get off the main road and into the countryside. Moving quickly but carefully he walked down the nearest side road and out into the nearby fields. He didn't really know where he was going but was drawn by a collection of buildings about half a mile away which he could see. On the spur of the moment he decided to head towards them. As he moved towards his objective he could see small groups of British, French and Belgian soldiers in the neighbouring fields. Most of them seemed to be heading towards the beaches and the sea. They didn't bother him but he kept the revolver handy just in case.

Walking through a field of tall grasses he let his hands gently brush the soft tops of the grass-heads. At that moment the war seemed to be a million miles away. He entered a small orchard and came upon a sight that not only rooted him to the spot but would remain with him for the rest of his life. The bodies of three small children were laid out neatly in a row. The marine sank slowly to his knees and was physically sick. Tears began to run down his face. He stared at their little bodies; they looked as if they were just asleep. There was not a mark on them that he could see. Someone had gone to the trouble of folding their arms across their chests, perhaps as a final gesture. It was quiet and peaceful in that field. High up above him in a nearby tree a bird began to sing. From the distance the sound of war invaded his thoughts. What madness this was, the young marine thought. After a minute or two, he pulled himself together, wiped his eyes and nose, and getting to his feet walked slowly on without as much as a backward glance.

As he approached the group of buildings to which he had been heading, he realised that it was, in fact, a farmstead, typical of that part of France. It had high walls, with a house, barns and stables that formed three sides around a central, cobbled courtyard. The fourth side included the entrance. It was a large brick-built gateway with heavy wooden doors. From the outside he could hear raised voices, shouting in English. Taking great care, he moved quietly towards one of the gates which was slightly ajar. Kneeling down, as he was less likely to be seen that way, he glanced quickly inside. What he saw shook him to his very being. Lined up against a wall was a group of young girls and two nuns. The latter were both dressed in long, dark blue, full length habits with large white headdresses. Confronting them were four British soldiers: one had a rifle, the others had all drawn their bayonets. Because they could not make themselves understood they had become aggressive and threatening. The young girls were not more than children really, perhaps thirteen or fourteen years old. They were crying and clearly very frightened. Both of the nuns were protesting in French whilst doing their best to try and protect their charges. The soldiers were getting increasingly angry. They wanted food, wine and anything else they could get their hands on. One of the soldiers had pinned a girl up against the wall, her chemise torn revealing her undergarments. She was terrified. His intentions were all too obvious. The other soldiers were beginning to egg him on. The situation was clearly getting out of hand. Dacre AJ decided that he had to act quickly. Since all the soldiers had their backs to him he realised that he had the advantage which, since he was outnumbered four to one, was going to be essential. Taking the weapon from his pocket, he stepped round the half-open gate and, raising the firearm, took aim and fired a single shot. The sound of the gun going off echoed from the walls of the buildings. The soldier with the rifle let out a howl of pain and dropped his weapon which clattered onto the cobbles at his feet. He clasped his injured arm. The nuns and the children screamed in unison as the other soldiers spun round, bayonets menacingly held at the ready. Dacre AJ took two steps forward. He noticed that one of the men had a single stripe on the arm of his battledress jacket. The corporal wondered where this man had come from. This wasn't supposed to happen and certainly was not part of his plan. He felt his legs begin to turn to jelly, his throat went dry and he thought he was going to be sick. He was suddenly very afraid. Dacre AJ adopted the classic two-handed stance, legs slightly apart, both hands holding the revolver as steady as a rock. He aimed the weapon at a point between the corporal's eyes.

'Your choice, Corporal! Drop your bayonets and go, or you, my friend, are a dead man!

The corporal's face turned ashen with fear. The menace in the marine's voice was enough to convince the little group of soldiers that it would be better for them to move on. One by one the men dropped their bayonets to the ground. Then without a word they turned and bolted from the courtyard as fast as they could. Dacre AJ watched them go until they were out of sight, then shaking slightly from the rush of adrenalin he put the revolver back into his pocket.

The two nuns and the young girls who had witnessed this in complete silence, burst into spontaneous clapping and laughter. The nuns crossed themselves. The older one walked towards the marine, a wide smile on her face. He started to reassure her in French but she held up her hand to stop him.

'It's alright, young man, we are both English,' she said.

Dacre AJ was completely taken aback by this revelation. She introduced herself as Sister Veronica and explained that originally she had come from the small fishing village of Shoreham-on-Sea on the south coast.

'It is between Brighton and Worthing, I don't expect you have heard of it?'

'Oh, but I have. Isn't there a Palmerston fort there known as the Kingston Redoubt, and didn't they use the beach for making some of the early films. Something about the light, I seem to remember.'

'Yes they did, how clever of you to know that.'

'My history teacher at school was very thorough,' he replied.

Sister Veronica then introduced her younger companion as Sister Elizabeth who was from Wivelsfield Green, a tiny village near Burgess Hill in Sussex.

'Sorry, I have never heard of that place,' replied Dacre AJ.

'Never mind, it is of no consequence except perhaps to those people who live there.'

The marine couldn't help staring at the younger sister who was very attractive. She had a stray lock of ginger hair peeping out from beneath her wimple that closely covered her head, neck and shoulders. Despite the situation, it seemed completely incongruous. She noticed his stare, and with a half-smile almost like an apology, she hastily tucked it away. The marine didn't know anything about nuns. In fact he would be the first to admit that he did not know anything about religion at all. He knew that his mother had been brought up in a Roman Catholic family but his grandfather, who had raised him after her early death, had lapsed. Dacre AJ knew that he had been baptised as a baby but that was as far as it went. Even at school, truth be told, he had learnt very little about religion and certainly nothing about his mother's faith. Despite this, he had developed a very strong sense of morality based on a clear understanding of what was right and what was wrong.

Both nuns were members of the Order of Saint Marie Madeleine Postel which was a teaching order. They had lived and worked in France for many years. The marine asked why on earth they had continued to speak to the soldiers in French. Sister Veronica's reply surprised him. It was, she felt, better for everyone concerned that the men believed them to be French. Had they known that they were English, she couldn't forsee what their reaction might be. They were clearly already in a desperate situation and she didn't want to exasperate the situation even more. The marine couldn't really make any sense of this idea but decided to let it go.

'Now what brings you to our little farm?' asked Sister Veronica.

Dacre AJ explained briefly his own situation and in particular that he was looking for some petrol. As luck would have it the farm had a generator which was petrol-driven and there were about half a dozen cans of fuel available. Dacre AJ was reluctant to take the two cans that were offered to him but the sisters were insistent. The girls, now fully recovered it would seem, even managed to find him a small handcart on which to carry his load. With much laughter and no little amount of fluttering of eyelashes at the handsome young man who had saved them, they tied the two petrol cans securely in place. Just as he was about to leave he took Sister Veronica to one side and explained that they would have to be very careful, not only of other retreating allied soldiers but also of the Germans who would soon be advancing. He also mentioned the three small bodies in the orchard. It turned out that the sisters had found them earlier in the day and had hastily laid them at rest. Later they would dig the graves and give them a proper Christian burial. Having said their goodbyes, they wished each other good luck. Dacre AJ then began to make his way back towards the beaches, dragging the small cart behind him.

Chapter 27

Dacre AJ dragged his precious load of fuel along the road that led to the beach. Several German planes flew overhead which he recognised as Heinkels. They released their sticks of bombs onto the beach as they dived, killing and wounding dozens upon dozens of men.

When the noise had died down, the marine saw a couple of medical orderlies trying to help the wounded, by using an old door as an improvised stretcher. He trudged on, past the debris of war: lorries of every description, abandoned stores, weapons, ammunition, even the wreckage of several aircraft and countless numbers of bodies.

He came across a soldier sitting by the roadside with tears streaming down his face. For some strange reason the man had no boots on his feet. Since the road was covered in broken glass he could go no further and certainly couldn't make the two hundred yards to the beach and the soft sand up ahead. Without a second thought, Dacre AJ offered to carry him on his back the short distance. The soldier was of slight build and probably didn't weigh any more than about nine stone. The marine carried him with ease. When they arrived at the beach, he gently put the man down. Whether through shock or exhaustion the soldier never said a word the whole time, not even a thank you. The marine shrugged his shoulders and decided to put it all down to experience.

In front of him he could see that much of the town and port of Dunkirk was ablaze, whilst shells were dropping into the sea close to the ships lying just offshore. More enemy planes, this time Messerschmitt 109s, flew overhead strafing the men on the beaches and the small boats at the water's edge. Dacre AJ took cover by flinging himself into the nearest hole he could find. As soon as it was clear he stood up and looked around only to hear and see a French burial party just a few yards away. He suddenly realised that he was standing in a grave. Quickly scrambling out, he continued on his way past acre upon acre of abandoned vehicles and equipment. There were piles of mailbags, all ripped open with their contents strewn for miles down the road. He couldn't help thinking of all of those soldiers whose letters would never reach them. He came upon a grocer's van parked by the side of the road, its rear doors swinging gently in the wind. Stopping to look inside he saw a heap of dead soldiers piled high on top of each other. The whole shoreline was awash with corpses, some terribly burned and mutilated others without a mark on them, killed, perhaps, by the concussion of exploding bombs as they waited to be rescued.

The day had turned grey and overcast, with a veil of mist and smoke swirling over the beaches. A stiff breeze was making the loading of the small boats at the water's edge difficult. The marine dragged his small handcart along the tideline and around the carcasses of several dead horses, their stomachs ripped open and their entrails scattered on the beach or lapping gently on the incoming tide.

An officer stood at the water's edge staring, but not seeming to see the chaos and carnage that surrounded him. Overhead, the Luftwaffe continued to fly past wreaking more death and destruction. A bomb dropped close by and exploded. The officer remained passive, unmoving. To the casual observer he neither sought cover nor flinched. He stood perfectly still like a rock. However, inside his head he screamed like a wild banshee. He had had enough. The three pips on his shoulders confirmed that he was a captain. His uniform was dirty and torn. He had not shaved for several days and couldn't remember when he had last eaten or slept. He vaguely wondered how he was going to get home to England but for some reason or other it didn't seem to be that urgent. The captain had served on Lord Gort's General Staff. It had been his job to help organise the evacuation from the beaches. He had even been given permission to return to Dover to see Admiral Ramsey and his staff in order to try to improve the movement of troops off the beaches but they had been too busy to listen. It had never even occurred to him that he should stay in England, so he had returned to Dunkirk. The situation there had become increasingly hopeless. How long ago had that been? He couldn't remember. The thick smoke that seemed to be everywhere suddenly cleared. Then, as if by some minor miracle, the fog cleared from his mind. Captain James Moulton had just spotted the *Gypsy Rose*.

The boat was at anchor about sixty yards from the shore. It looked as though she already had a full load of passengers yet the skipper seemed to be waiting. For what or for whom Moulton wondered. Suddenly coming towards him he saw a bedraggled soldier, wading along the shoreline, dragging a small handcart on which there appeared to be several cans of petrol. Then the penny dropped. Of course, that was why the boat was waiting: it was out of fuel. This could possibly be his chance to get home. The soldier arrived in front of him. He looked a big, strong lad and he wasn't even out of breath. Yet he seemed to be very young, no more than a teenager. What on earth was he doing here the Captain wondered?

'Can I give you a hand with those?' he shouted, as he pointed at the cans.

Dacre AJ looked at the officer and smiled. Amid all the noise and mayhem he, too, had to shout his reply.

'Thank you, sir, that would be a great help.'

The two of them then set about untying the cans from the cart. Dacre AJ couldn't help but notice the officer's shoulder flashes which said 'Royal Marines'. Dear Lord, he thought, out of the frying pan and into the fire. Holding the cans to their chests, the two men began to wade out towards the boat. Thankfully, the tide had not yet turned so the water was only a couple of feet deep. The owner, who was in the wheelhouse, gave them an encouraging wave. About twenty soldiers were sitting or lying about in the boat, some were wounded, some were asleep. All were completely shattered. The two men climbed on board. Mr Thomas immediately began to fill the fuel tanks. He glanced at the officer.

'Welcome aboard', he said. Then noticing the shoulder flashes he added without thinking, 'It's good to have another marine on board.'

Dacre AJ gave his skipper a really dark look but it was too late, the cat was out of the bag. Captain Moulton looked slightly confused.

'You have another marine here?' he asked.

The youngster realised that he would have to explain yet again why he was at Dunkirk.

'I am the other Royal Marine, sir,' Dacre AJ said quietly.

Moulton's mouth dropped open in surprise. He didn't know what to say. The youngster then proceeded to give the officer a brief overview of his situation. The Captain's eyes widened in amazement as the story unfolded. When the young marine had finished talking, Captain Moulton sat quietly taking it all in. The whole thing sounded like a 'Boy's Own' adventure.

'Well I must say that I am most impressed, young Dacre. You really are living up to the tradition of being a 'Royal'.

The youngster felt himself begin to blush from the neck upwards from embarrassment and from the officer's obvious approval.

'I hope we meet again. You never know, we may even end up serving together. I would be very pleased to have you in any unit that I command, and I really mean that. Now, as for the trip back to Dover I shall do my best to keep out of your way. You and the skipper, here, have clearly got things well organised. I thank both of you for managing to squeeze me in. I really wasn't sure how I was going to get back home.'

With that, Captain Moulton went below into the cabin where he found himself a small space. Holding a mug of tea and a half eaten sandwich he promptly fell into a deep and restful sleep.

The owner of the *Gypsy Rose* looked at his young companion.

'Well that didn't go too badly, did it? I'm really sorry about dropping you in it like that. I just didn't think!'

'Oh, that's okay. No harm done, I think. Anyway, we shall probably never meet up again. Our Corps works in that funny sort of a way: you never see the same people from one year to the next.'

Mr Thomas nodded that he understood then said, 'Anyway, well done in getting us the fuel. There's just enough to get us back to Dover. I had just about given you up for lost. What happened?'

The marine stood looking at their passengers.

'Nothing much. It just took longer than I expected, that's all. What about this lot?'

'They were already here when I got back, sitting quietly, waiting for us to get under way. Strange, though, no-one has said anything. They've sat in total silence just as they are now.'

Together, they hauled up the anchor, started the motor and began to guide the boat out into the deeper waters, the powerful engines growling, eager to be unleashed. More German planes flew low overhead. This time they were Dornier 17s with their distinctive twin-finned tail planes, bombing and strafing at will.

'We are likely to become a sitting target,' said the marine. 'I think we should break out the Bren gun and get a couple of these chaps to man it up on the bow. Are you okay with that?'

Mr Thomas looked up into the sky. There were dozens of planes, mostly German, swooping and diving everywhere.

'I don't think we have much choice, do we?'

Dacre AJ just nodded. He understood the owner's reluctance but the marine reasoned that needs must. He opened up the nearby locker in the wheelhouse and retrieved the gun and the boxes of ammunition. Now, he thought, I just need two soldiers to take charge of this. Moving through the boat he called out for volunteers. No-one responded. Some were asleep, some feigned sleep, others just plainly ignored him. He thought about waking the Captain but decided against it; Captain Moulton was clearly dead to the world. He then saw a sergeant who was just staring into space, almost in a trance. The marine shook him gently by the shoulder. No response. He shook him again, this time more forcefully. Slowly, the sergeant turned his head and looked up at the marine with eyes that appeared to be dead. He spoke almost in a whisper.

'Leave me alone! I have nothing left to give.'

Dacre AJ understood that it wasn't a case of cowardice. It was just that, as an individual, it can all be too much. If you are hungry, exhausted and shell-shocked, you do not want any more. The man was too far gone. After a long pause the marine nodded in sympathy and moved on. Two young soldiers sitting further forward in the cabin had been watching the exchange. One of them had been wounded. His arm was in a dirty sling that was heavily encrusted with dried blood. The elder of the two spoke.

'My pal and I can do that for you. We both know how to operate the Bren and even though he's wounded we can still give it a go, can't we, Taffy?'

His mate didn't say anything, just grinned broadly. The marine thanked them. They moved the light machine gun and a box of ammunition up to the front of the boat. Both men seemed to know what they were doing so he left them to it.

Up ahead of them, about seventy five yards away, another small boat took a direct hit from a low flying enemy plane and disappeared in a fountain of exploding water, debris and body parts. Mr Thomas eased back on the throttle of the *Gypsy Rose* as they approached the devastation. They were looking for any possible survivors although it seemed highly unlikely that there would be any. Suddenly Dacre AJ spotted a man in the water. He was struggling to keep afloat whilst waving and shouting for help. He was French. Without any hesitation, the marine dived into the sea and, with powerful strokes, was soon at the survivor's side. The Frenchman was clearly exhausted and allowed himself to be towed back to the boat without any protest. Willing hands pulled them both from the sea and blankets were soon draped around their shoulders. The French soldier turned out to be not only an officer but a general. His appreciation of the marine's courage knew no bounds. He hugged and kissed Dacre AJ on both cheeks. Then to everyone's amazement he took off a medal that was hanging round his neck and presented it to the youngster. It was the Legion d'Honneur.

Somewhat embarrassed the marine tried to protest but the General was insistent, 'Bravery' he said, 'had to be rewarded.'

Just as they were picking up speed, a flight of five Stukas flew overhead, heading for a couple of destroyers anchored about a mile off shore. Everyone on the *Gypsy Rose* held their breath as they watched the menacing gull-wing shaped planes peel off and dive at a steep angle, plummeting down onto the two ships, the banshee wail of their sirens drowning out the sound of their engines. Both ships were bracketed by the falling bombs but miraculously neither was hit. The decks of both warships were crowded with troops. An air strike on either one would have been a catastrophe.

Suddenly, Mr Thomas eased back the throttles once again. Coming towards them was an extraordinary sight, a man paddling a canoe. Dacre AJ shouted out to him that he was going in the wrong direction

'No' he replied, 'I have room for one more!'

With that he paddled on past them, heading inshore towards the beaches.

The marine decided to go down into the forward cabin to check on how the wounded were doing. One soldier, not much older than himself, was lying on one of the cabin bunks. He was bleeding from several wounds despite being heavily bandaged. Standing beside the soldier was another officer who was insisting that the injured man should give up his bed so that he, being an officer, could lie down. Dacre AJ began to remonstrate with the officer but he, a captain in the RAOC, was having none of it. Realising that persuasion wasn't going to win the argument the marine took out his revolver, cocked it and held the weapon none too gently against the man's temple.

'There are no officers on this boat!' he snarled.

The captain flinched, went to say something but thought better of it. Very reluctantly he backed off and, muttering under his breath, he retreated to a corner of the cabin, totally dejected and ignored by everyone. Breathing heavily the marine glanced around to see if anyone had witnessed his act of gross insubordination. It seemed that no-one had, or rather if they had seen anything they had chosen to ignore it. Even the Royal Marines officer had slept through it all.

As the marine went to climb back up into the wheelhouse, the French General, who had been sitting quietly huddled up inside his blanket, just winked at him. There was a hint of a kindly smile on his face.

'Vous avez absolument raison. Bravo,' he whispered.

Dacre AJ felt somewhat comforted by this genuine act of approval. It was good to know that his actions had been appreciated by at least one person.

An hour later, Mr Thomas helmed the *Gypsy Rose* into Dover Harbour. They tied up the boat alongside the harbour wall and began to unload their cargo of passengers. The wounded were helped ashore; the more serious were treated immediately on the quayside by doctors and nurses. Others were taken by ambulance, lorries and buses to the town's hospital or to the medical centre that had been set up in the tunnels deep beneath Dover Castle. Many of the walking wounded found themselves whisked away to any number of hospitals on the south coast or inland: to Folkestone, Margate, Canterbury or Maidstone. Soldiers were given hot food and drinks by the Red Cross. In the majority of cases it was the first that they had had for many days. Then they boarded the special trains that were waiting to take them to various parts of Britain. The dockside was a mass of men, rescuers and the rescued, all moving about in different directions in what could best be described as organised chaos.

Captain Moulton, now somewhat refreshed, went up to Dacre AJ.

'Don't forget what I said. I shall be on the lookout for you in the future. I hope we do meet up again.'

They wished each other well and shook hands. The youngster offered up his best salute which was immediately returned. Dacre AJ had taken an immediate liking to this man. Perhaps they would meet up again, he thought, one never knew what the future held.

'We need to re-supply', said Mr Thomas. 'You do the food and water, I'll see what petrol I can scrounge. Let's be as quick as we can because we need to get back to those beaches.'

About thirty minutes later, when the owner returned to his boat, he found two burly Military Policemen, distinctive in their white belts and cross-straps, talking to Dacre AJ. Mr Thomas noticed that the two MPs were wearing blue caps instead of their usual red. He wondered why.

'They've been sent to take us up to the castle. For some reason or other the Prime Minister wants to talk to us,' said Dacre AJ.

Mr Thomas just gave out a low whistle.

'Bloody hell!' he replied. 'Well, in that case we had better not keep the old boy waiting!'

Chapter 28

In the south east corner of the County of Kent stands Dover Castle. This magnificent building, going back to the 11th Century, overlooks the shortest sea crossing between Britain and mainland Europe. This is why the castle has always been of immense strategic importance. Within the famous white cliffs, hidden from view beneath the castle and safe from bombardment, lies a network of tunnels and rooms first excavated over two hundred years ago. This complex network of underground facilities had been adapted from the Napoleonic era when they had been originally built as soldiers' barracks and officers' quarters, an innovative answer to accommodating the troops necessary to man the castle's defences. However, by the end of the 19th Century the tunnels had been abandoned. During the 1914-18 World War, a central Fire Command Post had been constructed up on the hill overlooking Dover Harbour and the Straits beyond because of the excellent views. Later, the Admiralty sited a Port War Signal Station there for that very same reason. In 1939 the tunnels were re-opened and modernised because they were to be used as the Command Centre that controlled naval operations in the English Channel.

Vice Admiral Sir Bertram Home Ramsay RN, Flag Officer Commanding Dover was the man responsible for the oversight of *Operation Dynamo* and had chosen these tunnels to be his command centre. He stood looking at a large-scale map of the English Channel spread out before him on several trestle tables that had been hastily placed together. He was deep in thought. A number of WRNS, supervised by their officers, were moving small blocks of wood across the map between Dover and Dunkirk. Each block had the name of a ship printed onto a piece of white card: HMS *Havant*, HMS *Ivanhoe*, HMS *Saltash* and so on. The room was a hive of activity. The constant buzz of conversation was only interrupted by the ringing of telephones which seemed to be continuous. Admiral Ramsay was oblivious to all this noise. It was as if he was somewhere else, somewhere completely different and away from all this madness, this war. A young WRNS officer decided to interrupt his all too brief a moment of peace and quiet.

'Sir, the Prime Minister has arrived.'

Ramsay knew, of course, that Winston Churchill was due. They had had numerous telephone conversations over the previous couple of days. The Prime Minister, as always, had been very keen to know exactly what the situation was regarding the progress of the evacuation of the BEF from Dunkirk. He had made it abundantly clear in their last conversation that nothing on earth was going to deter him from coming down to Dover to see for himself.

The small convoy of two cars and a motor cycle outrider pulled up at the entrance to the tunnels. Mr Churchill always travelled light. He and his small party entered the Casement at road level and were escorted down the long steep, sloping zigzag tunnel that had been cut into the chalk. Down and down they went, more than two hundred yards, through brick-vaulted tunnels, past kitchens, sleeping accommodation and offices until they arrived at the Admiralty Operations Room. The Prime Minister was slightly out of breath but, nevertheless, clearly in good humour. He had, after all, spent the previous night at his own home at Chartwell with all its comforts and, of course, in the company of his dear wife, rather than at Number Ten or in the underground War Rooms in London. He was dressed in a dark grey, pin-striped three piece suit with a blue and white spotted bow tie. He walked with the aid of a stick in his right hand whilst in his left was an unlit cigar. A gold watch chain hung across his rather large stomach. On his head he was wearing his usual black Homburg hat. Behind him was his ever-watchful police bodyguard.

'Good morning Ramsay, and how are things progressing? Well, I hope? Perhaps you would be kind enough to bring me up to date with the current situation.'

'Good morning, sir. Well, the situation is as follows: Commander Day, our hydrographer, has worked out the three best routes from here to Dunkirk. You can see that they are clearly marked on our map here.'

The Admiral pointed to the sea routes known officially as X, Y and Z.

'Initially I put Captain Tennant plus twelve officers and one hundred and fifty ratings ashore at the port and on the beaches to try and organise the evacuation. Commander Stoppard RN who is my Flag Officer is in charge of all communications. Rear Admiral Wake-Walker RN is co-ordinating the movements of the recue ships from the Harbour Master's office. However, we are dealing with far more troops than we ever anticipated. Not only our own boys but also an increasing number of French and Belgian troops. Consequently, I have had to give Tennant some additional support. I have sent Vice Admiral Stephenson to take charge of the evacuation at La Penne and Vice Admiral Hallet to Malo-les-Bains. This seems to be working well.'

Churchill nodded his head in approval, 'You seem to have it all well organised,' he said. 'What about ships? Have you got enough?'

'Well, sir, destroyers are vital to my plan. Whilst they are not ideal as troop carriers they are fast and manoeuverable, so consequently they are difficult targets for the Germans to hit. In addition, their fire power is an invaluable asset especially with regard to their anti-aircraft role. The majority are either in the Mediterranean or in the Far East. Many of those on the Home Fleet are already committed to the Norwegian campaign or the protection of the Atlantic shipping routes which I am sure you will agree is a most vital role. However, Admiral Forbes, the Commander-in-Chief of the Home Fleet, released a number of destroyers to us here at Dover. They are mostly old but serviceable. But as soon as we began to take some losses, which was inevitable, either sunk or damaged, the First Sea Lord, Admiral Sir Dudley Pound, ordered eight of the more modern ships away from Dunkirk. I believe he did this in an effort to preserve the integrity of the home fleet for future unforeseen actions. Unfortunately this left me in a perilous situation with only fifteen elderly warships at my disposal. I did telephone to ask him to reconsider which I am pleased to say that he did. He has returned six of the destroyers for our use in evacuating the BEF.'

The Prime Minister had his eyes closed in concentration; he was clearly considering all the information that the Admiral had given him.

'It seems to me, Ramsay, that it was a good idea of mine when as First Sea Lord I managed to coax you back from retirement back in 1938. I cannot think of many people who could have achieved what you have managed to do in so short a space of time, eh! Now then what about the Merchant Service, how have they helped? What about that register of small boats? Has that been useful?'

'I have over one hundred and thirty merchant ships taking part in this operation. They include steam packets, cross channel ferries, coasters, trawlers and about forty Dutch schuits. As for the small boats, they have proved invaluable. There are dozens of them of all shapes and sizes. They have come from all over the country especially the south and east coast, from rivers and even the Norfolk Broads. They are mostly used to ferry the troops from the beaches to those ships waiting offshore. Their shallow drafts make them ideal for the job. However, there has been a high price to pay. Many have been sunk or severely damaged by the Luftwaffe with considerable loss of life.'

The Prime Minister shook his head in sympathy.

The Admiral continued, 'I have a small cabin just along the corridor from here. If you have seen enough for the time being, perhaps we might adjourn for some refreshments? After that I'll show you the view from the Admiralty casement balcony.'

Churchill readily agreed and followed Ramsay along the corridor. As they left there was a marked sigh of relief from all of the personnel in the Operations Room, the visit had gone well, so far.

Admiral Ramsay's room was far from what one would call comfortable. It contained just the basics: an old desk, several chairs, a small cot for overnight stays should the need arise, two wooden filing cabinets, an armchair from which some of the horse hair stuffing was trying to escape, a small bedside table on which stood two telephones. Behind the desk, pinned to the wall, was a large scale map of the south east of England and northern France. At the far end of the room was a large window that covered an entire wall. The individual panes of glass had been taped up in order to minimize splinters from shell or bomb blasts. Standing in one corner was an old but serviceable naval telescope. From here the Admiral would have had an excellent view over the harbour and beyond were it not for the taped up windows. Someone had brought a tea tray and a plate of biscuits which they had left on the desk. Both men sat down, the Admiral at his desk, Churchill on a nearby chair. Ramsay pulled opened a bottom drawer and brought out a large bottle of Navy rum. He poured a liberal tot into the two teacups and passed one to the Prime Minister who accepted it gratefully. Both men sat quietly, each lost in their own thoughts. The Admiral leant across and refilled Mr Churchill's cup. Churchill nodded appreciatively and looked around the room carefully assessing what he saw.

'Tell me,' he asked, 'what is it like living and working down here?'

'Well, sir, it is frequently damp and nearly always chilly. There are minimal comforts and only basic facilities. There is, of course, a lack of daylight and the constant background noise of the forced ventilation system can be a distraction but after a while you get used to it. Many of the passageways that have been cut from the chalk have uneven floors and more than one person has taken a tumble or two. All my staff, of course, work long hours, often with little or no sleep. That is to be expected. But thankfully no-one complains, they just get on with the job in hand, working together as a team.'

'Yes I see,' said the Prime Minister. 'What about your operational code name. I have been wondering where that came from?'

'Oh yes, *Operation Dynamo*. One of my junior officers thought that one up. It would seem that the room we are now using as the operational command centre once housed electrical plant equipment, dynamos and the like, to produce a supply of electricity for the castle. I hope you will agree with me that it seemed appropriate.'

Mr Churchill gave a deep chuckle and drained the last of his cup.

'Now, sir, if you have finished your refreshments perhaps you would care to follow me outside onto our balcony.'

The pot of tea and biscuits were left completely untouched.

The Admiral continued, 'Because we are so close to France, there is a constant danger of air attacks, so I must ask you to wear a steel helmet.'

Leading his guest outside to the Casement balcony, Ramsay equipped the Prime Minister with the necessary headgear and also loaned him a pair of powerful binoculars.

Winston Churchill scanned the horizon. Vast columns of smoke could be easily seen even without the use of binoculars. A huge number of ships were making their way to and from Dunkirk. The screech and thump of explosions and gunfire were clearly heard from across the water. The Admiral looked at his leader with interest. It was, he felt, good that the old man had come to see what was happening first hand. Now at least he could appreciate how difficult the operation was proving to be.

'The Royal Air Force have been flying hundreds of sorties to try and protect both our ships and the troops on the ground but the Luftwaffe are proving to be too strong for them. I am given to understand that the RAF High Command wants to retain some of its fighter capabilities for what will surely come next.'

Churchill looked up sharply.

'I presume, Ramsay, you are referring to the 'Battle for Britain'. Yes, I am certain that once France falls, as it will, Herr Hitler will undoubtedly give the order to invade our shores. In the meantime we must do everything we can in order to support our allies to hold the Germans at bay. Every day that we can gain gives us another day to prepare for the fight of our lifetime.'

The Prime Minister went back to using his binoculars. This time he was scanning the harbour down below, watching the frantic activity with considerable interest. Suddenly he stopped. He refocused on a small boat that was tied up alongside the harbour wall and was unloading a group of soldiers.

'Admiral! Do you see that small boat down there, the scruffy dark grey one, the one that is unloading its passengers?'

Ramsay scanned the harbour and eventually located the boat.

'I know that young man from somewhere. I cannot for the moment think where but I never forget a face. Can you send someone to fetch him and his companion, I should very much like to talk to them. Do you not think that would be useful? I am sure it would help us to get an up to date picture of what is actually happening over there and to be able to see it through their eyes would be most beneficial.'

The Admiral was going to say that the information he already possessed was actually well up to date and couldn't be improved on. However, he thought better of it. Clearly the Prime Minister was determined to meet these two men and besides, seeing the evacuation through the experiences of the crew of a small boat might indeed be helpful. He gave the necessary instructions and two military policemen were quickly despatched.

Chapter 29

The ride up to the castle took less than ten minutes. Dacre AJ recognised the road from his recruit training days when he and his squad mates had been on their way from Deal via Dover to the ranges at Lydden Spout. Mr Thomas who was still curious about the blue caps decided to ask one of their escorts about them. The sergeant explained that the red cap was worn for general policing and special investigations, whereas the blue was worn when guarding vulnerable locations such as the castle. The CMP also wore white caps when carrying out traffic control and green for field security.

Dacre AJ looked enquiringly at the older man who, to be honest, had previously shown little interest in anything to do with the army. Mr Thomas just shrugged his shoulders and silently mouthed, 'I was just curious'. The marine smiled a reply.

The military police vehicle entered the castle by the Constable's Gate which had been the main entrance to the castle for well over seven hundred years. The whole place was heavily fortified with gun emplacements and what looked like hundreds of troops. The vehicle they were in crossed a solid bridge that spanned a dry moat. High up above them loomed the brooding presence of the Great Tower, safe and secure behind its own massive fortifications. They stopped at a barrier, its red and white pole bright against the grey drabness of the buildings. A sentry checked their identity cards, whilst a second soldier kept them covered with his rifle and fixed bayonet. The barrier was lifted and they were waved through. A short drive took them through Peverell's Gate, then they followed the curtain wall and passed several smaller towers. The whole of the castle grounds had been converted into a huge defensive structure. Gun emplacements, anti-aircraft guns, machine gun posts and trenches were everywhere. Soldiers were guarding the essential buildings or manning the recently installed armaments. Yet more troops were digging additional defensive positions. Dover Castle was once again on a war footing.

Eventually they arrived at the entrance to the underground tunnel system. As they got out of the vehicle, Dacre AJ had a fleeting opportunity to glance across the town that lay below them, down in the valley. He was just able to make out the Redoubt on the opposite hill and behind that the Citadel. It was such a short time ago, he thought, that he and his squad mates had stayed there, yet it seemed like years.

Over the doorway to the tunnels was a large sign that said, 'VICE ADMIRAL, DOVER'. The two men were escorted down to the Operations Room where the Prime Minister and Admiral Ramsay were waiting for them. Mr Churchill stepped forward and shook hands with each of them. He spoke directly to the marine.

'Now then, young man, where have we met before? I was just telling the Admiral that I knew you from somewhere but that I couldn't quite place where.' This was all very embarrassing for Dacre AJ. He had been caught out by, of all people, his own Prime Minister. He took a deep breath and decided to reveal all.

'I am Royal Marine, sir! You presented me with my King's Badge in January of this year.'

Winston Churchill looked steadily at the youngster, his mind working frantically trying to place the event. Suddenly he broke into a broad smile.

'I believe I have it! I remember it now! I was the First Sea Lord then, Ramsay,' he said turning to the Admiral. 'Just let me see if I can recall your name.'

Dacre AJ was about to help Mr Churchill out by giving him his name and regimental number but the Prime Minister held up his hand to stop him.

'No, do not tell me. Wait, I have it! You're Marine Dacre,' he said. 'Am I correct?'

The marine broke into a broad smile.

'Yes sir, perfectly correct,' he replied.

'Well, Ramsay, what do you think of that?' said Churchill.

The Admiral was actually impressed by the Prime Minister's power of recall. This was, of course, legendary but he had to admit, if only to himself, that this little demonstration, this little conceit of the old man's, was nevertheless remarkable.

Admiral Ramsay stepped forward and drawing himself up to his full height (he was quite small when compared to the marine) looked the young man up and down.

'And what, may I ask, is a Royal Marine doing working as crew on one my small boats? Why are you not in barracks or on board ship?'

Dacre AJ swallowed hard, this was going to be a bit tricky, he thought. So without further ado he gave as brief an explanation as he could about being underage and having been given some leave so that he could do his bit for 'King and Country'. The Admiral, whilst somewhat mollified, clearly wasn't going to let this lie.

'I shall be checking out your story, young man, with your Commanding Officer. If I find out that you have not been telling me the truth, then you can stand by for a very 'short ring'! Do I make myself absolutely clear, Marine Dacre?'

Before he could answer, Mr Thomas stepped forward.

'I can vouch for him, sir!' he said.

Ramsay looked at him as if he had only just seen him for the first time. It wasn't an encouraging look, more of a steely glare.

'And who are you, sir, if I may ask?

'Leslie Thomas, at your service. I am the owner of the *Gypsy Rose*. I'm a civilian who just happens to have volunteered his boat to help with the evacuation. Marine Dacre joined me at Maidstone and together we brought the boat down here to Dover. Not only have we been heavily involved at Dunkirk but prior to that we carried out a night mission to Calais. It was this young man who actually brought back the Germans' battle plans for the capture of Dunkirk.'

The Admiral looked puzzled.

Mr Thomas continued, 'You can check this out if you like with your own officers. Might I suggest you start by asking Lieutenant Commander Copping? He was given the plans I believe.'

The Prime Minister had been listening to this exchange with a growing sense of impatience.

'Enough of this interrogation, Ramsay! All I can say is well done to the lad for using his initiative. I wish we had more men like him and, by Jove, we are going to need them! Now can we please hear what these two men have to tell us about their experiences at Dunkirk.'

For the next forty minutes or so, Leslie Thomas and Dacre AJ gave as much of a detailed report as they could. Nobody interrupted them. Almost everyone in the

Operations Room had temporarily stopped work. They were hanging onto every word that was spoken. For most, this was their only chance to really understand and appreciate what was actually happening on the other side of the Channel. There was a hushed silence as the appalling situation was gradually revealed and the desperate nature of the evacuation began to sink in. When they had finished their report there was silence, except for the ventilation system. One or two of the WRNS had tears running down their faces. Churchill broke the awkward silence. He was clearly quite emotional; his voice had an even deeper growl.

'I had no idea that it was so bad, did you Ramsay?'

The Admiral studied the two men with a look of absolute respect in his eyes.

'No, sir, I did not. The situation reports that I regularly receive do not, I am afraid, convey the reality of the situation.'

'Quite so, Admiral, quite so,' said the Prime Minister. 'I want to thank the two of you for being so frank and honest about your experiences. We are much obliged to you. What are your plans now?'

Mr Thomas spoke for the pair of them.

'We need to get back to our boat, sir. There is still work to be done. So if we could be given a lift back down to the harbour, that would be much appreciated.'

'Yes of course. I am sure that the Admiral would be only too happy to organise that. One last thing before you go. That medal hanging around your neck, young Dacre. Am I correct in thinking that it is the Legion d'honneur? How did you come by that?'

The marine had completely forgotten about the rescue of the French General. He briefly explained what had happened. Mr Churchill had a real twinkle in his eye.

'Well Admiral, I don't know what you think but I suggest we let Marine Dacre keep his medal, it will be good for morale if nothing else. I will speak to the French Government just to make things official. You know how touchy they can be over their awards. Then later, perhaps, we can get someone to present it to him more formally.'

Admiral Ramsay had his own views on this highly irregular award but decided to keep them to himself. One did not argue with the Prime Minister. Besides, the young man had performed well, but that, he reasoned, was what everyone expected of a Royal Marine.

Chapter 30

It took the *Gypsy Rose* nearly four hours to get back to Dunkirk. Navigation on the approaches to the beaches proved to be extremely hazardous because of so many sunken boats and ships. The whole sea seemed to be littered with blazing wrecks. From just half a mile out it seemed like a vision from hell, a scene that neither of the two men would ever forget. It was an awe-inspiring yet terrifying sight. Vast columns of smoke from the nearby blazing oil storage tanks were boiling up into huge clouds, the tops of which drifted away on the breeze into a great veil through which the sun tried to shine. On the beach it was utter carnage, much worse than they could remember seeing before. The sky was full of enemy aircraft which lined up and fell into dives, dropping bombs and firing their guns indiscriminately. There were corpses and body parts everywhere together with the screams and cries of the wounded.

Slowly and carefully Mr Thomas brought the boat in towards the beach, to one of the human piers which were now somewhat shorter in length. Numerous small boats were lining up waiting their turn to take on board a dozen or more soldiers at a time and to ferry them out to the larger ships waiting offshore. As they arrived at the head of the queue Dacre AJ noticed an army padre moving up and down the waiting column of men, directing, helping and encouraging them to be patient. They seemed to be inspired by his complete sense of calmness. The marine didn't see him again but he hoped that the padre had managed to get away.

On their third trip back to the beach they passed a number of naval whalers, each one manned by a single sailor. They had been towed in by a small steam boat and had been cast off about five hundred yards from the shore. However, they were struggling to make the final distance, so the *Gypsy Rose* gave them a tow. The sailors told them that the idea was to fill each boat to capacity and then get the soldiers to use the oars to pull them out to the waiting destroyers. The marine thought it was a good idea but that the plan depended on the troops being fit enough to row the whalers which, he knew from his own experience, was a difficult thing to do.

Arriving back at the beach, they saw dozens of dirty, wild-eyed, crazy soldiers rushing into the sea for the next boat. Time and again many of these smaller boats capsized. Some of the men, still laden with their equipment, were dragged beneath the surface of the water to their death. No-one stopped to help them.

Also, drunken soldiers, many of them still armed, appeared to be roaming everywhere. They were becoming a liability to the good order and discipline that seemed to prevail amongst the majority. But desperate times produced desperate measures. On the boat next to theirs, Dacre AJ saw two drunken squaddies hanging onto the stern. They just would not let go. Despite everything that the skipper tried to do, the boat wasn't going anywhere. A sergeant on the boat realising the situation, took out his pistol and shot both men through the head. The boat was then able to move off safely with its load of twenty evacuees. Further up the beach, a lorry had backed up to the water's edge and had begun to unload a number of small collapsible boats. To assemble these would normally not have been a difficult task. However, under these conditions the men whose task it was to assemble the boats were hampered and in danger of being overwhelmed by the dozens of soldiers who had gathered around in what was fast becoming a free-for-all. Seeing the predicament, the marine leapt from the *Gypsy Rose* into the water and splashed his way, the fifty yards, to help. Taking out his revolver from his pocket he fired two shots into the air as he charged into the tangled mass of heaving bodies. Luckily his timely arrival forced the mob back and allowed the boats to be assembled. When each was loaded they moved off, with the soldiers using their rifles and spades as paddles.

Meanwhile, the Luftwaffe was still flying up and down the beach, machine gunning and bombing at will. Dozens of men were hit, injured or killed. Running back down the beach, Dacre AJ took evasive action by jumping into a small crater about four feet deep which he assumed had been made by a bomb. The next second, he heard the whistling sound of another bomb coming down and thought that his time was up. It landed just a few yards away. The marine found himself completely covered in sand and badly winded but, thankfully, not wounded. Climbing out of the hole, he realised that he was completely covered in urine and excrement. The smell was awful. The crater had obviously been used as a latrine. As soon as the next aircraft had passed, he raced into the sea and plunged beneath the waves to wash himself off as clean as he could.

When he arrived back on the boat, Mr Thomas raised a questioning eyebrow at the state of his clothes.

'Just don't ask!' the marine said.

With yet another load of soldiers on board, they set off once again in the direction of the larger ships waiting out at sea. About half a mile from the shore they came upon a large motor yacht drifting aimlessly. It had a full load of about thirty soldiers on board. They had run out of fuel and no-one knew how to put up the sails. Mr Thomas steered the *Gypsy Rose* skilfully alongside so that Dacre AJ could go aboard to assist. Within fifteen minutes he had the sails up and set, and had given some of the men a set of basic instructions on how to sail.

Just as he was about to return to his own boat, someone called out, 'Can you show us the way to Dover?'

The marine gave a broad grin and pointed to the North West.

'Just follow all the other boats, you can't get lost,' he replied.

Despite the increasing efforts of all the small boats, there were still thousands of soldiers waiting on the beaches to be rescued. The *Gypsy Rose* picked up another load of passengers and set off. Unfortunately they attracted the attention of a lone Stuka dive bomber which came down at them. Dacre AJ had the Bren gun loaded and ready with a fresh magazine, pointing it out of the wheelhouse roof hatchway. Mr Thomas was at the helm.

'When I give the word turn as sharply as you can,' said the marine. 'Timing is going to be vital if we are to survive this attack!'

Mr Thomas just nodded in agreement; he knew that the marine was right.

Dacre AJ kept watch on the aircraft as it swooped in for the kill. At the very last second he called out, 'Hard a port!'

The boat turned sharply as the marine loosed off the entire twenty-eight rounds in the magazine. A bomb from the plane landed in the water close to their starboard side and exploded harmlessly. The German pilot flew around in a tight circle and lined himself up for another attack. Dacre AJ watched him carefully whilst automatically changing magazines. He was ready.

As the plane came in for the second attack he waited until the very last moment before shouting out, 'Hard a starboard'.

Mr Thomas swung the wheel with all his might. As the boat turned, so the marine opened fire with his gun. This time the bomb landed close on the port side. The *Gypsy Rose* rolled heavily from the explosion, whilst a massive water spout fell onto the boat soaking many of them to the skin. Dacre AJ had the satisfaction of seeing a thin stream of black smoke coming from the Stuka's engine as it passed. The pilot had decided that he had had enough and flew off in the direction of the land and safety. The soldiers on board gave a resounding cheer, only to have it stifled as they saw another fighter plane coming straight for them. The marine changed magazines and waited. Fortunately he had been told, by whom he couldn't remember, that when a fighter plane makes an attack, just a second or two before firing its machine guns the pilot has to lift the nose of the aircraft in alignment with its guns. Dacre AJ watched for that moment and as the plane was about to lift its nose he called out, 'Hard a port!'

Mr Thomas responded immediately. The bullets from the plane flew down past the stern of the boat less than a foot away, kicking up small splashes of water. The marine opened fire and clearly saw his tracer rounds strike the enemy's tailplane. Clearly hit but not fatally, the pilot waggled his wings as a salute and flew off.

'Victory to the winner!' cried Mr Thomas.

The marine gave a grim smile.

'This is a bloody strange war we're fighting,' he replied. 'One minute that German is trying to kill us all, then the next minute he's saying well done!'

'War brings out the best and the worst in us all,' said Mr Thomas.

'I suppose so. Still, it is a nice feeling having seen him off, even if it is only a small victory. Do you know what I mean?'

The owner of the boat looked carefully at Dacre AJ. Over the last few days the youngster had changed: he had become more assured, more confident and more hardened, which was to be expected given what they had seen and witnessed.

He replied to the question quietly, 'Yes! I know exactly what you mean. I think it is the small victories that keep you going when times are tough, especially when there is no end in sight.'

Chapter 31

Mr Thomas was worried. In fact he was very worried indeed. The fuel gauge of the boat was reading nearly empty. In all of the excitement he had lost track of how much petrol they had used. He had tapped the glass but it hadn't made any difference. The needle had stayed in the same place and had refused to move. In desperation he had even opened up the filler cap and, using a wooden dipstick, had checked the contents of the tank. He was not mistaken. There was less than a gallon left. He would have to tell 'his marine', for that was how he now saw the youngster. They were moored about a hundred yards offshore, waiting their turn to move into one of the lorry jetties. Dacre AJ was sitting on the roof of the wheelhouse cradling the Bren gun in his arms whilst he scanned the sky for a possible attack.

'AJ, I'm really sorry to have to tell you but we need more fuel.'

Mr Thomas paused and half expected the marine to make a comment or at least to swear. But on reflection he should, he thought, have known better. Despite their fairly brief acquaintance (they had actually only known each other only for a handful of days) the youngster had proved to be both completely unflappable and totally reliable, two qualities that Leslie Thomas admired above all else.

'That's all right,' replied the marine, 'Just drop me ashore and I'll see what I can scrounge. It may take some time, so I suggest you would be better to wait offshore. That way we might have a slightly better chance of surviving being attacked.'

'Yes, that seems like a good idea. And you, my young friend, make sure you don't go jumping into any more latrines when you have to take cover.'

Once on the beach at Malo-les-Bains, Dacre AJ moved towards the main boulevard as quickly as he could. Although it was still crowded with soldiers waiting to be taken off, no-one bothered him. On the spur of the moment he decided that being a 'civilian' was perhaps not a good idea, particularly since he had been told that the German army was already nearing the outskirts of the town. With this in mind, he liberated a battledress jacket. The shoulder flashes said 'Royal Engineers'. Its previous owner no longer had any need for it.

He would have to be quick if he didn't want to be rolled up in the German advance. Almost immediately he came across a petrol bowser, front end down in a ditch. He tried the main tap which was located at the rear of the vehicle but because of the steep angle nothing came out. Without further ado, he climbed onto the top of the bowser and opened the inspection hatch and looked inside. As he suspected, what fuel there was had gathered at the far end. He was just about to look for something, a tool or other implement which would help him get at the fuel, when a voice called out.

'You there! Get off that lorry right now!'

Dacre AJ looked down behind him. Two officers, one a major, the other a young lieutenant, both with CMP on their shoulders, were standing directly below him. Both men had their pistols drawn.

'Get off now or I shall be forced to shoot you!' said the lieutenant.

The marine slid off the bowser and ended up standing in front of both officers. He towered over them. He wanted to explain but they were not interested in what he had to say.

'Just what the bloody hell do you think you are doing?' said the major, 'You miserable excuse for a soldier! Get yourself down onto the beach with the other vermin who are trying to save their own skins! Now get out of my sight before I change my mind.'

With that, he waved his pistol under the marine's nose. Dacre AJ knew better than to argue with two men both of whom were armed. He moved off as quickly as he could and counted himself lucky not to have been shot. However, as he went he did question two things in his own mind: first, the stupidity of leaving fuel for the advancing enemy and second, perhaps more importantly, the comments made by the two military police officers. Like everything else in life, Dacre AJ knew that there were good officers and then those who were not so good. In fact within his limited experience most officers who held the King's Commission were, in the main, good. But these two MP officers were something else. Arrogant, vindictive and unpleasant were words that came to mind. Perhaps, he thought, that the military police needed to be like that in order to carry out their duties. He hoped not. However, the whole demeanour of these two made him very suspicious. Their very presence did not ring true. He couldn't put his finger on it but something wasn't right. He had heard from other soldiers that both the Belgians and the French had fifth columnists operating in their respective countries. He suspected it would be difficult to tell who they were. Indeed, in France there was a minority of people who were on the side of the Germans. They intensely disliked the Republic and all that it stood for. They tried to do everything that they could to weaken France in front of the assault by the Nazis. Some even felt that the fascists had got their priorities right, particularly in respect of the economy and nationalism. Many of these even went so far as to support the idea that it would be better to have a fascist regime rather than communism, or even the present system of government.

Further along the beach Dacre AJ came across two more Military Police NCOs who were doing their best to direct the massive number of vehicles that were arriving at the beach. They were fighting a hopeless battle. The marine took the bull by the horns and decided to share his concerns about the two officers. He spoke to the sergeant.

'That's strange,' the SNCO said. 'There's only me and my mate here on this part of the beach. We certainly don't have any officers here, that's for sure. They could possibly be German infiltrators in British uniforms. I have heard that they are all over the place. They've been parachuted in, so I've been told. Thanks for the tip-off, I'll look into right away.'

With that he disappeared into the sand dunes.

Chapter 32

Dacre AJ continued walking away from the beach. He had left the boulevard and taken a side road which headed inland. Unknowingly, he had moved towards the frontline where the retreating British Army were attempting to prevent the Germans from advancing. This was proving to be completely futile and the best they could hope for was to slow the enemy advance. The whole situation had been made more difficult because the Belgian forces had already surrendered on the northern flank. This meant that the Germans were able to come through the gap that had been vacated and were, therefore, coming in behind the hard-pressed British Army.

He stopped to watch a farmer using a very old horse to plough a field. It was such a strange sight. In all this chaos and death, the Frenchman had decided that it was the right time to work his land. Dacre AJ stood for a good couple of minutes, completely fascinated by the scene in front of him. That's a strange way of ploughing, he thought. The farmer appeared to be working down two sides so that it formed an arrow shape. The marine felt sure that in England the farmers ploughed up and down in straight lines, but he would be the first to admit that he was no expert. Suddenly from a nearby gateway a small group of British soldiers rushed across the field, rifles at the ready, and none too gently seized the farmer. They frogmarched him along the lane towards the marine. As they came up to him Dacre AJ asked the corporal in charge of the squad what was going on.

'He's a fifth columnist. See that shape he was ploughing in the field. It's an arrow pointing towards our Battalion Headquarters. When Jerry flies over, all he has to do is just follow the marker on the ground. He can't miss!'

'What is going to happen to him?' the youngster asked.

'Oh, I expect he will be questioned and then shot. From now on anyone found doing the same thing will be shot on sight, no questions asked.'

That was harsh justice thought the marine but given the circumstances what else were they supposed to do?

The marine strode on, checking the vehicles left by the roadside for any spare fuel but without any luck. He passed several lorries that had been left with their engines running. The black pools of oil on the ground underneath told him that they would eventually seize up. What a waste, he thought, although on reflection perhaps it was better than allowing them to fall into the hands of the advancing Germans.

Dacre AJ had not gone more than a mile down the small side road when he saw a handful of troops up ahead, about fifty yards in front of him, standing in the road. He suddenly realised that they were Germans from the shape of their helmets. Thankfully, they were just as surprised to see him, a lone British Tommy, and it took them several seconds before they opened fire. Their bullets ricocheted off the road in tiny puffs of dust right, where only seconds before, his feet had been. However, the marine dived through a nearby hedge into a neighbouring field and made a quick getaway. The Germans did not bother to pursue him: they clearly had more important things to do.

Moving cautiously on, the marine came across a badly wounded British soldier lying beside his motorcycle. He lay there unmoving, staring at his steaming entrails which had spilled from a terrible stomach wound. The man's revolver lay on the ground just beyond his reach. The youngster quietly approached the soldier, his shadow falling across the dying man's face. Without moving his head the he looked up, his eyes said it all. Slowly Dacre AJ reached down and picked up the weapon which he placed in the soldier's right hand. A look of tremendous gratitude spread across the man's face. The marine nodded and walked on. Seconds later a single shot rang out.

A little while later Dacre AJ met up with several Royal Engineers who told him they were from the 210th Field Company. The small group of three realised that they had to cross a lane between two buildings. Unfortunately, the Germans had the place covered for enfilade fire. It was clear that only one man could cross at a time and then he would have to take a chance. After a short discussion one of the sappers elected to go first. The others tried to give him what covering fire they could. He was about half way across when he was shot down and collapsed in the middle of the lane, dead before he had hit the ground. Seizing the opportunity presented to him, the marine sprinted across the lane and dived for cover behind the body as a further burst of machine gun fire took off the top of the dead soldier's head. Dacre AJ found himself covered in blood and grey matter. He waited for a few moments then, choosing his time carefully, he leapt up and dashed for the far side of the lane and the safety of the roadside ditch. Turning to face the others, he signalled to them to take their turn. Both men indicated that they were staying where they were. They clearly had no intention of risking their lives. They waved at him to go on. Rather reluctantly the marine gave them a thumbs-up signal and then disappeared into the welcoming safety of a nearby coppice. After a few yards he noticed that parts of the undergrowth had been trampled down, creating a sort of trail. It was then that he saw that there were red dabs of paint on some of the trees. Someone, he realised, had been very busy taking the time to guide the retreating troops to Dunkirk and the beaches.

Dacre AJ was now very concerned that he had become caught up in the retreat of the British Army, something that he had wanted to avoid. What he had seen and heard had convinced him that this was not an orderly withdrawal. It was panic, absolute panic. A number of soldiers he had met had told him all sorts of stories concerning the fact that some Germans were shooting their prisoners. Given what he knew of them he found this difficult to believe, although his opinion was largely based on his pre-war knowledge of the German people. However, his recent experiences over the past couple of days had taught him that you never could be sure of anything in war.

By late morning the weather had become quite warm. The sun was out in an almost cloudless sky. The young marine realised that he was very thirsty and there was a danger that he would become dehydrated. He needed water quickly if he was not to become ill. Fortunately, he came upon a damaged Bren gun carrier. Lying all around were the bodies of its crew. Several of them still had full water bottles which he liberated. Sitting in the shade with his back to a tree, he slowly drank some of the water, easing his parched throat. The water was warm and tasted brackish but it was a life saver.

On the spur of the moment he decided to review his situation before going any further. Firstly, he thought, he estimated that he was about three miles from the beach and that Dunkirk had clearly become caught up in the German advance. Secondly, he had so far failed to find any petrol despite his best efforts. Thirdly, he didn't have a weapon, other than the pistol which only had several rounds left in the chamber. Finally, he was hungry. Not, he thought, a very good situation to be in. He needed to do something about it. Springing to his feet, he moved across to the dead bodies and began searching their equipment. Their shoulder flashes told him that they were from the Royal Warwickshire Regiment. After twenty minutes or so he returned to the shade of the tree to check on his ill-gotten gains. Somehow or other he managed to find another full water bottle, a bar of chocolate which had begun to melt, two tins of bully beef and three packets of hardtack biscuits. In addition, he had found a .303 Lee Enfield rifle, although the magazine only had one round in it and the rifle butt had been splintered by a stray bullet. However, the working parts were sound and it would still do its job. Checking and cleaning his own personal weapon was the first thing that Dacre AJ did whenever he had a moment to spare. His training as a Royal Marine had taught him that. He checked the rifle's butt plate for the small brass tube of oil and the pull through. As he expected, both were in place, along with a small dirty piece of cloth, the four by two, so called because it was four inches wide and two inches deep. He had heard somewhere that experienced riflemen also carried a small flask of neat spirits for cleaning the firing mechanism. Apparently it never froze in cold weather and the spirits helped the firing pin to make a good contact with the round in the chamber. He then took the time to give the rifle a thorough clean, including the barrel. Better safe than sorry, he thought. The marine had also liberated four spare clips of ammunition, a Mills grenade primed and ready for use and a steel helmet that more or less fitted him. He had also managed to find a waterproof cape, slightly burnt around the edges, and a gas mask. He put his loot into a backpack along with the first aid kit from the carrier. Things were looking up, he thought. Now all he had to do was to find some petrol and then get back to Mr Thomas and the *Gypsy Rose*.

Checking the position of the sun in the sky with his watch, he was able to work out the approximate direction of due south. Feeling a lot more confident and nibbling on the bar of chocolate, he cautiously set off. At a crossroads Dacre AJ saw a concrete pillbox. A hastily scribbled sign on the wall outside said 'Battalion HQ'. Outside the building, seated on a wooden box at an old trestle table, sat the adjutant. In front of him stood a civilian prisoner, sandwiched between two burly soldiers with rifles and bayonets fixed. The prisoner was a small, weasely looking man, dressed in a smart brown suit. Instead of a tie he wore a red neckerchief. A sergeant was making his report.

'This Frenchman has been found in a nearby cottage that overlooks our lines. He was at a window with his Martini .22 rifle on his lap. On the windowsill there was a box of ammunition. The rifle barrel was still warm and on the floor there were a number of spent cartridges.'

The NCO then turned and snapped his finger. A soldier standing nearby brought the rifle and ammo to the table.

He continued, 'We have questioned him, sir, but he refused to answer.'

The officer looked the man up and down, then fired off half a dozen questions in fluent French. The prisoner looked straight ahead defiantly and refused to say anything. The adjutant shrugged his shoulders.

'Just get rid of him, Sergeant,' he said at last.

The prisoner was led away and out of sight into a neighbouring field. Shortly afterwards two shots were heard.

The marine continued on his way. He didn't know what to make of the summary execution. Clearly there was a lot more going on in this area than he knew.

He had been walking for only about ten minutes when rounding a bend in the road Dacre AJ came across a group of soldiers under the command of a captain and a sergeant.

They had taken up a defensive position beneath a hedgerow that looked across a wide, open field. The Germans were on the far side of the field in a wood. Their tanks were clearly visible. The marine found himself a place amongst the row of soldiers. No-one asked him who he was or where he had come from. It was enough that he was there, fully prepared to fight alongside them. One or two of the men were dozing in the warmth of the sun. They all looked absolutely exhausted. Suddenly there was movement on the far side of the field. The German infantry, with their tanks in support, were beginning a slow advance across the open ground towards them. The sergeant, crouching down, ran along the line of soldiers telling them to hold their fire as they were pulling back to a farm about five hundred yards to their rear. Grabbing his precious possessions, Dacre AJ quickly followed the others at a half run, making sure that he kept his head well down below the top of the hedges that bordered the fields. As soon as they reached the farm, the officer ordered everyone to take up defensive positions. They needed no second bidding. They began to knock holes in the walls of the wooden barn which was already heavily pitted by shrapnel. Suddenly, enemy mortar rounds began to land nearby. Someone shouted out that 'Jerry was coming!'

The soldier kneeling next to Dacre AJ, an older man, said, 'Come on, lad, I think we should find somewhere a bit safer than this wooden building.'

With that, the two of them went to the far end of the barn where, just outside, they found a small outhouse. They went in and immediately began taking out some of the bricks from the walls to make loopholes. On the other side of the farm there were some stables and a few cowsheds. Other soldiers had had the same idea. Within minutes the whole farm was well defended.

The Germans arrived in force shortly afterwards and a fierce fire fight took place. The enemy, largely in the open, took heavy casualties but they persevered and their greater numbers began to tell.

Towards midday, the captain came round to say that ammunition was running low. He also asked the men their opinions as to whether they should surrender or carry on fighting. Some of the soldiers had said to fight on, others wanted to surrender. Dacre AJ and his new 'oppo' both agreed that they should fight on since morale, despite everything, seemed to be pretty high. The captain disappeared only to return twenty minutes later to let them know that there was no point in wasting human life and since they couldn't hold out much longer he had decided to surrender. He then gave them the order to cease fire but he added that if anyone felt they could get away then they were at liberty to give it a try. The young marine looked at his army colleague.

'I suggest we stay here for a bit and see what happens, but I have no intention of surrendering if I can help it.'

Both men sat on the floor with their backs to the wall. Dacre AJ opened the two tins of bully beef with his jack knife and passed one to his new-found friend.

Meanwhile back in the barn the sergeant had been persuaded to tie a dirty white towel onto the end of his rifle. Cautiously, he opened the barn door and began to wave the flag. Unfortunately, a young soldier at the far end of the barn suddenly started shooting at the Germans. Fearing that this was a British trick they returned fire immediately, killing the soldier in the process. The sergeant desperately continued to wave his flag. The Germans eventually stopped shooting. Some of their officers and NCOs began to cautiously approach the barn doors. Looking through one of the loopholes, Dacre AJ had a clear view and could see that these soldiers were not the ordinary Wehrmacht troops. These Germans were a Waffen–SS regiment. He could clearly see the SS flash on their uniforms and the 'Death's Head' badge on their helmets. They seemed to be well equipped and most of them had automatic weapons. The marine suddenly had a bad feeling about the situation.

Dacre AJ estimated that there must have been about fifty British soldiers in the barn. They were all marched out, disarmed and stripped to the waist. All their personal possessions, including watches, were taken from them. The senior German officer then ordered the first five prisoners to be taken into the neighbouring field. The young marine couldn't actually see what was happening because of a high hedge that blocked his view but he clearly heard the order to open fire which was immediately followed by the sounds of automatic weapons. The young marine was suddenly afraid, very afraid. His fear fed on the desperate need to escape, to get as far away as he possibly could from what he had just witnessed. Never in all his life had he known such dread. The blood pounded in his ears and tears came rolling down his cheeks. He slumped back down onto the floor, staring blankly ahead, but seeing nothing. He was horrified and sickened by what he had witnessed.

'The Germans are shooting our chaps from the barn,' he whispered.

'What?' replied the soldier.

'Those bastards are murdering our mates,' he said in a louder voice.

'Where? Show me! Let me see?'

The soldier pushed the marine out of the way and squinted through the loophole for himself.

'Oh my dear Lord, you're right! The bastards! Look out there are two of them coming to check out our building.'

Both men froze, their hearts beating so loud that surely they would be given away. At the last minute the two Germans were called back by their comrades.

'Blimey that was close and no mistakes,' the older man said.

Dacre AJ wiped the tears and the snot from his face with the back of his hand. He mentally shook himself. He couldn't be doing with this! His tough and uncompromising training as a Royal Marine automatically took over.

'We need to get away from here as fast as we can,' he said. 'Otherwise they are going to find us and then we will meet the same fate as the others.

Just then it began to rain, light at first then within minutes it had turned into a real downpour. Dacre AJ took one last look through the loophole and immediately wished he hadn't. He saw several German soldiers prepare their stick grenades which they then threw into the barn. This was followed by more machine gunfire and other grenades. Eventually everything went quiet.

'Time for us to be going,' said the marine.

It had occurred to him that maybe they should have gone back to the barn in order to see if anyone was left alive but with only a few rounds of ammunition between them he reasoned that it would have been suicide.

Together, they made their way outside into the pouring rain. They were both quickly soaked to the skin. Nearby there was a ditch where, on their hands and knees, they crawled away as quickly as they could. With the rain continuing to fall, the ditch had soon become a torrent of water. Both of them were soon covered in mud from head to toe. As they crawled along they went past a soldier of the same regiment sitting on the bank. He was covered in blood with a hand over a wound in his chest. The marine gave him a cursory look. The empty eyes said it all. He was dead. Eventually, they found shelter in a pigsty and crawled inside out of the rain. There were two pigs inside who grunted at the intrusion. Both men were shivering violently. The smell was pretty unpleasant. However, the warmth from the animals' bodies helped the soldier and the marine to keep warm. Dacre AJ shared the last of his meagre rations with his companion.

'We could stay here for a bit,' said the soldier.

'I can't,' replied the youngster. 'I have to get back to the beach with some petrol. People are depending on me.'

'I think I will stay here,' said the older man. 'Will you be okay on your own?'

Dacre AJ nodded. 'I'll be fine!'

They wished each other well and shook hands. Pausing at the doorway, the marine turned and said, 'I don't even know your name.'

'It's Keeping, Malcolm Keeping, but I answer to 'Mal'.

'Well good luck to you, Mal. If we ever get through this lot we must try and do something about what we have witnessed here today.'

'Too bloody right, mate! You watch out for yourself, young 'un.'

With that the marine ducked out of the doorway into the rain. Keeping low, he ran as fast as he could away from the building. He hadn't gone more than half a dozen paces when he found Mal Keeping hard on his heels.

'A man can change his mind, can't he?' he panted. 'I have decided to come with you. You seem to know what you are doing.'

Together they sprinted through a nearby field of corn, the wet stalks snatching at their clothing. Behind them, and some way off, they could hear German soldiers shouting.

Almost immediately the air was full of what seemed to be angry bees, spitting past them. They were being shot at! Together they dashed forward, weaving from side to side, heading for a nearby stagnant pond into which they both jumped. Mal told the youngster to keep his head down. He needed no second bidding. He took shelter in some reeds on the pond's edge.

Keeping struggled to reach the far side, but the muck and weed held him back. One of the SS troops had seen him. From about fifty yards away he raised his rifle and fired a single shot. The bullet struck the soldier, the back of his head disappeared in a fine red mist. He was killed outright. The young marine watched Mal's body slide under the water and out of sight. Dacre AJ remained out of sight, huddled amongst the reeds. Fuck, he thought! What a waste of a good man, so near yet so far from safety. He shook, both from the cold and from the shock of the sudden turn of events. One minute Mal was there, living and breathing, the next he was gone. The youngster was convinced that he was next. He huddled even closer to the reeds, not that they offered him much protection. Nothing happened. After about thirty minutes, he ventured out from his place of safety. It was all clear. The Germans had chosen to move on.

Chapter 33

After about half an hour, Dacre AJ came to the outskirts of Dunkirk. In a roadside ditch, beneath a large hedgerow, he saw a group of about twenty elderly men and women, clearly refugees, who had taken shelter. He stopped and asked them what they were doing and why they were there. Somewhat surprised that he spoke their language fluently, they explained that the Boche had put detonators on the road so they couldn't go any further forward for fear of setting them off. One of the elderly men pointed to where the detonators were. More than a little surprised that the man had used the word 'detonator', Dacre AJ walked the few feet to take a look for himself. They looked like ordinary blue pencils to him. He bent down to pick one up.

One of the refugees who had followed him grabbed his wrist and said, 'No! No! Explosive! This is a trick of the Germans. These are very dangerous, they will explode!'

Dacre AJ took a long hard look at the detonators. They still looked like pencils, even the ends were sharpened and he could clearly see the lead inside. Gingerly, he bent down and picked one up. The group of refugees shrank back as one, fearful of an explosion. Well, thought Dacre AJ, it looked like a pencil and, holding it up to his nose, it smelt like a pencil. Checking that all was clear he threw it over the hedge into the neighbouring field. Nothing happened. They were pencils! He picked up the remainder and presented them to the leader of the group. There was much embarrassed laughter and apologies. Everyone wanted to shake his hand. After about five minutes he wished them au revoir and bonne chance, and continued on his way chuckling to himself. It took him a few minutes to suddenly stop and realise that he had actually taken a terrible risk in picking up the rest of the pencils. A more devious enemy would have scattered some real detonators amongst the pencils. The thought made him shudder and break out in a cold sweat. He would have to be more careful in future.

The rain had stopped and the sky had cleared, although there was an oppressive atmosphere. It was now mid-afternoon. Taking what he hoped was going to be a short cut to the town, Dacre AJ moved in a southerly direction, crossing a railway line on his way. Shortly afterwards he came across one of the many bridges that crossed the canal. He tried to remember its name but his schoolboy geography failed him. The bridge was crowded with refugees, mostly women and children, who were moving in the direction of the town. He crouched down behind a nearby wall because he had spotted German infantry in their field grey–green uniforms on the far side. German tanks and armoured fighting vehicles were queueing up, waiting to cross over the bridge. Clearly they were unable to do so because of the mass of civilians. Indeed, a number of the German soldiers had moved into the crowds and, at first sight, appeared to be urging them on with their rifle butts and fixed bayonets. Dacre AJ watched them carefully. Then it suddenly dawned on him that the soldiers were actually using the civilians as a shield. They were not interested in moving them out of the way at all. In fact, it was the exact opposite. They wanted them there in order to cover their advance to the far side. Suddenly there was an ear splitting explosion when at least half of the bridge disintegrated into a mass of flying timbers, splinters and bodies. Somebody had deliberately blown it up, enemy soldiers and civilians alike, presumably to try and stop the Germans from advancing. Dacre AJ was shocked by what he had just witnessed.

About fifty yards in front of him but still on his side of the canal, he spotted three British soldiers hiding behind some scrubby bushes. The Germans on the far side of the canal had also seen them so that bullets and shells immediately began to rain down on their position. Other German soldiers, who had already crossed the canal further west, were cautiously moving along the main road towards the British trio in an effort to outflank them. All at once the three soldiers jumped up and started running towards the marine as fast as they could. They were Royal Engineers, a warrant officer and two sappers. Heads down and bodies hunched over, they charged past Dacre AJ. The warrant officer caught sight of him at the last moment.

He half turned and shouted at him, 'What the fuck are you waiting for? Come on you idle bugger get your arse moving!'

The marine needed no second telling. Leaping to his feet, he sprinted after them as fast as he could.

The small group dashed around the corner of a building and immediately came under attack from a lone German sniper hiding on the first floor of a nearby house. One of the sappers fell to the ground, dead, shot between the eyes. He never knew what had hit him. The others returned fire at once. The sniper was hit several times and, clutching his chest, rolled out of the window and fell the twenty feet or so to the ground below. He was mortally wounded and in great pain. He just lay there calling for his 'mutter'. The warrant officer looked the German over.

'There is nothing we can do for him, that's for sure,' he said grimly.

'Well we can't just leave him,' said the marine.

'Why not?' replied the WO. 'He's just killed one of my lads.'

'Because we can't, that's why. If he were a dog or a horse in that much agony, we wouldn't hesitate to put it out of its misery.'

'Well if you feel like that why don't you shoot him,' said the remaining sapper.

The warrant officer interrupted both of them. 'Look, we can't stand here all day discussing this. Either you shoot him and put him out of his bloody misery or we leave him. It's as simple as that. Now make up your damned mind. But you'd better be quick about it. His mates won't be far away.'

Without hesitation Dacre AJ took out his revolver. He checked the cylinder. There were just three rounds left. He was sure this was the right thing to do. Holding the gun to the German's temple he gently squeezed the trigger. The WO nodded his head in approval.

'That was well done, youngster. Be thankful that there were no other witnesses around who might accuse you of a war crime rather than a mercy killing. Now, if you're finished, let's get the hell out of here.'

With that they ran on hoping it was in the direction of the sea. They left both bodies lying together in the companionship of death, amongst the dirt and the rubble.

After a couple of hundred yards, the soldier leading the group ducked into a doorway of a deserted, bombed-out building. Everyone was breathing heavily but the two soldiers were absolutely shattered. Clearly they were not as fit as the marine.

The warrant officer was the first to speak, 'Bloody hell that was close and no mistakes!' He looked the marine up and down. 'And just who the hell are you?'

Dacre AJ explained briefly who he was and what he was doing in Dunkirk. The WO turned to his sapper.

'Hear that, Chalky, this lad might be our ticket home to Blighty.'

The WO then explained that he and his men had been amongst the last of the British troops defending the north bank of the canal. Their task had been to blow up as many of the bridges as they could.

'My officer made it quite clear to me that we were to make sure that no-one was to cross over those bridges and he meant no-one. Unfortunately that included the women and children who Jerry was using as cover.'

The marine thought about this for a moment or two and then decided not to question the morality of their orders. Even he knew that in war difficult decisions had to be made, often involving the life and death of the innocent,

Just as they were getting ready to move on, a figure suddenly appeared in the doorway. The daylight behind him initially made it difficult to identify his features. However the shape of the helmet said it all. He was a German soldier and he wasn't alone. He spoke in remarkably good English.

'Please put up your hands and surrender. For you, Tommy, the war is over!'

Chapter 34

The three British prisoners were sitting on the pavement outside the building with their backs against a wall. They were guarded by two pairs of German Field Police dressed in their long, black, leather overcoats and steel helmets. Machine pistols were slung across their chests. Their motorcycles with sidecars were parked nearby. The marine was listening discreetly to the conversation of the guards. He did not want to give away the fact that he could understand their language but he didn't like what he was hearing. Two of the Germans wanted to shoot the prisoners and be done with it. They were doing their utmost to convince their comrades. Thankfully, the others were not convinced that it was a good idea, at least for the time being.

Dacre AJ quietly asked his two companions if they had any cigarettes since he didn't smoke. The warrant officer reached into one of the top pockets of his battledress jacket and took out a crumpled packet of Woodbines and an old well-used brass lighter. He passed them across to the youngster. Dacre AJ stood up and took a couple of steps towards the nearest guard. He mimed smoking and at the same time said, 'Zigaretten, zigaretten? The guard agreed but refused to take one when he was offered the packet. Meanwhile, the two field-police who were the farthest away suddenly mounted their motorcycle and side car and, without a word to their fellows, started up the bike and rode off. The marine sat back down and gave his attention to the two remaining guards.

Then out of the corner of his mouth he said, 'I am going to have a go at one of these guards. When I do, make sure you two take care of the other one, understand? This might be our only chance of getting away!'

With that he got up and began walking towards the first guard. He started to undo his trousers saying, 'Toilette bitte?'

At first the German hesitated, then understanding the Englishman's need he agreed, waving him to a nearby doorway. The youngster dropped his trousers and began to squat down. The guard looked towards his mate, making some crude comment about the English and their toilet habits. In doing so he had taken his eye off the marine, which was all the excuse Dacre AJ needed. With a ferocious roar he launched himself the short distance onto the unsuspecting German, trapping his machine-pistol against his body. Despite the surprise, the guard reacted quickly. Wrapping his arms around the marine's waist and using Dacre AJ's own momentum, he twisted around so that the marine was carried backwards. Being already off balance, the German's weight forced him to the ground. He was momentarily dazed as his head hit the pavement. The guard was on him in an instant, his hands scrabbling for the marine's neck and eyes. The second guard seeing his companion under attack unslung his weapon as he ran forward to help. However, he hesitated to open fire for fear of hitting his friend. This was just what the other two wanted. They immediately leapt into action bringing the second guard to the ground and pummelling him into unconsciousness. Meanwhile, the marine was in serious trouble. The guard had one hand around Dacre AJ's throat and was squeezing as hard as he could. The other hand was on his face going for his eyes. That was the German's first mistake. The second mistake was that his thumb had somehow got into the side of the youngster's mouth. Dacre AJ bit down as hard as he could and had the satisfaction of hearing the bone crack. The German let out a huge cry of pain. The marine seized his chance. Using all his strength, he managed to roll them both over so that he was now on top. It was his turn. He found the man's jugular and was applying as much pressure as he could. His adversary, realising that he was losing the fight, reached down to one of his boots and had pulled out a large trench knife. The next second, in a final desperate effort, he thrust the blade right through the marine's left hand. Dacre AJ cried out in agony and shock. Despite the unbelievable pain, he still had his hands around the soldier's throat. Drawing on his last reserves of energy, he managed to maintain his grip. Such was the effort that the sweat from his brow dripped onto the German's face. Eventually the soldier finally went limp. Totally exhausted, Dacre AJ rolled away from the dead body onto his knees and was violently sick. The other two ran up to him, the sapper began applying a bandage that he had taken from the first aid kit on the motorcycle. The warrant officer looked him over.

'You okay?' he said.

The marine nodded.

'Was this your first time?'

'What?'

'Was this the first time you've killed someone up front and personal?'

'Yes!'

'Well despite what people will tell you it doesn't get any easier, take it from me. Now, I suggest we get out of here before anybody else arrives.'

Dacre AJ looked at his injured hand. Blood was already seeping through the hastily applied bandage. It hurt like hell.

'I think I can find my way back to the beach,' he replied through gritted teeth.

With that he led them off at a brisk trot through the back streets and narrow lanes that made up that part of the old Dunkirk town.

Turning a corner, the small group came across an old and battered Citroen car, stopped at a barrier. There were two men it. The elder of the two had been seriously wounded in the chest whilst his right arm was hanging by just a thread of muscle and flesh. He and his son lived nearby and had been trying to get home when they had been attacked by an enemy plane. The son had emerged completely unscathed. The old man was sobbing and moaning terribly. Together, the soldiers carried him gently from the car and laid him down by the roadside. They tried to make him as comfortable as they could. Dacre AJ agreed to take off the remains of the shattered limb which he did with his jack knife. However, the old man's injuries proved to be too much for him. He died quietly with the son holding his hand and the three Englishmen kneeling close by, unable to do any more. With tears in his eyes, the son urged them to get away saying that he would take care of his father's body. They needed no second bidding.

When they arrived at Malo-les-Bains, the beach was still a scene of complete pandemonium. Some drunken French soldiers were looting cafes, shops and homes, blazing away at anything that moved with their rifles. Enemy planes were still flying overhead, bombing and strafing the sands. A number of small boats had been riddled with bullets and had sunk. Taking the Engineers with him, Dacre AJ made his way back to the petrol bowser that he had discovered earlier in the day. He still had to get some fuel or else the *Gypsy Rose* was not going to get home. Urging the others to find some empty petrol cans, he went in search of a pick axe which he found strapped to the back of a nearby truck. Returning to the bowser, he was pleased to see that the others had managed to find three large cans complete with screw tops. Taking the pick axe he flexed his shoulders and with one mighty swing punctured a neat hole in the side of the bowser. A long, thin stream of fuel came spurting out which allowed the soldiers to fill the cans. The marine checked his hand. It was still bleeding and extremely painful. When all was finished he picked up one of the cans, told the other two to do likewise and to follow him down to the water's edge.

At that very moment the beach came under heavy enemy mortar fire, the shells landing everywhere on the beach. Horses grazing on the grass in the nearby dunes were killed and others were wounded. Their screams of pain and fright were unnerving. An officer passing by detailed some of his men to shoot the wounded animals and to unhobble the others and set them free.

As Dacre AJ and his two companions ran down the beach to the water's edge, another burst of mortar fire landed nearby. A captain who had been standing nearby directing his men was surprised to see one of his arms drop to the ground, blown clean off. He continued giving orders to his men whilst others attended to him, applying dressings and a tourniquet.

As they reached the sea, the marine had a quick look back at the chaos all around them. Striding down the beach towards one of the small boats he was amazed to see a soldier carrying an English longbow and on his back a quiver of arrows. The warrant officer saw what the marine was looking at.

'Do you know who that is?' he asked.

'No, I don't', replied Dacre AJ.

'His name is John Churchill. In the pre-war Olympics he won the gold medal in archery. I actually saw him shoot.'

How totally bizarre the marine thought. Only an Englishman would consider going to war with a weapon that had been used at Crecy and Agincourt.

Dacre AJ could just make out the *Gypsy Rose* lying about a hundred yards from the shore. She seemed to be all in one piece which was a blessed relief. He had wondered if they might return to the beach only to find her another casualty, at least badly shot-up or, heaven forbid, sunk. Without hesitating he plunged into the water with his can of petrol clasped to his chest. The sapper followed his example. The warrant officer hesitated before sheepishly calling out that he couldn't swim. Quickly the marine showed him how to hold the petrol can as a float. Together they all began paddling their way out to the boat. The warrant officer was struggling and clearly in danger of drowning. The marine grabbed a handful of the soldier's collar and, with every ounce of strength that he had left, he kicked out violently in an effort to get both of them and the much needed petrol to the boat. It proved to be too much. He wasn't sure when he realised that they were not going to make it. The thought came upon him just as all his strength suddenly seemed to ebb away. Dacre AJ vaguely remembered being told that when you are about to die your whole life flashes before you. This was not so for him. What he did experience was like watching a slow motion film, but without the sound, of his final day. The pictures, although somewhat fuzzy, were clear enough for him to see the various incidents in which he had been involved: the two military police officers; crossing the narrow lane; the farmer ploughing his field; the attack on the barn and the atrocities committed by the Germans; the death of Mal Keeping; the group of elderly refugees; the canal bridge being blown up; shooting the wounded German soldier; his capture and escape; the old Frenchman in the car and finding the much-needed petrol. It was all there in amazing detail. When he met his Maker he hoped that he wouldn't be judged too harshly. He had done what needed to be done in the best way that he could. Then the cold sea water closed over his face. He could feel the salt on his lips and in his mouth and throat. Totally exhausted he surrendered peacefully to the inevitable.

On the *Gypsy Rose* Mr Thomas had been watching as the situation developed. He soon realised that Dacre AJ was in trouble. As quickly as he could he brought the boat in towards the men in the water. Using a boat hook, he managed to drag Dacre AJ to the side where willing hands pulled him and his companions aboard as well as their precious cargo of fuel. As soon as the petrol tanks were topped up, Mr Thomas powered up the twin engines and set a course for Dover. They had another full cargo of troops to deliver to Blighty.

Down below in the cabin the two Royal Engineers, wrapped in warm blankets and clasping mugs of hot sweet tea, counted their blessings. The warrant officer looked across to where the marine was having his hand re-bandaged.

'I just want to say thank you 'Royal' for saving my life. I thought I was a goner then!'

Dacre AJ smiled and nodded in acknowledgement.

'That's okay, it's all part of the service. To tell you the truth I thought we were done for as well! Anyway what's your name?'

'Ted, Ted Makepeace,' he replied.

They shook hands

'Good to meet you, Ted. You just take it easy for a while. All being well we should be back in Dover in a couple of hours.'

With that the marine climbed up the short flight of steps into the wheelhouse. Mr Thomas looked him up and down.

'Are you alright?' he asked, concern in his voice. The marine gave him a lopsided grin.

'I'm a bit battered and bruised and my hand hurts, but other than that I'll survive.'

Dacre AJ then decided to confide in the older man exactly what had happened when he witnessed the soldiers being massacred in the barn. He valued Mr Thomas's opinion and would welcome his advice. The marine already had a notion of what he should do but he wanted to hear what the older man thought. His guidance was simple and to the point. As soon as they arrived back in Dover, the marine should report the massacre to the proper authorities. Mr Thomas said that not only was it the right and proper thing to do but that it was also his duty, particularly on behalf of all those men who had been murdered.

Mr Thomas gave a long and heartfelt sigh. He thought that both he and his marine had had enough experiences and dangers over the last few days to last them a lifetime.

'Last trip I think, AJ. What do you say?'

'I agree, let's call it a day. I think we have done our bit. Maybe it's time we went home!'

Chapter 35

The signal 'Operation Dynamo now completed' was circulated by the Admiralty at 1423 hours on the 4th of June 1940. However, not all of the British Expeditionary Force had been evacuated from France. There were still more than one hundred and forty thousand British soldiers south of the River Somme. Some had never even known about the evacuation. In the meantime, the Prime Minister, Winston Churchill, in a bid to re-enforce the British support for France and with the express purpose of slowing down the Third Reich's advance, sent another expeditionary force across the Channel during the second week of June 1940 to fight alongside their French Allies. This Second BEF was commanded by Lieutenant General Alan Brooke. Despite this appointment, Churchill was firm in his belief that France was about to surrender. Yet his warnings were ignored. Consequently, British and Canadian soldiers continued to be shipped across the Channel. As it turned out, this movement of troops was wholly unsuccessful in helping the French to save Paris and ultimately the rest of France from German occupation.

General Weygand, the French Commander in Chief, needed some convincing that the 'Battle for France' should continue. The odds were now heavily stacked against him in favour of the advancing Germans. They had over one hundred and four divisions available to them for their Operation Fall Rot or Case Red, the code name for the attack south which was intended to break through the allied line along the River Somme. To prevent this, General Weygand had only forty-five divisions including all the units of the Second BEF. Their task was to hold a two hundred and twenty-five mile line. An impossible task! The German strength was added to by their growing air superiority. Although Churchill had agreed to send some additional RAF squadrons, it was not enough to make a difference. The French asked for even more air support but the Prime Minister had to refuse. He knew that a battle for Britain was coming and they would need all the squadrons they could muster in order to defend England.

Back on the ground, General Weygand seemed to have lost both the will to command and to continue the fight. The wide front allocated to the British, in particular to the 51st Highland Division, showed all too clearly the weakness of the allied position and, it must be said, the French Command. It was an impossible task against such a well-equipped and professional army. Only strong points could be held, which left gaps elsewhere through which the Germans were able to penetrate with disastrous results. In the end the 51st were surrounded, cut off and therefore forced to surrender. As a result of the overall situation, Paris fell to the Germans on the 14th June. Consequently, the French Government had no choice but to surrender.

The order was given for the newly arrived Second BEF to be evacuated, code name Operation Ariel. The ports of Cherbourg, Saint-Malo, Brest and others were to be used. At Saint-Nazaire the huge Cunard liner *Lancastria* was bringing home more than six thousand soldiers, civilians and crew when it was sunk by German aircraft. More than three thousand, five hundred people were killed. It remains the worst maritime disaster in British history.

Mr Thomas and Marine Dacre AJ did make one final trip back to Dunkirk on the day after *Operation Dynamo* was officially ended. The Prime Minister and Admiral

Ramsey had decided to ask for volunteers from the company of small boats to return once more with ships of the Royal Navy and the French Navy to evacuate any survivors of the French Army who had been left behind. Over four hundred soldiers, including some of the 28th Infantry Regiment were successfully saved and brought back to Dover despite heavy German opposition. Two days later, those self-same French soldiers were landed back in France to bolster General Weygand's army.

Epilogue

The *Gypsy Rose* returned to Maidstone on the River Medway in Kent. Dacre AJ and Mr Thomas shook hands and said their goodbyes, firm in a mutual friendship that had developed during a period of unbelievable intense adversity, and went their separate ways. Rather surprisingly, despite everything that they had endured together, they never kept in touch or met again.

After the fall of France, General Weygand had been one of the first French leaders to call for an armistice with the Germans. Yet he refused to co-operate with the invaders, which disqualified him from serving in the Vichy Government. In October 1940 he was sent to North Africa to command the French forces in Algeria. He opposed General Rommel and his Africa Korps, so consequently he was brought back to France in 1941 where he was arrested. He remained in custody for the remainder of the war. Afterwards, he was accused of collaboration with the Nazis by the French government and imprisoned. He was eventually exonerated and released in 1948.

After Dunkirk, Vice Admiral Ramsey was appointed Allied Naval Commander, Expeditionary Forces. In October 1943 he was given the task of organising the transportation of Allied troops to the beaches of Normandy for the June 1944 invasion of France which was one of the great achievements of World War II. General Eisenhower said of him that no-one else could have organized such a large-scale landing. By then he was a full Admiral and had been knighted. He was unfortunately killed in a plane crash in January 1945.

Lord Gort never commanded a field force again. Churchill considered making him Commander-in-Chief, Middle East. However, General Brooke, who had criticised him so harshly over his command of the BEF 1939-1940, vetoed the idea. He was, nevertheless, given the Governorship of Malta and played a major part in helping the island to withstand the German siege. Subsequently, he went to Palestine as the High Commissioner. He became a field marshal but died from cancer in March 1946.

General Ironside was encouraged to resign from his post of Commander in Chief, Home Forces. He had been criticised, perhaps a little unfairly, about the number of troops he had provided for the defence of Britain. Nevertheless, he was made a field marshal and a peer of the realm.

General Sir John Dill's career as a military commander declined after Dunkirk, although he was made a field marshal. Churchill referred to him as 'Dilly-Dally' and had little time for him. He retired as Chief of the Imperial General Staff in December 1941. Later, he successfully led Britain's staff mission to Washington. Although he did not get on with Churchill, he was, surprisingly, very highly thought of by the Americans. He died in November 1944.

General Alan Brooke was highly praised for his performance as Commander in Chief of the Second BEF in

France and rightly so. In December 1941 he was promoted to Chief of the Imperial General Staff until the end of the war. Unlike those who went before him, he was quite prepared to stand his ground against the Prime Minister and would not be bullied. Churchill respected him for that. Brooke was made a field marshal and a viscount after the war had ended.

Anthony Eden, the First Earl of Avon, had earned a reputation as an opponent to appeasement in the 1930s, at one time resigning from his cabinet post as Foreign Secretary. He was appointed Secretary of State for War by Winston Churchill in 1940 and became a close confidant and adviser to the Prime Minister. In 1942 he was again appointed to the post of Foreign Secretary. He later became Leader of the Conservative Party and then Prime Minister in 1955. He resigned due to ill health following the Suez Crisis in 1956 and died in 1977.

Winston Churchill led Britain through the war years from 1940–1945. Although quite elderly at the time, he was a robust and pragmatic leader. He took on the dual roles of Prime Minister and Minister of Defence. His steadfast refusal to consider defeat, surrender or compromise helped to inspire British resistance, especially during the difficult and dark days of the war when Britain stood alone against the Germans. He is regarded as one of the greatest wartime leaders and without doubt played a major role in leading the Allies to victory in World War ll. He lost the post-war election in 1945 but was re-elected in 1951. In 1953 he was awarded the Nobel Prize for Literature. He died in 1965 and by order of Her Majesty Queen Elizabeth II he was given a state funeral.

It was not unusual for Royal Marine officers like Captain James L Moulton to attain posts outside their corps. Moulton had spent much of his earlier career flying, both for the navy and for the air force. In the summer of 1944 Moulton, then a lieutenant colonel took command of the newly formed 48 Commando RM. Marine Dacre AJ joined the unit after his arduous duties as a naval frogman clearing the beaches. During *Operation Overlord* and the Battle for Normandy, Dacre AJ was promoted twice in the field, once to the rank of sergeant then later to captain and company commander, specifically on the orders of Colonel Moulton.

After the war Moulton went on to attain the rank of MGRM Portsmouth. In the late 1950s and early 1960s he was Chief of Amphibious Warfare (CAW). In 1962 he became instrumental in involving Marine Dacre AJ in Operation Saint George.

Much of the Royal Marine Commandos' present day capabilities are directly due to General Moulton.

On his return to Dover, Marine Dacre reported the massacre to a senior army officer from Intelligence. The Lieutenant Colonel listened very carefully to his story, making a series of notes in a diary.

When the marine had finished the officer said to him, 'Now look, son. You are not to tell anyone about this. I know about it and you know about it. I shall make my report to those in higher authority. You might like to know that we have known for some time that the SS do not take prisoners. However, you must keep this to yourself. What we don't want to happen are stories like this getting out and inciting our lads to seek vengeance, when and if they have the opportunity to do so. Is that clear? When we have won this bloody war, and make no mistake young man we will win come what may, then, and only then, will we be able to start on the road to seek justice for those soldiers who have been murdered in cold blood by the Germans. Do you understand what I am saying?'

Dacre AJ did understand, perfectly!

Some of the soldiers from the massacre in the barn, although wounded, did actually survive. In 1945 several of them returned to the farm and retrieved some of the bullets fired from the Germans' automatic weapons. They also managed to obtain an affidavit from the French authorities concerning the massacre. Several years later, the German officer in charge was brought to trial charged with war crimes. He was eventually executed.

Other massacres of British soldiers who had surrendered during the BEF's retreat were also recorded as having taken place, for example those at Wormhoudt and Le Paradis. However, not all the perpetrators were brought to justice. It has been suggested that some of the main culprits lived well into old age and even received a pension from the West German Government.

In 1946 Marine Dacre AJ informed the War Graves Commission of the possible location where Mal had been killed. His remains were eventually recovered from the pond. Private 4087259 Malcolm Keeping of the King's Own Yorkshire Light Infantry was finally interred at the military cemetery at Dunkirk. Later that same year, the marine obtained permission to visit France. Whilst he had only known Mal for a short period of time, he nevertheless felt it an obligation and a matter of honour to see for himself the soldier's last resting place. As a mark of respect he laid a single white rose at the graveside. Because Mal was from the mining community of Ravensthorpe near Dewsbury in Yorkshire, Dacre AJ thought that this was a fitting tribute for a Yorkshire lad.

Mr Leslie Thomas returned to his film processing laboratory. He was responsible for producing many of the wartime information and propaganda films that were so essential at that time. He and his wife lived quietly in their home in the London suburbs of Ruislip. They had two children, both boys. It took him nearly a year to restore the *Gypsy Rose* back to her immaculate pre-war condition of varnished wood and bright metalwork. However, he never went back to France again. In 1947 he rather surprisingly sold the *Gypsy Rose* which, apart from his family, had been the love of his life. He never gave a reason for the sale. He tragically died in 1952 as a result of a brain haemorrhage caused by the infamous great smog.

Warrant Officer Edwin (Ted) Makepeace of the Royal Engineers made a full recovery from his ordeal at Dunkirk. In 1941 he was sent to India and later took part in the campaign in Burma. After the war, he joined HM Prison Service as an engineer and rose to the position of Inspector of HM Prisons. He married and had four children. He died in 1986 from cancer.

Royal Marine Dacre AJ went back to his barracks at the Chatham Naval Base. No-one ever asked him where he had been or what he had done whilst he had been on compassionate leave although it was noted on his service record. Three months later he was summoned to Admiralty House in London where, in front of the Prime Minister, Mr Winston Churchill and the Adjutant General of the Royal Marines, General Sir RFC Foster, he was formally presented with the Legion d'Honneur by the leader of the Free French Forces, Colonel Charles de Gaulle.

A week later, Dacre AJ was transferred to the small elite detachment of Royal Marines that was responsible for the safety and security of the Prime Minister in London. It was rumoured that Mr Churchill had asked for him personally.

In 1942 Dacre AJ, along with several hundred other marines volunteered for training in the newly formed Commandos that the Royal Marines were assembling. In that same year he took part in the infamous raid on Dieppe, codenamed Operation Jubilee. Some people have likened that particular action to a naval version of the charge of the Light Brigade. But that, as they say, is another story.

Appendix

Appendix A	Daily Evacuation Records at Dunkirk	
	Date	Lives Saved
	26-May	4,247
	27-May	5,718
	28-May	18,527
	29-May	50,331
	30-May	53,227
	31-May	64,141
	01-Jun	61,557
	02-Jun	23,604
	03-Jun	29,641
	04-Jun	27,689
	Total number of lives saved	338,682
Appendix B	The total number of ships and boats involved in the Dunkirk evacuation were 693.	
Appendix C	The number of ships of the Royal Navy that took part was as follows: 42 destroyers, 36 minesweepers, plus several flotillas of motor torpedo boats. Of these, 50 were lost or damaged at Dunkirk.	

Appendix D	The number of Merchant Navy and private vessels that took part was as follows: 77 trawlers, 40 Dutch schuiten, 35 passenger ferries and 26 yachts. Other vessels: 440. Approximately 200 small boats were sunk and another 200 were damaged.
Appendix E	The Royal Air Force flew over 660 sorties but sustained heavy losses. During the 'Battle for France' they lost a total of 959 planes of which 477 were fighters. The RAF strength of 1078 frontline aircraft had been reduced to just 475. 60 pilots were killed.
Appendix F	During the battle for Dunkirk, the Luftwaffe flew 1,882 bombing missions and 1,997 fighter sorties.
Appendix G	The number of soldiers killed at Dunkirk or at sea by enemy action was 3,500. The number killed, wounded or taken prisoner during the three week campaign in Flanders was 68,111

BEF	British Expeditionary Force
Bootneck	Naval Slang For Royal Marines
BREN Gun	Light Machine Gun, .303 Calibre Ammunition
CIGS	Commander In Chief General Staff
CO	Commanding Officer
CPO	Chief Petty Officer RN
CSM	Company Sergeant Major RM
Crab	RN/RM Slang For Dirty Person
Eating Irons	Knife, Fork And Spoon
First Drill	Senior Drill Instructor RM
Heads	Toilets
HE	High Explosive
HM	His Majesty (King George Vl)
Hussif	Housewife, Iepack Containing Needle And Thread And Darning Wool
JNCO	Junior Non Commissioned Officer (Corporal & Lance Corporal)
Make & Mend	Time Off
Matelots	Sailors
MC	Military Cross
NAAFI	Navy, Army, Air Force Institute

OC Provost	Officer Commanding (Eg A Company Of Men) Regimental Or Barrack Police. Also Used For Military Police
PTI	Physical Training Instructor RM
PWI	Platoon Weapons Instructor RM
QMS	Quarter Master Sergeant RM
RAF	Royal Air Force
RAOC	Royal Army Ordnance Corps
Rear Party	Small Group Of Men Who Guard A Barracks Whilst The Main Force Is Away
Royal	Slang For A Royal Marine
CMP	Corps Of Military Police (Not Royal Until 1946)
RSM	Regimental Sergeant Major (Highest Non-Commissioned Rank)
Sapper	A Royal Engineer
Schoolie	Education Officer RN
Short Ring	RN/RM Slang For Serious Trouble
Sick Bay	Naval Hospital
SNCO	Senior Non Commissioned Officer (Sergeants And Above)
Tracer	A Bullet That Lights Up When Fired

Bibliography

By Sea and Land. Neillands Robin, Pen & Sword 2004

Dunkirk Evacuation 1940. Osbourne Henry John, WW 2 People's War BBC

Dunkirk, Fight to the Last Man. Seburg-Montefiore Hugh, Penguin Books 2007

Dunkirk, The Incredible Escape. Geb Norman, 1990

Dunkirk, The British Evacuation 1940. Jackson Robert, Cassell 2002

Fighting Talk. Inglis James, Pier 9 2008

Forgotten Voices of Dunkirk. Levine Joshua, Ebury press 2010

My Life My War. Hallias Bernard, WW2 People's War BBC

The Bowman of England. Featherstone Donald, Pen & Sword 2003

The Illustrated History of the 20th Century. Matthews Rupert, Ted Smart 1994

The Royal Marines 1919-1980. Ladd JD, London 1980

The Royal Marines. Moulton JL, Sphere 1973

The Royal Marines. Thompson Julian, Pan 2001

The Second World War. Taylor AJP, Penguin 1989

1940 The Fall of France. Beaufare Andre, Cassell 1967

The War on Land 1939-1945. Lewin Ronald, Vintage 2007

Historical Notes

Whilst some of the characters portrayed in this novel such as Marine Dacre AJ and his fellow marines both at Deal and Plymouth are fictitious, there are, of course, others who were real people, for example Churchill, Eden and Admiral Ramsey, who were and still are part of our history. I have deliberately taken the decision to mix fact with fiction in an effort to try to recreate a sense of the period as well as, hopefully, a more interesting story.

Whilst it is true that there were no Royal Marines' units at Dunkirk, one officer, a Captain JL Moulton RM did actually serve on Lord Gort's staff as a GSO 3 officer. In fact he was one of several officers who were responsible for organising the evacuation of the troops from the beaches at La Penne and Dunkirk.

The character of Leslie Thomas has been based on my father who, according to family folklore, did three or four trips to Dunkirk in his boat *Gypsy Rose* although I can find no actual evidence to support this. Nevertheless, I rather like the idea that he may have done this of his own accord. The Royal Engineer Warrant Officer, Ted Makepeace, is modelled on my father-in-law who was not only at Dunkirk but was responsible for destroying some of the bridges that crossed the canal outside the town. Like many old soldiers he rarely talked about his experiences, but I do know that he was one of the last off the beaches, and furthermore was saved from drowning by an unknown person. I like to think that perhaps amongst all the chaos, death and destruction that took place on the beaches all those years ago, that it would have been a wonderful coincidence if my father had saved the man who was to become my father-in-law.

The training of Royal Marines in 1939, both at Deal and at Plymouth, is based on actual recorded evidence by former marines, many of whom are no longer with us. At Dunkirk, the adventures that Dacre AJ experiences are based on actual events as witnessed by soldiers and sailors who were there at the time.

Despite their absence from Dunkirk, the Royal Marines did play a role in the final 'Battle for France' albeit in a minor way. On the 11th May 1940 the Grand Chatham Division hastily assembled two hundred marines. At Dover they embarked in two destroyers for the Hook of Holland. There, they secured the port prior to the Queen of the Netherlands and the Dutch Government being spirited away, practically from under the noses of the advancing German army.

On the 23rd May, another hastily gathered company of marines left Chatham for Boulogne. Their task was to provide cover for the naval parties that were demolishing the port installations. They returned to Chatham the following day, safe and sound.

On the 25th May a further two platoons consisting of just over eighty marines under the command of Captain Courtice RM were landed at Calais, which was held by the British 30th Infantry Brigade. Here, they took part in the bloody and gallant final stand. When it was all over only twenty-one marines were lucky enough to have escaped. The remainder were either killed or wounded and taken prisoner.

For anyone who would like to know more about the Royal Marines, particularly this period in their Corp's history, you could do no better than to read Julian Thompson's excellent book The Royal Marines – From Sea Soldiers to a Special Force. It is both informative and well written.

The events of the Battle for France and the evacuation of the British Expeditionary Force (BEF) from Dunkirk in 1940 are well documented for anyone who wishes to find out more, particularly as this year is the 75th Anniversary of the start of the Second World War.

Finally, despite all the help I have received in writing this adventure story which takes place in such a key part of our history, any mistakes or faults, historical or otherwise are entirely of my own making and for which I apologise.

J.G. White
Nottingham
2015

Dear Reader,

Thank you for reading Never Surrender, my second book about Marine Dacre AJ.

I hope that you enjoyed it as much as I did in writing it.

Now I want to tempt you with the first couple of chapters of my next book DO or DIE. This story is set in 1942. Winston Churchill is the Prime Minister. Britain has its back to the wall as the war in the North Atlantic takes a fearful toll. There is an overwhelming need to break the codes that the German submarines are using.

Against this background, Royal Marine Dacre AJ trains as a commando. Later that same year he takes part in the ill-fated raid on Dieppe in France. Some commentators have likened this operation as the Royal Navy's very own 'Charge of the Light Brigade'.

I hope you enjoy the beginning of the story. If you do, then be sure to read the rest of the book; you will not find it disappointing.

With my best wishes,

J.G. White
Nottingham 2015

DO OR DIE

BY J. G. WHITE

Chapter 1

'Good morning, sir. You wanted to see me?' Anthony Eden, newly appointed to the post of Minister of War, stood facing his prime minister. The old man looked exhausted. Churchill sat hunched in his chair behind the long conference table in the Cabinet Room of number ten Downing Street, the official residence of the Prime minister of Great Britain. Winston Churchill was staring morosely at some official papers that were spread out before him. One of his favourite cigars, a Corona, was clamped firmly between his teeth. A cloud of pungent smoke hovered in the air above his head. He removed the cigar before speaking. Eden noticed that his hand was shaking very slightly. Churchill pointed to the papers in front of him.

'These are the final numbers for *Operation Dynamo*,' he said. 'We didn't do too badly all things considered. The navy and that armada of small boats managed to rescue more of the BEF than we ever hoped for. It was a miracle, Anthony, a bloody miracle.'

Churchill paused, re-living his own visit to the Port of Dover in 1940. He and Vice Admiral Ramsey had, at the height of the evacuation, interviewed two men from one of the small boats that had already completed five trips across the channel. What a salutary lesson that had been for both him and the Admiral; official reports and messages could not, they had learned, compare to the actual experience of being there in person. The two men, one of whom was a serving Royal Marine under the age of eighteen, had shocked and horrified everyone with their brutal honesty about the conditions on the beaches at Dunkirk.

Anthony Eden nodded his head in agreement and said, 'There was also BEF 2. That went quite well.'

Winston Churchill looked up sharply.

'Yes,' he growled in response, 'But at what cost? We had to sacrifice the whole Scottish Brigade in order to save the remainder of the force. What a damn waste of good men.'

Both men sat silently reflecting on what might have been.

'You know, Anthony, I may have misjudged the situation in France. I should have known that our French allies were going to collapse under the German onslaught.'

The Minister of War looked at his Prime Minister. This was the closest he had ever known Churchill admit that he may have been wrong.

'Well, that is all behind us now, sir. We must move on and face the future. The rearming and re-equipping of the army is going well. The 'hostilities only' call-up is proceeding as planned. Aircraft production is exceeding our initial predictions and the Royal Navy still controls the Channel and the North Sea. The Royal Air Force is well prepared to defend our skies should Herr Hitler decide to invade our shores.'

'Not 'should' Anthony, not 'should' but when! We are the only country standing in the Fuhrer's way to his complete domination and occupation of all Europe. He will come. I feel it in my water. But to do that he first has to control the skies with his Luftwaffe. Mark my words, Anthony, it will be a close run thing.'

'I agree with you, sir, but only time will tell.'

'Quite so, Anthony, quite so! Anyway, that is not why I have asked you to come and see me. I do not intend that we should sit on our backsides and wait for the invasion. I have given this a lot of thought and have decided that we must take the fight to the Germans. Somehow or other we must attack and harry the enemy as much as we can, albeit on a small-scale of course. What do you think of the idea?'

Eden sat quietly for several moments with his eyes closed trying to imagine in his mind the picture that Churchill had of these attacks.

'You mean rather like a fly or a mosquito that can be really annoying?'

'Yes! Yes, you have it! Just like a mosquito. I must say that I like that idea. Small stinging attacks that annoys the hell out of the Germans and, like that damned insect, you do not know where it is going to attack next.'

'I think it is a rather good idea, sir. We shall need a special force of men, volunteers perhaps, who are highly trained and can deliver these raids, perhaps like a storm from the sea. You will, of course, have to convince the Chiefs of Staff, but that shouldn't be too difficult.'

'I hope you are right, Anthony. Anyway I have arranged to see them all tomorrow afternoon at two thirty in the underground war rooms. You will be there of course?'

'Yes gladly, Winston. I wouldn't miss this meeting for all the tea in China!'

Chapter 2

Royal Marine Dacre AJ was standing perfectly still. He was on guard duty outside the main door to the conference room that was located deep beneath Whitehall in London. It was 0715 hours. His shift had begun at 0600. He and his fellow marine took it in hourly turns to guard the door or man the small cubbyhole that served as the guardroom. It was here that they kept the ledger for visitors to sign in and where they managed the key board. The Prime Minister had already been at work for over an hour

Standing on your feet for a long time was not an easy thing to do. However, there were little tricks of the trade that a sentry could do to help pass the time and perhaps, more importantly, prevent his leg muscles from developing cramp. Dacre AJ had just finished counting the bricks on the wall opposite him, there were two thousand and fourteen, and was part way through a discreet and invisible set of exercises when the conference room door opened. Winston Churchill stuck his head out. He checked the corridor in both directions, then addressing the marine said, 'Come inside will you please?'

Although it was phrased as a request, it was in reality an order. Dacre AJ followed the Prime Minister into the conference room and quietly closed the door behind him.

'Sit down and take the weight of your feet. Remove your cap. Make yourself as comfortable as you can.'

This was not the first time that Winston Churchill and the young marine had sat and talked. This strange alliance had begun shortly after the marine had been transferred to the Royal Marines Detachment that guarded the Prime Minister. They had first met, albeit briefly, back in 1939 when Churchill, then the First Sea Lord, had been guest of honour at the Depot RM in Deal when the King's Squad had had their passing out parade. Mr Churchill had presented Dacre AJ with the much coveted 'King's Badge', instigated by King George V in 1919 for the best all-round recruit. They had met again in 1940, during *Operation Dynamo*. The marine, although fully trained, was underage and unable to serve with his company. He had volunteered to crew one of the small boats. Together with the boat's owner, Lesley Thomas, they had taken the thirty-five foot motor cruiser, *Gypsy Rose,* to Dunkirk to help evacuate the troops from the beaches. Impressed by the young man's initiative and zeal, Churchill had personally asked for the youngster to join his detail of 'Royals'. Their first conversation had taken place late one evening when the Prime Minister had enquired as to how the marine was settling in.

Other conversations had followed, often in the early hours of the morning when no-one else was around. Gradually, this very unusual relationship between the young marine and the old man had developed, borne out of mutual respect and understanding. Churchill had soon realised that this youngster was no ordinary bull-necked marine. He was bright, intelligent and well educated. He had been to a good public school in the outskirts of North London at Mill Hill. He was a gifted linguist in Italian, French and German and was an outstanding sportsman who excelled in canoeing and mountain climbing. Churchill often wondered what this young man was doing in the ranks. Clearly he should have been an officer. However, the

Prime Minister supposed that was the marine's business and he must have had his reasons.

Dacre AJ had found it difficult at times to comprehend how this clandestine association had developed. Whilst he would be the first to admit that he enjoyed their regular meetings, he was intrigued that the Prime Minister of Great Britain should actually seek his opinion on a whole range of military and other matters. After all, he had absolutely no experience or wisdom of years that would give any substance to what he might say. He found the whole thing totally perplexing.

In one of their earlier conversations, Winston Churchill had let it slip that as the Prime Minister he was surrounded by people who either told him what they thought he wanted to hear or were too afraid to tell him what he really needed to know. Once, perhaps after too much brandy, Churchill had casually mentioned that there were, perhaps, only five people that he could really count on to tell him things as they really were. One of those was this young marine!

The Prime Minister looked directly at the marine. Dacre AJ held Churchill's gaze. He was not in the slightest bit intimidated by the great man.

'Well, my young friend,' growled Churchill, 'What do you know about the Boer War?'

The marine thought for a moment or two, martialling his thoughts.

'Not too much, sir. I know that it took place in South Africa between 1897 and 1902. I understand that you served there in the army and then later as a war correspondent. I believe you were captured but later escaped. I also know that the British Army learnt some hard lessons at the hands of the Dutch Boers, particularly with regard to their irregular forces. I seem to recall that most of these men were farmers who were mounted on horses and were excellent shots with the rifle. They could live off the land almost indefinitely. They would attack and harry the British at will and then disappear, only to re-appear later somewhere else. Some of our generals considered them to be an ill-disciplined rabble because they would not stand and fight in the traditional manner. But having said that, they were very effective and nearly cost us the war.'

Churchill stared at the young marine intently.

'You seem to be remarkably well informed. How is that?' he asked.

'My history teacher at school happened to be a Welshman. He was particularly interested in the African Wars. I think he had an uncle who had fought at Rorke's Drift.'

'Ah I understand. What a battle that must have been! However, in the early days of the Boer War things were going so badly for us that England was soon drained of men to cope with the increasing demand. Fortunately there was no shortage of volunteers. However, their training left a lot to be desired. It became so bad that in some instances these volunteers became more of a hindrance than a help. On more than one occasion the Boers sent derisive notes to the British Commanders asking them not to clutter up the field of battle with such men because they were getting in the way of both sides. There were even several instances when the Boers sent whole detachments of these captured raw recruits back across the lines. Talk about adding insult to injury!'

'I didn't know about that, sir.'

'No, well not everything gets into the history books. But I was there and I saw for myself. Anyway, enough of that, I digress. Do you recall what General Botha of the Boers called his irregular troops?'

'No, sir, I'm afraid I do not.'

'He called them 'commandos'.

Dacre AJ had a suspicion that he knew where this conversation might be going.

Churchill continued, 'Even though we may be facing the fight of our lives if Herr Hitler and his Nazis decide to invade our island, I think we must take the fight to the enemy, much like the Boers did to us. It has been suggested to me by Lt. Col. Clarke that we will need a special force of highly trained soldiers. Lt. Col Clarke is on the CIGS staff and has lived in South Africa for a number of years. The idea is that they should deliver a series of lightening attacks on the enemy coastline. I think that we should call these forces 'Commandos'.'

Dacre AJ sat quietly for a few minutes thinking through what the Prime Minister was proposing. It had occurred to him almost immediately that the Royal Marines would be perfect for this role. Their long history of being the Royal Navy's sea soldiers would make them ideal. After all, they were used to carrying out small-scale operations on land from the navy's ships, which was reflected in their Corps motto, *Per Mare Per Terram*, which meant by sea by land. However, at the last minute he decided not to say anything, particularly since Mr Churchill had on this occasion not asked for his opinion.

The Prime Minister sat staring at a spot on the wall behind the marine. He was deep in thought. With a slight start Churchill realised that the marine was still sitting quietly in front of him.

Curtly he said, 'That is all, young man. You can return to your duties.'

Dacre AJ stood up, put his cap back on and snapped up his smartest salute, longest way up and shortest way down. He did a sharp about-turn and marched to the door in order to return to duty in the corridor beyond. As he opened the door, Churchill looked up from the papers that covered his desk, his spectacles were perched on the top of his head, the overhead light reflected off the lenses.

'Thank you very much for listening to an old man rambling on,' he growled.

The marine just nodded and quietly closed the door behind him. There was just a hint of a smile on Dacre AJ's face.

Have you read *Operation Saint George* by J.G. White,
published by Austin Macauley?

You should! Here is a brief overview:

In April 1962, Royal Marine Dacre AJ with twenty-two years of experience as a commando is suddenly sent from his unit 43 Commando RM in Plymouth to the Depot RM in Deal, Kent.

Dacre AJ is a most unique marine, a marine's marine. He has seen service all over the world and is the most decorated marine in the Corps. Surprisingly he has always turned down the chances of promotion, preferring to stay as a marine first class. With his extensive experience of combat and having served with distinction in the SBS, he is now in the twilight of his career. His task at the Depot RM is to retrain and revitalise a tired and dispirited handful of marines for a gruelling competition, which requires this small group to be super-fit in a way that only commandos can be and which, against all the odds, he manages to achieve.

Meanwhile, the Sultan of Brunei flies into the UK on an unofficial visit. He wants urgent talks with the British Government regarding the increasing threat to his country from neighbouring Indonesia. His only son, the Crown Prince, is at that time undergoing some intensive training with the Royal Marines. An audacious plot to kidnap the prince and then kill him and the Sultan is undertaken by the IRA at the behest of the President of Indonesia.

The situation is well beyond the abilities of the local police and even Special Branch. Can HM Forces possibly help? The only problem is that there are no Special Forces available in the UK at that moment and time is of essence.

Failure to rescue the prince and to prevent the two murders is not an option that the government is willing to consider. The political consequences and the resulting instability in the Far East would be such not seen since the fall of Singapore in 1941.

Interview with the Author

When did you begin writing, and did you always envisage being an author?

I started writing my first book *Operation Saint George* about three years' ago. For the first couple of years I wrote in secret, not even my wife new. I would spend a couple of hours here and there. I never considered myself a writer, it was more of a hobby than anything else. When the book was finally finished my family encouraged me to try and get it published, which I did at my very first attempt. I was very lucky.

What do you hope people will get from reading your books?

I try to set out with the idea of writing a book that I would enjoy reading. I want people to have a thoroughly good read, to really enjoy the story, to get into it, to be part of it and perhaps be a little more informed particularly from a historical perspective. I rather like the idea of someone saying 'Well I never knew that!'

What advice would you give to budding writers?

Firstly, to read widely as many different genres as possible. To be a good writer I think you need to be a good reader.

Then try to write about what you know and places that are familiar to you. Use your own experiences when you can. Try to imagine yourself actually being there, particularly when developing things like conversation. Plan well but be flexible. Write and keep on writing. It is better to have something down on paper rather than nothing. I cannot imagine anything worse than having a blank sheet of paper in front of you and not knowing what to write. Spend your time and energy on good research, it is a good investment.

What other authors have inspired you?

I have always liked adventure stories. As a youngster it was *Biggles* by W E Johns. Later it was Ian Fleming's James Bond books. Now I really enjoy Patrick O'Brien for his sea-going sagas. I also really like all of Bernard Cornwell's books particularly his series on Sharpe. Then there is Douglas Reeman, Allan Mallinson and Simon Scarrow, all brilliant authors in their own fields.

What do you like to do when you are not writing?

I like hill walking, gardening, reading and DIY. I have four children and four grandchildren and enjoy spending time with them. I also enjoy the cinema, going to the theatre and concerts. I am also fortunate enough to be able to travel and often go abroad. We have a small caravan which we have towed all over England & Wales and also the Continent.

Do you feel your background has helped you in your writing?

Certainly my nine years as a Royal Marine has helped, particularly with my first book. In the 1960s I was in barracks at Deal, Portsmouth and Plymouth, as well as overseas in the Far East. Many of the places I have used in my first book are well known to me such as Whitstable, Maidstone, London and Nottingham. I have lived in all of them and therefore, know the geography of each pretty well.

Do you do a lot of research before you start writing?

Yes I do. I spend months reading and checking the internet making endless pages of notes in longhand. I am very particular about trying to get my facts right. I am constantly updating the script when I discover a new piece of information that I can use. I am always conscious that a diligent reader somewhere will pick me up on an error so I do my best to be as accurate as possible. It is, of course, extremely time-consuming but I always enjoy every moment of it.

How do you write, pen and paper or computer?

I am a pen and paper person. I have an excellent old fountain pen which is a joy to use. I then edit the first draft usually in red pen. When I am satisfied with the result, I then type the whole manuscript onto my computer (two fingers only), print a hard copy and edit that. I then put the script to one side and leave it for several weeks, maybe even months. Then I do a final edit.

Do the characters in your books relate to your own life?

Yes, to some extent they do. My main character, Marine Dacre AJ, is very loosely based on an amalgam of myself and other marines that I have served with, but, to be completely honest, more of them than me. He has an Italian background as I do and his father was an Australian as is my step-father, but we are also different. I was never very good at foreign languages at school so I decided to make him fluent in several, something that I could never manage. The only thing I was good at was sport so we do have that in common. Dacre AJ is also an expert at weapon handling and I was pretty good in my time. Other characters are based on people that I knew as a youngster. So, for example, in *Operation Saint George* the woman with glasses in the pie shop in Woolwich was modelled on my grandmother whilst the two elderly sisters who live by the sea at Tankerton in Kent were actually my next door neighbours.

Is your first book 'Operation Saint George' a true story?

I am often asked this question. To quote a famous fictional politician, 'You might think that, I couldn't possible comment.' I leave it up to the readers to decide for themselves, although an answer is actually in the book itself. Nevertheless I take it as a great compliment when people say to me, 'I never knew this sort of thing happened back in the 1960s.

What feedback have you had from people who have read your first book?

Since its publication there have been some great reviews which you can read for yourself on Amazon, by complete strangers as well as friends and family. They have made some very positive comments which for a first time author have been very encouraging because, as we all know, it is extremely difficult for a 'new kid on the block' to get recognised. Many people have asked me if there is going to be a second book and if so when will it be published? These requests have given me a real boost to my need to carry on writing, so if you are reading this then you have your answer. Hopefully another one will follow.

JG White is available for readings, talks and book signings. For further details about a possible appearance please contact his publisher.

J.G. White Supports the Rural Libraries of Cajamarca

I am very pleased to support the Rural Libraries of Cajamarca which is located in Northern Peru.

Established by my brother-in-law, Padre John (Juan) Medcalf RIP in the late 1960s, it is an independent charity that has changed the lives of the campesinos through knowledge, the promotion of cultural identity and literacy. Briefly, the scheme involves groups of volunteers carrying books on their backs, and sometimes donkeys, relaying them over the Andes to outlying villages. This system of carrying books from one community to another covers thousands of square miles and serves thousands of people.

Despite the lack of government support, (why would they want an educated workforce?) the RLC is totally funded by voluntary overseas contributions. This allows them to continue and develop their main aim which is to provide communities with a multitude and variety of books thus improving their skills, their literacy and knowledge.

Having been to Cajamarca with my wife and daughter to see for myself how successful the scheme continues to be, they now write and publish many of their own books. I am more than happy to ask you to consider supporting this worthwhile project.

To find out more about the RLC, visit their monthly blog on http://bibliotecasruralescajamarca.blogspot.co.uk/ which has the facility to translate into English or email doustks44@hotmail.co.uk.

J.G. White
Nottingham